T0123524

THE RAID
TOWARD PRAGUE

THE RAID
TOWARD PRAGUE
MAY 1945

HARRY JACOBS

THE RAID TOWARD PRAGUE
MAY 1945

Copyright © 2018 Harry Jacobs.

All rights reserved. No part of this book may be used or reproduced by any means, graphic, electronic, or mechanical, including photocopying, recording, taping or by any information storage retrieval system without the written permission of the author except in the case of brief quotations embodied in critical articles and reviews.

This is a historical novel based upon real events. All characters, names, incidents, organizations, and dialog are based on the author's imagination and/or on actual occurrences.

iUniverse books may be ordered through booksellers or by contacting:

iUniverse
1663 Liberty Drive
Bloomington, IN 47403
www.iuniverse.com
1-800-Authors (1-800-288-4677)

Because of the dynamic nature of the Internet, any web addresses or links contained in this book may have changed since publication and may no longer be valid. The views expressed in this work are solely those of the author and do not necessarily reflect the views of the publisher, and the publisher hereby disclaims any responsibility for them.

Any people depicted in stock imagery provided by Getty Images are models, and such images are being used for illustrative purposes only.
Certain stock imagery © Getty Images.

ISBN: 978-1-5320-5292-7 (sc)
ISBN: 978-1-5320-5293-4 (e)

Library of Congress Control Number: 2018907549

Print information available on the last page.

iUniverse rev. date: 06/28/2018

CONTENTS

ACKNOWLEDGMENTS

Ed Elkes, who edited this book, is the key to bringing this story into print. He closely reviewed the chapters and made valuable changes and additions.

An old friend, Major General John E. Murray (Ret) provided the impetus to write this.

My wife, Selma Jacobs, was patient with me when I spent countless hours on this project.

Audrey Hatry, a friend for many years, read the entire manuscript and offered valuable changes and additions.

Beverly Eddy, a distinguished author, made numerous suggestions.

Charles Pinck, President of the OSS Society, actively supported me in the book's development.

John Gannon, Deputy Director (Ret) of the CIA, provided valuable insights.

Steady assistance was provided by Dan Gross in finding valuable source material at the National Archives.

Michael Kirkland has been most helpful in providing support with correspondence and obtaining data.

Background data on 1945 Czechoslovakia was made available by Steve Goodell.

I am in indebted to historians at the State Department, Pentagon, Army War College, and the Roosevelt and Truman libraries. They made significant documents and information available.

FOREWORD

THE RAID BY THE U.S. Army behind the Line of Demarcation in Czechoslovakia in May 1945 captured a treasure of intelligence on the Russian Army. Although the Russians were allies, the United States had become aware of Russian post-war goals contrary to American policy for the future of Europe. Key people in the Pentagon, the State Department, and the Office of Strategic Services had to adjust to reality. The United States had to be prepared for a military conflict. This evolved into the Cold War.

The Cold War is commonly supposed to have started with the Truman Doctrine or the Berlin Airlift or some other celebrated stroke of statecraft. Not so. From newly declassified military archives emerges the hitherto untold tale of how the Americans, only hours after V-E Day, waged and won the first skirmish of the Cold War by swiping the Red Army's most vital secrets from right under the Russians' noses.

The die for this mission was cast soon after May 8, the day that Hitler's Third Reich collapsed. That's when American commanders learned that a Wehrmacht intelligence headquarters on the Eastern Front had collected files with extensive data on the Soviet Army Order of Battle, including the strength and equipment of each individual division. The trouble was, the German headquarters was encamped deep inside the region in Czechoslovakia assigned by the Allies to the Red Army and Soviet Units were already on the move, headed into that area.

The Americans had to think fast. And they had to think small. A sizeable task force would risk detection by the Russians. Entrusted with the mission was a team of the U.S. Fourth Armored Division, which had crossed the old Czech frontier by war's end.

In addition to the May 8, 1945, operation, there was another U.S. Army effort to obtain hidden German Army intelligence in Czechoslovakia. It took place on February 9, 1946. It is covered briefly below. This book deals extensively with the 1945 event. The rest of the Foreword is concerned primarily with the background and actions of both events.

Between May 1945 and February 1946, the U.S. Army mounted two highly classified operations in Czechoslovakia, which was later split-up into the Czech Republic and Slovakia. The purpose of both actions was to acquire information the Germans had collected during World War II on the Russian Army, as well as other intelligence. In light of the deteriorating relations with the Soviet Union, the American Army urgently wanted to get its hands on this material. To date, no public information has been released on the first operation, which occurred on May 11, 1945. It was an official Army action, and there is tangential evidence that it was launched at the instigation of highly placed military and civilian officials in Washington. The United States, through the National Archives, has released a comprehensive file on the second operation, which took place on February 9, 1946. The documents had remained classified "Top Secret" until released by the National Archives over four decades later.

Regarding the first operation, on May 8, 1945, General Eisenhower, the Commander of the Supreme Headquarters Allied Expeditionary Forces (SHAEF), declared the end of World War II in Europe. All U.S. Army units were ordered to halt at the Line of Demarcation which had been agreed to between Eisenhower and Marshal Zhukov, of the Soviet Union. The American government, through Eisenhower, had negotiated this agreement, even though numerous high ranking officials in Great Britain and in the U.S. had urged the Army to go farther into Czechoslovakia. This would have preempted the Russians from seizing most of the country, including Prague, its capital.

In the previous weeks there had been intense discussions between Churchill, Truman, Stettinius, the Secretary of State, General Marshall, the Army Chief of Staff, Eisenhower, and their subordinates. As early as April 23, Stettinius told Truman that the British stressed that we should liberate Prague. About that time Marshall communicated to Eisenhower that the British Chiefs of Staff urged the relief of Prague by Allied Forces rather than by the Soviets. Marshall added his comments that he did not want American lives exposed for political purposes. Eisenhower responded that he agreed. Churchill himself strongly believed that the American Army should move on to Prague. He sent a message on April 30 to Truman advocating his views. In a final effort, on May 7, Churchill wired to Eisenhower directly that he should not be inhibited to advance to Prague.

On May 4, General Bradley, Commander of the Twelfth Army Group, had already told General Patton, Commander of the Third Army, that Eisenhower's orders were for him to enter Czechoslovakia but to go no further than up to the Line of Demarcation. This finally stopped Patton from going to Prague, for which he had lobbied Bradley relentlessly. To assure that everyone in the Army understood, Eisenhower issued an order that the Army, including the OSS (Office of Strategic Services) which was within the Army structure, was prohibited to engage in any actions behind the Line of Demarcation.

Never-the-less, Eisenhower's edict was bypassed by staff members at SHAEF and at subordinate Army field commands. On April 25, SHAEF ordered the Twelfth Army Group and the OSS European headquarters in London to strengthen the OSS detachment in the Third Army in order to enable the Special Operations Executive (SOE), the British secret intelligence service, and the OSS to conduct small scale operations designed to aid the Czech resistance. This was the first time that the SOE and OSS were authorized re-engage in Czechoslovakia since December, 1944, when the Germans captured fifteen allied agents who had entered from Austria. All were tortured and killed.

The OSS took full advantage of the SHAEF message of April 25 by dispatching teams into Czechoslovakia to contact Czech resistance. For instance, in early May, Gene Fodor, who became well known for his travel guides, led a team from Pilsen, at the Line of Demarcation, to Prague. The OSS teams were equipped to communicate with the London office either by direct radio or by way of radio to over-flying OSS planes.

Major General Donovan, head of OSS, had long harbored suspicions of the Soviets' long range intentions. He regarded the Soviets as an intelligence target and notified General Marshall that his staff was preparing a study on Soviet intentions and capabilities. In a memorandum to Truman on May 5, 1945, Donovan warned the President that "we cannot possibly wait for Russia to reveal her full policy before we take certain measures of security."

After graduating from the basic course at the Military Intelligence Training Center, Camp Ritchie, Maryland, in November 1943, I underwent combat training at Camp Sharpe, near Gettysburg, PA. Until the end of December, 1944, Camp Sharpe was used to prepare selected personnel for commando operations behind the German lines to gather intelligence. Beginning in January, 1945, Camp Sharpe became the training center for psychological warfare teams.

Upon completion of an advanced course at Camp Ritchie in February 1944, I was sent to Great Britain to attend a special orientation at a joint British/U.S. intelligence school in London. Then I was assigned to the Military Intelligence Service at SHAEF and was subsequently attached to the G-2 section of the Fourth Armored Division, which had recently arrived in England. I remained in this assignment throughout the war, from Normandy to Czechoslovakia.

By May 1945 the Division, which was part of the Third Army, had halted its advance into Czechoslovakia at the Line of Demarcation. Early in the morning on May 11, I was called to report to the G-2. He had received a priority message to send my team immediately to a site near Prague, where the former German Army Headquarters for the Eastern Front was located. We found the German Headquarters in the vicinity of Neveklov and Benešov. It was guarded by Czech Partisan forces. Our orders were to seize pertinent intelligence data on the Russian Army and bring it back with us. Showing the Czechs a note from the Czech Liaison Officer with our division meant we had no trouble entering the German compound. We took a truck and trailer containing the records we sought, plus two *Wehrmacht* Officers who had worked with that data, as well as one soldier to drive the truck. The Partisans at first would not let us take the truck and trailer back with us, but finally, by threatening to call for assistance, we were able to proceed. After evading a number of fire fights, we reached our lines before nightfall. I described this raid in greater detail in "Operation Strakonice: In Pursuit of the Soviet Order of Battle", in the April, 2001, issue of The Journal of Military History.

The origins of the order for this mission remain a mystery. Except for a copy of the message to the Division's outpost at the Line of Demarcation authorizing to let us proceed, no other information has been found in the relevant files at the National Archives, nor do The Army's World War II files released to date touch upon this operation.

In recognition of the successful conclusion of this action, I was awarded the Bronze Star for Heroism in August, 1996. This came about through the efforts of General Hal Pattison, the last Commander of the Fourth Armored Division, who had personal knowledge of the May 11, 1945, action.

I believe that the original source revealing the existence of the extensive intelligence on the Russian Army at the German Headquarters may be traced to OSS operatives in the Prague area and their Czech counterparts. It later surfaced that a German intelligence officer, who had surrendered to the U. S. 26th Infantry Division, had urged, when he was interrogated, that the U.S. Army seize the German Army files on the Russian Army. Possibly this German officer had previously passed this information to OSS personnel he had encountered while fleeing toward the American lines.

The second operation on February 9, 1946, was also highly classified. With the release of the Army files on this incident, the history of this raid can be readily reconstructed. A major omission in the documents made available by the National Archives is how and where this mission originated. The only reference on this is a denial that Washington had been involved. The Pentagon took the position that it was cooked up in the European Theater of Operation. Fourteen Army personnel participated in a raid on a sealed cave near Prague. Three of them were seized by the Czechs.

The troubles about this second American raid started soon after it had occurred. The Czech government sent a démarche to the American Embassy in Prague citing the violation of its sovereignty. They demanded the immediate return of all the material which, according to the Czechs, included data on sophisticated radar equipment.

On February 19, 1946, a conference was held at the State Department (State) with the Operations and Plans Division (OPD) of the War Department to determine what action should be taken in response to the Czech government's complaints. The Pentagon went on record that it had no advance knowledge of the action. State conveyed its opinion "that the Czechoslovak government could very well claim the raid to be an act of war." The Pentagon position was much less dramatic. Finally, agreement was reached that State inform the Czechs that the War Department would conduct an investigation. The United States would also apologize about the manner in which the action was carried out. The end result of the diplomatic steps was to achieve the following objectives: No publicity, retention of the seized documents, release of the three captured soldiers, and reestablishment of cordial relations.

Following the meeting on February 19, the Pentagon requested the European Command to barter the seized material for the release of the three soldiers. Return of the documents would be made upon approval by highest U.S. authority, presumably the President. Washington also wanted information from the European Command on the specific data seized during the raid. The papers were to be microfilmed as rapidly as possible.

A memorandum to Lt. General John E. Hull, Chief of OPD, dated February 20, 1946, listed the documents "removed," such as German counterintelligence correspondence; papers belonging to Himmler, von Ribbentrop, Frank, and Funk; *Gestapo* papers; and President Beneš' files from 1918 to 1938. The memo also cited that the Paris edition of the New York Herald Tribune had information on the raid. An American war correspondent had accompanied the American task force. The memo expressed the hope that "every action has been taken at your end to prevent publicity." Whether the European Command succeeded in keeping the story under wraps was not covered in subsequent War Department papers.

A memorandum sent by the War Department on February, 21, 1946, to the European Command reflects the concern about how the incident should be handled. It informed the European Command that no press release was authorized. A referral to Secretary Byrnes of the State Department was being made and a briefing of General Eisenhower had been scheduled. At that time, Eisenhower was the Army Chief of Staff.

What is interesting is that both internal and external Pentagon documentation did not address the Czech demand about radar equipment. One can only speculate that the Czech allegation was based on something they had become aware of. The Czech government had no prior knowledge about the cave and its contents raided by the Army. If they had, they would have already removed its valuable contents. The Czech assertion about radar data must have come from their interrogation of the American personnel they had captured. How the U.S. Army learned about the cave is also not touched upon in the Pentagon papers on the raid. Presumably they learned about it from U.S. intelligence personnel, including OSS agents, who had worked closely with Czech Partisans during the war.

In an effort to downplay the incident, the State Department issued a short innocuous press release on February 23, 1946: "On February 11, 1946, an American military detachment from the American occupation forces in Germany entered Czechoslovakia and proceeded to remove, to the American Zone in Germany, a number of documents which were found concealed in a hillside south of Praha. The detachment sought these documents because they were informed that the documents would throw light upon the pre-war plans of Hitler and give information as to the conduct of the war by the Nazi government.

"Although this American detachment entered Czechoslovakia with passes issued by the appropriate Czechoslovak liaison officer, this expedition had not been given approval by the Czechoslovak government, which has protested this action. The American Government has expressed its deep regret to President Beneš, and has ordered an immediate return of the documents to the Czechoslovak government."

The United States apparently succeeded in its efforts to avoid wide publicity on the raid and the subsequent interactions with the Czech authorities. The only exception was when Congressman A. J. Sabath of Illinois wrote a letter to the Secretary of War on March 1, 1946, expressing surprise that the Army had removed certain documents from

Czechoslovakia. He wanted information on who had issued the orders and the reasons therefore. A response was prepared for the Secretary of War indicating that the Army, after an "exhaustive investigation," concluded that it had acted in good faith. The draft response asserted that these documents were essential to the occupation of Germany and the prosecution of Nazi war criminals. It also stated clearance had been obtained from the Czech mission in Germany, but the Army had failed to notify Prague through the American Embassy. This draft was prepared by the G-2 of the Army on March 7, 1946. No information is included in the released files at National Archives of what was actually sent to the Congressman.

None of the released Pentagon papers contains a description of the February 9, 1946, operation. However, the American Ambassador to Czechoslovakia provided the State Department with a summary of what had occurred. The Air Attaché at the Embassy had requested the European Command in December, 1945, to take aerial photographs of the surroundings near a river bank 30 miles south of Prague. What had caused this request was not mentioned. Then, in late January, 1946, the Military Attaché was contacted by the G-2 of the European Command to get permission from the Czechs for the entrance of a detachment of 14 American soldiers. The reason for the request was not stated in the Ambassador's memo. The Ambassador believed it was in connection with the photographs. The European Command was informed by the Embassy that the Army detail must report to the Military Attachés' office. The group, however, did not follow up on this, but went directly to the site. There they used explosives to gain entrance to the cave and left for Germany with what they had found. The Czechs had discovered the excavation operations. They seized three of the soldiers, including a Captain who was an explosives expert. The Czechs told the Embassy they found documents which indicated that the highest American authorities knew about this. The Czechs asserted that the material included information about "the latest in radar technology". The Ambassador complained that bypassing the Embassy had placed the Military Attachés' office in an embarrassing position.

A review of the declassified documents at the National Archives poses some question marks, such as; why the Embassy was bypassed, did a war correspondent take part or not take part, and was the inventory released of the material taken complete?

The continued non-release of any information on the first operation which took place on May 11, 1945, is puzzling. Nothing was uncovered at the National Archives and at the Central Intelligence Agency which had custody of the OSS records until they were transferred to the Archives. A review of Donovan's own OSS papers shows nothing about the operation. The OSS involvement probably was at the SHAEF and Third Army levels.

This leads to the conclusion that the records are in custody of the Pentagon. None are with the Army's Chief of Military History. They may be in a place in, or controlled by, the Pentagon where highly-classified WWII documents are still kept. They may never be released because of the high degree of sensitivity involved in the planning and execution of the operation.

It is in the realm of possibility that among the data in the sealed cave recovered by the U.S. Army in February, 1946, were some records on research conducted by the Germans on atomic weapons and rocketry. The War Department's response to the Czechs' complaints, after they had discovered that it had occurred, asserted the finding of only historical information. The Czechs demanded the delivery of all contents in the cave. After microfilming the data, the Czechs were informed that everything was being returned. Reading between the lines of the War Department's documents leads to the conclusion that the entire inventory was not included in the returned data. The rationale for the declassification and release by the Pentagon after over 40 years is not known. It may be that the manipulation of the 1946 response to the Czechs, and to the Congressional inquiry, would not cause any problems after so many years had passed.

Gaining a comprehension of the Russian military capability became an urgent requirement. By fortuitous circumstances, the U.S. Army discovered the availability of the German Army's vast collection of intelligence on the Russian military. This data was at the German Headquarters for the Eastern Front, which had retreated to an area near Prague. An Army intelligence team was ordered to go behind the Line of Demarcation to locate the site and seize the information which proved invaluable in the future. This was the origin of the successful raid.

Due to the unavailability of records on the circumstances upon which the May 11, 1945, operation was initiated, this book is published as a historical novel. It is based upon actual events and on storyline narrative. The latter reflects the author's efforts, over a period of several years, and research, and the necessity for the introduction of fictional events to provide a cohesive plot.

The main character in this book, Kevin Keefer (Keef), as well as others, appeared in the author's previous work, *The Pentagon Brank*, a mystery covering an espionage affair in today's Pentagon.

CHAPTER 1

MIS FORT MEADE

AFTER AN INTENSE INVESTIGATION into the security problems in the Office of the Joint Chiefs of Staff (JCS) finally came to a conclusion, Lieutenant Colonel Bob MacMerial, my boss, the Executive Officer of the Army's Military Intelligence Service (MIS) detachment at Fort Meade, gave me a few days off. Due to the ramifications of the events that transpired over the many months the JCS project took, major organizational changes in our group were contemplated by MIS.

Lieutenant Colonel Alicia Gouperz, our Commanding Officer, got canned. She was lucky to get off easy. Being involved with a rogue Russian spy network was her undoing. No decision had been made for a replacement. Bob MacMerial was scheduled to attend a senior course at the Army Intelligence Center, Fort Huachuca. Bob had worked closely with me on the investigation, which had been ordered by the Chairman of the JCS. That was, indeed, a very sensitive assignment. JCS wanted to keep it under wraps. It all began when I had received a mysterious letter posted in Germany. Why the letter was addressed to me personally was a mystery which I was determined to resolve. The writer implied that there was a major security breach in the military side of the Department of Defense. Bob and I concluded that the problem was in the JCS. Alicia, Bob, and I went to the JCS to let them handle this hot potato. However, JCS requested our headquarters, the Army Intelligence and Security Command (INSCOM), to conduct the investigation.

The job landed in my lap. It was pretty much a solo proposition, although Bob MacMerial supported my efforts 100 percent. As a warrant officer in an MIS detachment I did not have a lot of clout to pursue this investigation. But as I was actually working at the direction of JCS, my ranking in the military scale did not matter. The MIS hierarchy above Bob MacMerial also got into the act. They felt an assignment for the JCS required their participation. Personally, I could have operated without their meddling, but, of course, I had to cooperate.

My investigation took me to a lot of places. I made contact with important individuals throughout the government and VIPs abroad. It quickly dawned on me that I was in a unique position for an ordinary warrant officer. I grew into this assignment. I actually enjoyed it. Most of the time, I was not in uniform. My contacts viewed me as representing the JCS. However, I did not let this unique position change my work ethic. I realized that I, Kevin "Keef" Keefer, had landed in a prestigious environment and I might as well enjoy it.

Bob was groomed for a new assignment at INSCOM. Yours truly was under consideration for a big promotion and assumption of the Executive Officer spot in our office. Our long-time secretary, Eloise, was leaving the Army. She was slated for a civilian job at the Pentagon. To beef up our detachment, Henry Kelly, a Special Agent working out of the MIS office in Munich, which was being closed, was transferred to us. This was a plus. I had good experiences working with him while I was snooping around Europe on the JCS case.

As things actually work out in the Army, proposed personnel changes do not always take place. INSCOM decided to designate Bob MacMerial to run our office. I declined my proposed promotion because it would mean I had to give up my warrant and climb the career ladder of the regular officer corps. My rationale was that I was comfortable with being a Warrant Officer. By becoming a Captain or Major I would receive a sizeable pay increase, but the negatives outweighed the positives. It would involve attending career development courses, possible transfers to other Army branches, and constant pressure to keep a clean slate.

Eloise had recommended Amy, a clerk in the Fort Meade administrative office, to take her place. Amy had handled my travel orders. I had no problems with her. In fact, she enjoyed kidding me about – as she put it – my popularity with the girls. This, of course, she got from Eloise.

I devoted my off-days to taking care of the things at home I had neglected. The kitchen needed cleaning badly and the yard required a lot of time for upkeep. In the morning of the third day of my leave the phone rang, interrupting a snooze. A female voice queried whether this was Kevin. When I confirmed, she asked whether I remembered her, Carla, and our having met in Prague a few months ago. Now I recalled talking to her at the Uhelny Trh square when I was sight-seeing in Prague. She was the production manager of a small film company shooting scenes dealing with espionage operations. In the course of our conversation, after she had found out that I was in the intelligence game, she asked me to become a technical advisor to work with her during the editing phase. I had responded that I was intrigued, but would have to get approval from the Army. I gave her my phone number in case she really wanted me to come.

"Kevin, oh, I forgot you like to be called 'Keef,' can you visit Prague for about two weeks as soon as possible? I need your expertise."

"Carla, I would be glad to come. However, as I had explained to you, I need the OK from my superiors. I will get to work on this right away. I will call you in a few days."

"Thanks, Keef, waiting to hear from you."

Carla had slipped my mind. She was getting on in years yet her figure and all accoutrements were in the right places. She did not get embarrassed when I looked her over when we first met. As if to discourage anything further, she had mentioned that she was waiting for her boyfriend. However, she was very pleasant. She arranged with her driver to take me on a quick tour of some of the sights in downtown Prague.

I called our office at Fort Meade to get the ball rolling. An unfamiliar voice answered.

"Is this, by any chance, Amy who replaced Eloise?"

"Yes, it is, and you are Kevin Keefer. How can I forget you? You are the most popular bachelor on the post."

"Amy, let's get one thing straight. I am a Warrant Officer, addressed as 'Mister.' You know that, you wrote my travel orders. We are an informal office, but we are still in the Army and must retain decorum."

"Mr. Keefer, I apologize. I just like to kibitz a bit. I have not had a chance to talk extensively with Colonel MacMerial. I am sure he will provide me with his policies on how he wants the office to run."

"Amy, I think we are on the same page now, and will get along just fine. Is our boss there?"

"He called a while ago. He is taking the day off."

"Thanks, Amy."

I thought I'd better call Bob at home. He was in. We joked around a bit before I told him about the call from Prague. I reminded him about having included, in my trip report, a note about Carla's invitation. He told me I deserved a break and he would OK a two-week leave; but first it was the Standard Operating Procedure (SOP) to get concurrence from the Pentagon. He would get back to me.

Bob called me a couple of days later. "Keef, it looks good! My inquiry was bucked up all the way to DOD, the Defense Department's Public Affairs Office. Their Motion Picture Production Branch went to work on it. They found out that the Prague outfit is reputable. The movie being processed deals with some aspects of U.S. Army intelligence operations. The Pentagon thinks it would be a good idea to keep tabs on what they are doing. You being requested as a technical advisor is a stroke-of-luck opportunity for the Army to have an input. In fact, the Army is placing you on two weeks of detached service."

"Bob, they wanted to pay my way and reimburse me for my stay. May I still accept this?"

"No, tell them you have some other Army matters to attend to and you will go on military travel orders. As they are small outfit, with limited capital, this should be welcome news. Besides, you will not be under any obligations. You can probably be more influential to see that the Army is being portrayed in a favorable light. You are a fine B.S. artist, so do a good job!"

"Bob, thanks for the compliment! So my ability to shoot the breeze is being recognized! When do you want me to leave?"

"Suit yourself; call Amy to get going on the travel arrangements."

Immediately I contacted Amy. I explained the situation and asked her to cut me travel orders and get me on a flight to Prague in a couple of days. She should advise me when all arrangements were completed. The next morning she called me.

"Mr. Keefer, you are all set. Your orders are for two weeks. As Prague is a hardship post, your travel expenses are the maximum. I took the liberty to call an acquaintance at the Adjutant General's office who handles travel policy and priorities. She checked with the motion picture group at the DOD. They know all about your proposed trip. They recommended that you are put on a business class flight. They said this would make a good impression on the film company."

"Amy, I see you are on the other side of the same coin as Eloise. Thanks for getting me on business class. The seats are much better and you get free drinks. Now what are the details?"

"You will leave day after tomorrow on board a United flight from Dulles. I tried to get you on Lufthansa, but they were filled up. I faxed you the details. I already sent you the orders plus the plane reservations."

"Amy, how come you checked Lufthansa first?"

"Mr. Keefer, I remember that Eloise related to me that you had such good experiences with Lufthansa."

"Anyway, thanks. See you in two weeks or so."

Doggone it! I wondered what else Eloise told her. Well, I should not be surprised. These girls like to gossip. That reminded me, whatever happened to the stewardess I had met on a Lufthansa flight? She was very pleasant and helpful when we got to Munich.

I checked the fax machine which Bob MacMerial got for me. It saved lots of time and energy previously expended by a million phone calls and trips to Fort Meade. The travel orders looked okay. The flight reservations were confirmed. Trip to Dulles was arranged. A phone number of a commercial limousine service was included, with a note to call them in case they did not pick me up on time.

We have had a number of robberies in the neighborhood. I called my next-door neighbor, asking her to keep an eye on my house while I was gone. Then I went into Silver Spring to buy a gift for Carla; my father taught me it does no harm to butter up anyone with whom you expect to have a relationship or do business. I chose a nice manicure set. Next I called Carla, providing her my travel schedule. She was delighted. Her driver would pick me up upon arrival.

CHAPTER 2

SURPRISE IN PRAGUE

THE TRIP WAS UNEVENTFUL. The limousine pulled up on time. Processing at Dulles was relatively smooth. The plane was only half full. The food was good. Most of the passengers were businessmen. The ladies on board were pre-occupied with all sorts of computer gadgets. I glanced at a few magazines, but soon fell asleep. Upon arrival I was whisked from the line, thanks to my government passport. As I approached the exit, I saw a guy holding a "Keef" sign. He took me straight to the hotel, would pick me up the next day after breakfast. The hotel turned out to be the same one where I had stayed the last time I was in Prague during the JCS investigation. I recalled the dining facilities were okay and there was a small swimming pool.

In the morning I was picked up by Gunther, the same driver who had shown me the sights the last time I was here. He remembered me and seemed happy to see me again. Carla gave me a big hug. We went into the trailer office. She asked me to review a lengthy summary of the plot of the movie.

It took me about two hours to absorb it. I immediately realized why Carla wanted my assistance. The plot covered a group of resistance fighters in the Prague area during World War II. Because of the ferocious punishments of the German Security Forces, the SS, such as destroying houses and executing their inhabitants, the Czech Underground limited its overt activities. They concentrated on data mining instead. They worked closely with agents of the Office of Strategic Services (OSS) who had been parachuted in and merged into the general population. The OSS operatives were organized into small teams whose main job was to keep tabs on the identification and location of German Army units and pinpoint armament factories. The information acquired was periodically radioed to OSS headquarters in London. This data was used for Allied air raids. The Germans quickly realized what was going on. A cat-and-mouse game developed between special SS units and the OSS teams. The agents constantly moved around to become elusive targets. The film concentrated on one of the teams.

Luckily, I had done some research on the OSS-Czech Underground relationship. I was prompted to understand what had happened in the last days of the war when my father was on the mission behind the Line of Demarcation. The script of the film was fairly realistic. A major correction I recommended was to substitute "OSS" for "Army Intelligence." Whoever developed the narrative was not aware that Army Intelligence did not actively participate in the OSS activities. It was exclusively their game. I also urged Carla to delete or reduce Czech destructive actions because they did not happen often. However Carla kept several such incidents in. They were needed as part of the story line.

I asked Carla why she wanted me to stay for two weeks. She laughed.

"Keef, you don't know anything about the movie business. I need you to support me in convincing my co-workers of the changes we must make."

Carla wanted me to stop by every morning for a couple of hours to attend her staff meetings. In the afternoon I was free. Her driver would take me around. As it happened, the get-togethers in her trailer were interesting. Her associates sometimes asked me questions about the OSS. When I told them that some were military personnel while others were civilian volunteers, they incorporated disagreements and jealousies to make the movie more challenging. They asked me whether any of the OSS were females. I responded affirmatively. They included a woman who had emigrated to the States from Czechoslovakia before the war. Even though she was married, two male agents competed for her favors. Carla concurred, noting you can't make a film without romance.

The following afternoon, I phoned the American Embassy. Colonel O'Rancher, the Military Attaché, and his wife, Lucy, were on vacation. They had been very cooperative the last time I was in Prague. I had been looking forward to seeing them again. In anticipation of my call, they left word that Anna Protiles, my father's old girlfriend, had passed away. That was a blow!. She had been very helpful in obtaining a solution to the JCS case.

I was resting in the hotel pool when the idea popped into my mind to make an effort to locate somebody who had been active in the Underground. For my own edification, I wanted to find out how they actually operated. I have to admit what I told Carla and her co-workers was what I knew from second-hand sources, but it would be nice to get the real facts.

The next day, I asked Carla whether Gunther, her driver, would be available in the afternoon. She called him and told him to take care of me.

I took him for lunch. After we had gossiped about our family lives, I shifted our conversation to my father's experiences during the last days of the war. I told him what had happened when my father was in Strakonice at that time. I knew very little about the details. My dad had mentioned in passing how he ended up on a highly classified mission beyond the Line of Demarcation. He had told me this venture had developed as a result of a tip-off that came from the OSS in Prague.

"Gunther," I said, "I was wondering whether any of the Czech Underground people who worked with the OSS at that time were still around. I sure would like to talk to any of them. Do you have any ideas about how this could be accomplished?"

As I had been relating my father's activities to Gunther, he displayed increased interest. "I think I may be able to help. One of my friends has an uncle who was active in the Underground. My friend once mentioned that the uncle worked with American agents. The uncle is getting old, but his mind was still clear." As soon as I asked him to call his friend to find out if I could talk with his uncle, Gunther took out his cell phone. They spoke in Czech for about five minutes. Being ignorant of the language, all I could decipher was "OSS." The driver explained that his buddy would try to get a hold of his uncle. In the meantime, we decided to do some sight-seeing. About two hours later, his friend had positive news. I was to meet the uncle's niece to explain what I was after.

This puzzled me. The uncle had worked with OSS and presumably spoke good English. Why did I have to be screened by a third party?

I expressed my thoughts to Gunther. He laughed, saying not to wonder about this. The uncle had been indoctrinated into security-consciousness and has never lost it in all those years. He is suspicious about the motives of people who wanted to talk to him. That is why he wants his niece to check me out. It is quite probable that he had had bad experiences with some newspaper guys who misquoted him.

In the intelligence business there are all sorts of angles one encounters. One needs patience to attain results. I asked Gunther to call back and make the arrangements. After several calls he told me the young lady would meet me at a popular restaurant at lunchtime the following day. She would be there at noon and wear a red rose on her jacket. Her name was Anezka. She was in her early thirties. He had not met her. She was supposedly very responsible. We would get along.

After spending the next morning with Carla and her crew I walked to the nearby restaurant. I soon saw a young lady with the red rose. She had a friendly face. She smiled as we exchanged greetings. Her English was accented but fluent. After we ordered, she mentioned that she worked as a loan officer in a bank. She was on her lunch hour and only had limited time. She basically wanted to know about me, especially why I was in Prague. She did not know Carla. I briefly explained my father's role in World War II and that I wanted to find out more than he had related about his venture behind the Line of Demarcation.

Anezka was all ears. She would talk to her uncle. If he was agreeable, I would meet him. I gave her my cell phone number. When we got up, I could not help saying how pleased I was to have met her. I insisted on treating her for lunch. She laughed, saying "Mr. Keefer, you are a charmer." Giving me a hug, she left, waving her right arm. Hmm, I said to myself, if I only was younger, I could really go for her.

True to her word, Anezka called me the next day. Her uncle was surprised about my request. He asked her to find out more about me, my relationship with my father, how I got into Army Intelligence, and some other questions. She doubted there was enough time to get all these details during her lunch hour.

"I have a payback for the delicious lunch. I would like you to let me treat you to a home-cooked meal tonight. Are you available?"

"I would love it, but let's go out for dinner at a quiet place where we can talk."

"Thanks for the offer, but I would much prefer for you to come to my apartment where we would not be pressed for time. Please come around seven tonight; bring a healthy appetite! I will phone Carla the address and directions."

On the way back to my hotel, I stopped off at a men's store to buy a decent shirt. My pants were okay, but I had brought only two shirts which needed washing. The salesman was very nice. I asked him what kind of wine I should bring to a dinner invitation. He recommended Ludmila, a popular white wine. A nearby shop would have it.

Around 5:30 I asked the front desk to call a cab. The clerk pointed out there were always taxis waiting near the entrance. He told me it was only a ten minute ride to my destination. So far I was able to charge all my expenses on my Army-issued credit card. I believed these expenses were a legitimate part of my Army-sanctioned trip. In the past Bob MacMerial had urged me to use the card when I was on official trips. If there was not much activity on the card, the Army would take it away. The budgeteers would be upset when they had projected the expenses for our office and came up short. Soon enough they would cut our budget. Yep, this is another reason I did not want a regular commission. Instead of an action officer, I would become a bean counter.

Sure enough there were several cabs near the hotel entrance. When I got into one I gave the driver the address and asked him to stop at a flower shop on the way. I bought a nice red rose which the sales lady taped on the wine bottle.

I pushed the doorbell button for Anezka's apartment. Anezka was standing near the elevator when I got to her floor. She wore a Czech peasant dress which really fitted her nicely. I presented my little gift to her. She was really surprised and kissed me on the cheek. I hugged her and it went over very naturally.

It was a small apartment. There was an eating alcove in the living room next to the kitchen. The table was all set. Anezka went to the fridge to get a bottle of Pilsner. I asked her why we did not drink the wine I had brought. She educated me on what drinks would go with what dishes. I asked her where she had acquired her culinary expertise.

"Keef, when I was in college, at Charles University, I worked every summer to make some spending money and …"

"Pardon me, Anezka, how come you addressed me as Keef?"

"When I contacted Carla to give her my address, she informed me that you like to be called 'Keef' rather than 'Kevin.'"

"Of course, I should have told you everybody knows me as 'Keef.'"

"As I was saying, one summer I worked in a tavern in Bavaria. I waited on tables and also learned some cooking. There they told me most people prefer beer rather than wine with what we will eat tonight."

"Oh, Anezka, did they make you wear a *dirndl*?"

"No, but one of the waitresses wore a Bavarian peasant dress which I believe is a *dirndl*."

"That must have been in the same place I was taken when I was on the job in Passau last year. It was supposed to be the best eating place in the area. What a coincidence!"

"Yes, Keef, what a sign that we were destined to meet each other. But, talking about restaurants, I smell the dishes in the oven are ready to be tasted."

The entrée consisted of beef goulash with bread dumplings. The Pilsner was a good choice. For dessert, apple strudel graced the table. Everything was delicious! I helped clear the table.

We sat on the couch and Anezka announced, "Now we can talk business."

I described for her my father's role as an intelligence agent during the war. I detailed the mission he was on to seize the German Army information on the Russians and the OSS role in prodding the Army to go after it. My father rarely talked about his experiences in the war. While he described how they went to the German Army site near Prague, he was very circumspect about the mission. He said one of his life's ambitions was to discover just how it originated. He said he was doing research on it.

So now that I was here I had to take the opportunity to find somebody who worked with the OSS who may know something about the background of all this. I hoped her uncle was familiar with the OSS activities in late April/early May of 1945 or knew someone who may be able to clear things up for me.

"Keef, I will relate what you just told me to my uncle. I am off work tomorrow and will see him. I will call you about his reaction."

We chatted for a while on the sofa while sipping some brandy. She became very animated and once in a while our elbows touched. I was feeling very comfortable with her. After a while she turned on the radio, telling me there was a station with good dance music.

"Anezka, last time a lady asked me to dance with her I got into trouble."

"What happened?"

"This woman bit me on the ear."

"What? I don't believe it!"

"Yes, while we were dancing she moved very closely onto me, kissed me and then chewed on my left ear!"

"Where did this happen?"

"While I was on business at a resort in West Virginia, I went to a dinner-dance at a local country club. I was introduced to this lady and this is what happened."

Anezka then asked me to show her the ear. I responded that it had healed by now, but she insisted. I pointed to the left ear lobe. She leaned over me, stroked the ear and -- what do you know -- she kissed the spot lightly. Of course, this maneuver had some impact on me and I kissed her in return. She turned slightly flushed, and pulled me up to dance with her.

First there was a foxtrot and then a rumba. Then another foxtrot, a very slow one, came on. She moved closer to me. I noticed she was not wearing a bra. I could feel her nipples. Well, I am sure she noticed something rising between my legs. Her rate of breathing increased.

As if something snapped in her mind, she walked me back to the couch, but did not sit down. Instead, she finished her drink. She had calmed down; telling me it was getting late. She drove me back to the hotel. I was puzzled by how quickly she had switched gears. But, I said to myself - as I often had before - you can't figure out women. Before I could open the car door when we arrived, she pulled me over and gave me a deep kiss. Now I was even more confused. Her last words were that she would call me tomorrow after she had seen her uncle.

I was just about ready to leave the trailer the next day when Anezka called. She asked me whether I had a good sleep. I told her my system had been somewhat in turmoil, but eventually things got back to normal. She giggled, saying that she had "never encountered anyone who had this reaction to food I prepared."

Now it was my turn to grin. I told her what had ailed me was not my stomach, but the area below it.

Then she abruptly changed the subject. Anezka related her conversation with her uncle. We would see him at home in about an hour from now. She would pick me up.

I changed clothes thinking if everything went well at the uncle's, I would take her out for dinner. I called the Embassy and talked to the Military Attaché's secretary. We had met when I was there the last time. I asked her if she could make reservations for two in the Colonel's name at the executive dining room at Charles University. It was a very plush place. Colonel O'Rancher and his wife had taken me there on my last night in Prague on my previous visit. I asked her to call me. She told me she would make it in the Colonel's name. I could spin a story when he did not show up with me.

Anezka came early. She had to wait a few minutes while I got ready.

"My, my, you did not have to put on your Sunday suit. My uncle likes everything informal."

"My, my, you did not have to wear your best dress, either."

"Who says I want to impress my uncle?"

When she had finished, I leaned over and gave her a good hug.

Her uncle lived in a small house in one of the suburbs. He was well into his 80's but appeared to be in good health. He introduced himself as Eduard. He asked me to repeat what I had told Anezka about why I was in Prague, about my job in the Army, and my relationship with my father. I emphasized that I was intrigued by my dad's mission behind the Line of Demarcation. He always told me he wanted to know the details behind the origin of the mission.

"Since he is no longer with us, it has become my quest to find out how it happened. I sincerely hope you might be able to shed some light on this."

Uncle Eduard then took me by my hands and said, "You remind me of your father. I had never met him, but we had many telephone conversations. I know we were both committed to confidentiality. I am not surprised that he did not tell you about his contacts with me."

My facial expression must have reflected my utter amazement. I was close to my father. It is true he did not talk much about World War II. But I thought I had a complete picture of his mission in Czechoslovakia at the end of the war. After Dad died I went through his papers, but I did not come across anything about contacts after the war with either agents of the OSS or the Czech Underground. He kept papers on practically everything. He preserved all sorts of minutia. Why was there nothing on contacts with the Underground? Had he destroyed them for security reasons or by accident?

Uncle Eduard gave me a few minutes to digest what he had related.

He said, "I will try to clear this up for you. First of all, let's see how he first got in touch with me. He reached me by phone through somebody he knew who had been with OSS in Europe. This man connected him with one of the former OSS guys who had served in Czechoslovakia. I had worked closely with this person. He called me, explaining why your father wanted to contact me. He told me that your father would phone me. I heard from him a few days later.

"Your dad explained what he was after. He said he was trying to discover who had ordered the raid behind the Line of Demarcation. He was wondering whether Eisenhower had anything to do with it. We had many lengthy conversations. He described his trips to the National Archives and how frustrated he was to find nothing there. He finally got some real leads. Somebody who had worked in the CIA, and before that was with the OSS, informed him that he was quite sure that the ball got rolling in Washington. Apparently some officials were eager to get data on the Red Army. Just how this all evolved was a mystery to him as well as to me.

"According to your dad he had a tough time getting anything in Washington. Even the Pentagon had nothing. He knew some people in the Historical Division. They told him they could not find anything. He read many books written about the war. Somebody mentioned he should check with the Presidential Libraries which have a lot of data on this period. He was delighted to get tidbits of information from the Eisenhower and Truman Libraries. These skimpy clues implied there had been discussions within and between U.S. Government agencies about getting military information on the Russians. That's about all I know. He worked diligently to follow up leads. Unfortunately, he died before he could complete the project.

"Now I am greatly surprised that you know nothing at all about this. It just dawned on me that he may have kept separate files on the project. I remember that one time during his calls the electric power went out in his neighborhood for several days. He told me he had to work in the basement where he had an old desk and an empty filing cabinet. I guess it was warmer down there and he had daylight from a window. Apparently, he started to like to work down there. I recommend your checking if you still have the desk and the files. If so, you may find a lot of answers. Good luck!"

After my father died, I had to clear out his house so it could be put on the market. After the funeral, my daughter Jennifer stayed with me to help me move a few things I could use in my house. The items I took were his office equipment, mainly the desk and a small cabinet, which contained all of his current papers. On our last walk-through, Jennifer urged me to also take an old desk and a file cabinet which was stored in the basement of his house. She said if she ever came back to the Washington area, she might be able to use them. They were old, but still serviceable. There was the old desk down there. It was empty. There was no filing cabinet. I wondered what happened to it.

I would try to find out where the cabinet could be. Perhaps the cabinet did contain data my father had gathered when trying to find out about the origin of the raid in Czechoslovakia. If he really worked in his basement, as Uncle Eduard had told me, perhaps I would hit a gold mine. We will see.

It was getting late. I noticed that Uncle Eduard looked tired. I thanked him for the extensive briefing. He told me if he could help me further, not to hesitate to call him. I went into the adjacent room where Anezka was reading a book. I told her about our fruitful conversation and thanked her for making it possible.

"Anezka, let's depart. Your uncle looks like he needs a nap."

When we were in the car, I again thanked her. Would she like to join me for dinner?

"I see you are wearing your Sunday best. I heard of a nice place. I think you would like it."

She acted as if she was surprised. I doubted this. Why was she dressed up?

Anezka apparently read my mind. She said she always wore her best when she visited Uncle Eduard. He was old-fashioned. Even she complied with his wishes about visitors showing respect by dressing properly.

I mentioned that I had called the Embassy for a recommendation in case we could celebrate a successful interview with her uncle.

"One of the secretaries suggested going to the executive dining room at Charles University. The Military Attaché was a steady customer there. I asked the Attaché's secretary to make a reservation. I figured I could always cancel it. So, Anezka, would you like to go there?"

"Keef, this is a wonderful idea. I have heard about this place. I know you had to be a member of the staff to get in or else be someone the University President had spoken for. I hear it has excellent food!"

"Anezka, I am glad you endorse the Embassy's recommendation. So, let's go for it!"

It looks like it was a good choice. When we reached the university, a guard directed us to a small parking lot near the faculty facilities. The maître'd checked the reservation list. We were shown as guests of the American Attaché. He explained that the Embassy had called him to say that the Attaché was delayed. We should go ahead, rather than wait for him. Apparently, the sponsor of guests had to accompany them. That girl at the Embassy knew all the ins-and-outs. I must thank her.

After we were seated, we each went to the restroom to freshen up. I was already at our table when Anezka reappeared. She looked charming and I told her so. I asked her to make the dinner selection for both of us.

"I see the special for the day is venison steak with *Spätzle*. What a surprise! This was one of the main features of the place I worked in Bavaria during the summer. I want to see whether it is as good as what was served there. Are you game?"

"What a coincidence. That was the meal we had when they took me to that place in the Bavarian Forest. Let's try it, but don't tell me I have to drink beer, I want some wine."

She laughed. When the waiter took our order, I asked why Charles University served a typical Bavarian dish. He explained that the chef was a Bavarian. It was featured at least once a month. Most of the professors loved it.

"You will like the taste."

I asked him what wine would go well with it. He pointed to a row of cabinets at a wall. He explained that most of the steady guests kept a selection of wines in their cabinet. We should go over and select one in the Colonel's cabinet. Anezka asked him to pick one out for us which would go with our dinner.

The food was excellent. I thought it was even better than what was served in Bavaria. Anezka agreed. We loved the meal and the wine. She was disinclined to order dessert. I agreed; enough is enough.

I could tell that Anezka enjoyed both the food and the company. She took my arm as we walked to the parking lot.

When we got into the car, Anezka said she really did not want dessert anyway. She had baked a cheesecake the way she had learned in Bavaria. She was anxious to find out how well she had succeeded. Did I have room to try it?

"You should know that if there is an offer like this, I can't refuse. I'd be delighted to taste it and give you an expert opinion."

After we had entered her apartment, she asked me to excuse her while she quickly changed into something more relaxing. I asked her if I could take off my jacket and remove the tie. She said to go ahead and make myself comfortable. I sat on the couch, glancing at some magazines on the end table. As it turned out, her quick change took 15 minutes. She came out in a colorful house dress and a rearranged hairdo. I gave her an admiring look; I'm sure she noticed.

She suggested we sit down and gossip, unless I was ready for dessert. After talking to Uncle Eduard, it occurred to me that maybe there was somebody in the Czech Ministry of Defense who knew whether there were any retired records on the Underground/OSS activities. Did she have any contacts who might be able to help? She doubted that her uncle had any connections. She thought I should approach the Military Attaché to see if he could get any leads. He must have some friendly acquaintances with whom he deals. I thanked her for an excellent suggestion.

I told her how much I appreciated her interest and help. Carla had mentioned the completion date of the editing process was not far off. I could return to the States in a few days. She and her staff had already planned a farewell party. I hoped to be able to spend more time with Anezka. Maybe if she had the time, she would show me some of the countryside.

Anezka said she would be delighted to spend more time with me. However, she was on the audit team of her bank. They were scheduled to visit several bank branches in the provinces. They would probably start tomorrow and would not return before I had left.

While we were sitting there, I felt that I was getting tired. I did not want to appear like an old man. I asked Anezka for a big favor; could I take a quick shower to become rejuvenated?

"I noticed you were getting sleepy. After all you had a busy day. You are most welcome to shower. Let me go into the bathroom, take out my stuff hanging there and fix the shower curtains."

I followed her to see if I could help. After having removed some underclothing which was hung up to dry, she climbed on the rim of the tub to straighten out the shower curtain. I noticed that she was losing her balance as she was grabbing the curtain rod. I quickly stepped up, using both hands to support her. I noticed her dress had become loose, exposing part of her body.

As I pulled her off the rim I inadvertently touched her breast. When she finally got down and turned towards me, I could not resist hugging her tightly and kissing her. She was flushed and I felt the firmness of her nipples against my chest. She did not say anything or attempt to withdraw. Instead, after unbuttoning my shirt, she started to breathe rapidly and kissed me fervently. I think we both had reached a point-of-no-return. Who needs a shower when one is fully alert and highly stimulated?

Anezka pulled me into her bedroom. I completed removing her dress, unbuttoned the bra and kissed her from head to toe. At the same time she pulled down my pants and gently stroked my organ, which had already come to life.

As she was dragging me toward the bed, I removed the rest of my clothes. Nothing was said between us. We were fully occupied exploring each other's bodies. I don't remember exactly what happened on the bed. I left all the initiative to her. The climax came when she was moving rapidly on top of me. When we were lying side-by-side, I started to tell her how good I felt. But she put her finger on my mouth. I soon drifted off into a deep sleep. When I woke up I checked my watch and saw that it was already three o'clock in the morning.

Anezka was also stirring. I turned to kiss her when I felt her right hand stroking my body. I still was not fully alert and gladly would have gone back to sleep. But she was wide awake and wanted me again. After playing with me for a while, finally she succeeded in getting me a hard-on. This time I slowly explored all the niches of her body. She became very animated and pulled me on top of her. I slowly penetrated her. She suddenly cried out, "Now!"

Around seven in the morning, I woke up and heard Anezka working in the kitchen. This time I got into the shower and came out like a new man. After I dressed I went into the kitchen. Anezka was fully dressed. She smiled and gave me a hearty kiss. She hoped I had recovered and was ready for breakfast.

After we had stacked the dishes, we went down to the car. When we reached the movie trailer, Anezka hugged me. I gave her my home phone number, inviting her to visit me. She said, "Perhaps I can make it. I have always wanted to visit America."

My last days at the trailer passed quickly. Carla had a deadline to meet. I spent most of the day with her on the final touches. On the day before I left, she and her crew cooked up a buffet on tables outside the trailer. Everyone had brought a dish. I tasted a variety of Czech specialties.

The next morning Gunther picked me up for the ride to the airport. I thanked him for all the help he had extended. As I was leaving the car, I pressed a bunch of dollar bills into his hand. He appeared embarrassed, but I insisted.

At the airport, I remembered that I had forgotten to thank the secretary at the embassy for getting me into the executive dining room at Charles University. I called her and, while chatting, I inquired why Lucy, the Colonel's wife, was still in the States. Her response revealed that Lucy and the Colonel had been separated since last year. Apparently, they had been drifting apart for some time. Lucy was now working at the State Department in Washington.

I had an uneventful flight back; picked up a cab at the airport and soon was back in good old Silver Spring.

CHAPTER 3

SECURITY CONCERN

I WAS SURPRISED HOW neat everything was inside my house. I expected to see a lot of dust on the furniture and mail strewn around the front door. Instead, there was a lived-in look, everything neat and clean. I found the answer to this puzzle on the kitchen table. My neighbor left a note explaining when she checked the house she was appalled by the mess. She hoped I would not mind sending her cleaning lady over to straighten things out.

I should have told her about my having neglected doing these chores before I went away. I didn't have the time then. I was going to do a thorough job when I got back.

It was late in the afternoon, and I was getting hungry. The car started up all right. First I went to the grocery to buy some basics, then I stopped off at my favorite Italian restaurant where I enjoyed a good meal. At the nearby county liquor store I bought a bottle of the same brand of white wine my neighbor had served when I had dropped over for a drink a few weeks ago. I went over to thank her and, before leaving, I squeezed a twenty dollar bill, for the cleaning woman, in her hand.

After putting the groceries in the fridge, I hit the hay. I slept soundly. The next morning I called my office to check in. Amy welcomed me back. Apparently my lecture on office manners had sunk in. This time there were no uncalled-for remarks. Bob MacMerial had just arrived.

I quickly brought him up to date on my lightning fast, but successful, career as a movie production expert. I related the rewarding visit I had with the former member of the World War II Czech Underground who had known my father.

After telling Bob about my dad's as yet unfound files for this period, I asked for a delay in my return to duty. I needed a few days to search for the missing file cabinet. I was so curious I did not want to delay it.

Bob was aware of the close relationship I had had with my father as well as his record as an intelligence operative during the war.

"Keef, I fully understand your anxiety to see what is in those files. You should get the time to review them. However, unfortunately, I can't spare you right now. Something has come up. As they say, the files won't run away. As soon as this priority situation has been cleaned up, you may take all the time off you need."

"Bob, I agree with you. This can wait. Do you want me to come in right away?"

"No, come in tomorrow morning. You and Henry Kelly, the fellow you worked with in Munich, will be on this case together."

"Ok, Bob, see you tomorrow. Make sure the coffee is hot!"

Henry Kelly and Bob were already imbibing when I arrived. Handing me a cup, Bob said, "Let me get right to the point. Yesterday I had a call from the G-2 of the Army Central Command at Fort McPherson in Georgia. They need our help in running down a potential problem involving a soldier attached to a reserve unit at Camp Blanding, Florida.

The G-2 said, "I know you are puzzled about why I contacted you. Let me summarize. Our MIS detachment is currently involved in a complicated investigation. All their personnel are tied up. I called INSCOM for help. They referred me to you.

"I have faxed you the details. Hope you can help us out. I will be in touch in case there are any new developments."

Bob then proceeded. "Here is what he sent me. Read it and we will see what comes next."

He handed us copies of the fax.

"Sgt. James Hunter is a member of a reserve unit at Orlando, Florida, which trains a couple of times a year at Camp Blanding, near Jacksonville. Hunter was called for active duty about eight months ago by the Army Central Command. He is an expert on special weapons. They shipped him to Afghanistan where he served as an instructor for a company which has been earmarked to remain there for a while.

"Hunter was there for six months. According to his efficiency rating he did a good job. Upon his return to Central Command, he was given a special assignment. This came about when the G-3 received a call from a friend of his, Major Smythe, who is serving as an advisor to Army reserve units in Brooklyn. Major Smythe wanted someone who had special weapons experience to spend a week with one of the reserve units being called for active duty.

"Hunter went to New York. Although they had arranged quarters for him, he declined, saying he would rather stay with friends. While Hunter was with the reserve unit, he was observed to be in contact with individuals who had been under surveillance by the FBI's New York counterintelligence section. The nature of the involvement is not clear. Was he being recruited by this group? Was he already a member? Was he not involved at all and just friends with one of its members? These are the questions we need to have answered.

"In the meantime, Hunter has been released from active duty and has returned to reserve status with his unit in Orlando."

"Well," Bob told us, "this is the ball of wax. We will get right on it. You, Keef, will go up to New York to talk to Major Smythe and the FBI. When you return, we will plan the next move. It is likely that you and Henry will have to go to Florida to wind this up.

"Keef, you are off to New York tomorrow. Amy has made train reservations and she also reserved a room for you at a hotel in Brooklyn."

On my way out I checked with Amy. She had all the papers ready. A cab would pick me up at 8:30 to make the 10 o'clock train at Union Station. Amy also included the location of the Army base and Smythe's phone number.

The trip to New York was uneventful; no attractive females in sight with whom I could chat. I struck up a conversation with a gentleman sitting next me. He was a businessman, telling me he had been in Washington to check on the status of a government loan for a client whose company just got into energy conservation in the construction trade. Rather than risking a run-around at the Federal agency, he went up the Hill to see his Congressman. He hoped for an answer in a few days. I remarked that I was going to Brooklyn to check up on some personal matters. I asked him if the hotel where I planned to stay had a good reputation. He related hearing that the hotel had had some problem with room service, recommending my staying at a guest house which he used for his visiting clientele. It was near a subway stop.

I decided to follow his advice and went there instead of the hotel. I was shown a room which appeared OK. It featured a comfortable couch, a desk, a phone, a fridge, and a sink. The shower and toilet were down the hall. The woman who showed me the room told me that as there were only three guest rooms on the floor, accessibility to the toilet should not be a problem. I would have preferred bathroom facilities in the room, but except for this, I liked what I saw.

After I had settled in, I called Major Smythe. His line was busy. I left my number with the switchboard. He called me back.

"Mr. Keefer, thanks for your call. My friend at Central Command buzzed me yesterday, advising me to expect to hear from you."

"Major Smythe, should I come down to see you tomorrow?"

"Mr. Keefer, I would be glad to meet you. However, the little I know about this case, we can discuss over the phone. You should talk to the FBI agent. I called him this morning to tell him that you were coming here. As I told Central Command, I had no problems with Sgt. Hunter. He was always on time and had a good rapport with the unit he was instructing. There was nothing unusual until the FBI called me.

"Allan Graham, the FBI agent, told me how they became interested in Sgt. Hunter. The Defense Security Service, which investigates potential problems involving national security in companies holding Federal contracts, was keeping tabs on a group of individuals in the New York area who had been nosing around several firms engaged in the military hardware business. Thus far the Service had not yet determined who is behind this group. The Service suspects the most likely purpose is to sell information to industry competitors or to foreign governments. Perhaps there is also a connection with a foreign intelligence organization.

"At any rate, it seems that Sgt. Hunter was friends with a member of the group. Hunter met this individual for lunch, according to a

Defense Security Service agent who was shadowing this group. Hunter was in uniform. The agent decided to tail Hunter. When he saw that Hunter was going into the Brooklyn Army base, the agent called me to alert me of Hunter's friendship with one member of the group under surveillance. I then got in touch with my friend at Central Command, recommending that somebody should keep an eye on Hunter. Anyway, that's all I know. You should get in touch with the FBI agent for further details."

After concluding our conversation, I called the FBI. Fortunately, Allan Graham was at his office. I explained who I was and why I had come to New York. He suggested I meet him for lunch tomorrow at his building. I should call him from the lobby.

I did not realize how late it was getting. I had noticed a Hungarian restaurant down the street. After checking with the receptionist at the front desk about this place, I went there. The food was excellent, even better than my favorite place in Silver Spring. I had a sampler for dinner, topped off with a bottle of Mexican beer. Back at my room, I watched a cowboy movie on TV and soon went to bed.

The next morning, it was time to shed my travel fatigue. A good long shower was called for. I put on the robe hanging in the closet and went down the hall. The door was closed, but not locked. I went in and lo-and-behold there was a young woman standing, drying herself off. I quickly exited. I waited about ten minutes before re-entering.

I got dressed and went down to the dining room to try out breakfast, which was included in the room rate. I surveyed the room before entering. The only guest at the table was the female I had encountered in the shower. She was clean-looking, not bad looking, but much too young for me. I asked her whether I could join her, and she nodded. I apologized for barging in on her. She laughed, saying that it was her fault. She had forgotten to lock the door.

I started a conversation about how she liked the food. She responded that it was OK, better than what was served at the cafeterias. She had scrambled eggs with bacon on the side. I ordered the same. We talked a bit about innocuous things, such as the weather. As we were getting up from the table, I told her I needed exercise, would she like to join me for a run in the nearby park? She brightened up. Yes, that was a good idea. She needed to get off her butt. We agreed to meet in twenty minutes at the front door.

As we got going, I could see that she was a regular runner. After about twenty minutes, we took a break on a bench. She told me her name was Alice. She worked for a computer outfit in Richmond, Virginia, and was here on business. I mentioned I had come up from Washington to interview some people to staff a planned New York office. On the spur of the moment I thought I would bring up my contact with the Brooklyn Army base.

"Alice, I am staying in Brooklyn because an acquaintance had told me about a soldier at the base who impressed him. He suggested that I interview him. He was a reservist who lived down South, but was looking for a better job. Regretfully, he had completed the assignment and left for his home today. So I missed him."

"Mr. Keefer, that is really interesting. Carrie, a girl who works with me in Richmond wanted to introduce me to her brother, James, who was on a temporary assignment at the Brooklyn Army base. My friend, by the way, recommended that I stay at this place. But I got tied up with my job. I did not have time to meet him."

"Alice, what good luck that I ran into you! Is the last name of your friend's brother, by any chance, Hunter?"

"That's him! What a small world this is!"

"Where does James live? Maybe I will contact him. I am scheduled for a business trip to Florida when I get finished here."

"His home is in Orlando. You'll probably find him listed in the phone book. If you ever see him, tell him I regret not having the time to check in with him. I am sure his sister had alerted him that I might contact him while he was in New York."

We then ran another ten minutes before returning to the guest house. I thanked her for keeping me company. I suggested she relate our meeting to her co-worker so she could let her brother know that I might call him. We hugged before we parted.

The following morning I slept late. After taking another long shower I had a leisurely breakfast. I decided to do a little sight-seeing. I paid my bill and took the subway downtown. The New York subway rider is strictly a mind-my-own-business entity. He either stares straight ahead or hides behind a newspaper. I had an hour to kill before my meeting, so I walked around window-shopping.

Allan Graham was waiting for me in the lobby. He was a middle-aged trim individual dressed in the FBI uniform, the dark business suit with a conservative necktie. His shoes were spick-and-span, reflecting the sunlight as we passed a window. He took me to what he called a private dining room, which was actually an area off the cafeteria. A waitress showed up as soon as we sat down. Allan ordered for both of us, namely the daily special; a veal stew, side-ordered with French fries. I declined a beer and settled for iced tea. Allan took the day's special, a draft.

While we were eating, Allan described what he knew about Sgt. Hunter. "While the Defense Security Service was investigating the group's interest in defense industry companies, I checked up on Hunter's activities in the New York area. The FBI took this on to ascertain whether Hunter was by any chance involved with anyone engaged in espionage. We followed him for several days to see who his contacts were. Other than people he was working with or training, he was not in touch with anyone except, of course, the guy he was staying with.

"We weren't able to eavesdrop on his conversations with his friend. Thus far, there is only a suspicion that he may be feeding military information to his friend or that he could be an active key member of the group the Defense Security Service is concerned about.

"Usually, when someone in the military is under suspicion, the FBI depends on the Pentagon to make a preliminary check. That is why Major Smythe at the Brooklyn Army base contacted the Central Command and you got involved. We can cut out a lot of red tape by your staying in touch with me directly, including what, if anything, you uncover."

"Thanks, Allan, I get the picture. It is, of course, our business to know if, and when, a soldier is under suspicion by a civilian agency. I am glad I came up here, even though I was of the opinion that much of the information I gathered here in New York could have been transmitted by fax and by telephone. However, I personally prefer to make person-to-person contacts.

"I also got a lucky break by running into someone who has some personal knowledge of Sgt. Hunter."

I then related my encounter with Alice, who was supposed to date her friend's brother, namely Sgt. Hunter.

Allan said, "It was a lucky break meeting Alice. It should greatly enhance your approach to Sgt. Hunter. You just have to dream up a good cover story for the trip to Orlando.

As we were leaving the cafeteria, Allan wanted to treat me. I responded that I had heard the FBI was always short on funds. So we split the bill. I told him to relate to his supervisor how he was saving the Bureau's cash. I had heard that FBI employee efficiency reports covered the smallest details. Allan laughed heartily and thanked me for looking out for him. Before leaving, I asked the waitress to get me a doggie bag with a turkey sandwich and potato chips to take with me on my trip back to Washington.

I took a cab to Penn Station and hopped on a train leaving for Washington.

I planned to make a draft of my doings in New York on the train. To keep the bureaucracy happy I would include all the expenses I had incurred. Bob MacMerial would be pleased if I walked in tomorrow with the trip report ready for Amy and her computer. I got in late, took a cab home, briefly checked the mail, which included the usual bills, and went to bed.

CHAPTER 4

TRAIL LEADS TO ORLANDO

I WOKE UP LATE the next morning. When I called Bob, he answered the phone. He told me that Amy was running errands on the post.

"Bob, I had an interesting trip with some leads to follow up on. If you agree, let me fax my trip report. Amy can finalize it. After you have read it, and you concur, I will fly to Orlando tomorrow. Ask Amy to cut travel orders and arrange for the flight. Return trip should remain open. Also, authorize my renting a car there."

"Glad you got back in one piece. I am tied up with meetings all day. That's what happens in the government when you are the boss. Of course, you may run down to Orlando. Amy, as you know, handled travel at the Post G-1. So we are in good hands as far as that goes. Other than being negligent as far as military courtesy goes, she is getting into the groove. She will call you later."

Late in the afternoon, Amy buzzed me. "Welcome back. I finished your trip report. Colonel MacMerial had a little time and glanced over it. He asked Henry Kelly to go with you to Orlando. The Colonel thinks there will be enough work for both of you. I booked two tickets on a flight departing from National at 10:00. A car will pick you up at 8:30. Agent Kelly will meet you at the airport. I will fax the details to you."

"Thank you, Amy. Also, don't forget we need a car."

After we had boarded the flight I discussed my trip to New York with Henry. When we get to Orlando I would call the major who I had dealt with in the Army Chief of Staff's office in the Pentagon. I mentioned him in my final report on the investigation that I pursued last year for the Joint Chiefs of Staff (JCS). The major told me at our last meeting that he was being transferred to G-2 of Central Command at Fort McPherson in Atlanta.

"Yes, I remember him from reading your report. Why would he know anything about the potential problem with Sgt. Hunter in Orlando?"

"You may recall that I mentioned in my report how the major finally became very cooperative in spite of his friendship with Lt. Colonel Alicia Gouperz."

"I don't recall all of the details. Fill me in on Colonel Gouperz."

"She was our detachment commander, but was working with G-2 in the Military District of Washington. When I was picked by the JCS to check out their problems concerning the security leaks, Alicia became directly involved. Finally, she was kicked out of the Army because of her adverse involvement in the JCS case."

"Yeah, now I remember. She was being blackmailed by a former Russian agent."

Upon arrival in Orlando, we picked up the vehicle Amy had ordered, a medium-sized sedan. Amy had used her noodle to get us something better than a smaller car. We went over to the Travelers' Aid Desk to get a recommendation on a centrally located motel, a medium-sized one with a restaurant on the premises.

Life keeps getting more and more complicated. The rental office at the airport no longer provides the car in front of the terminal. Now you have to take a bus to near the airport exit to pick it up there. Ours was ready. It was spick-and-span, but had a few dents which I pointed out to the rental agent. He showed me the agreement I had signed. It noted the dents.

After exiting the airport road we finally got to I-4 which took us downtown. Soon we approached the motel. They gave us the military rate and we signed up for a week. The room was pleasant enough. We were getting hungry. The dining room was only open in the evening, but there was a coffee shop.

After coffee, I called the information desk of Central Command. After explaining to the operator who I was, I told her I needed to get in touch with the major who had been transferred from the Pentagon to G-2. She did not know who I was talking about and connected me with G-2. A female sergeant answered. I gave her the same story. She knew right away.

"You want Lt. Colonel Al King. He just a got a promotion. I'll connect you."

"Al, this is Kevin Keefer from MIS in Washington. Do you remember me? We had several meetings at the Pentagon when I was on a JCS case. Congratulations on the promotion!"

"Of course, I remember. What prompts your call?"

"I, and another agent, Henry Kelly, had to run down to Orlando to investigate a security problem. Your office had requested assistance from the Intelligence Command at Fort Belvoir. They passed the buck to us.

"It involves Sgt. James Hunter of an Army Reserve unit in Orlando. He was sent to New York on temporary duty to advise a unit in Brooklyn on special weapons."

"Oh, yes, I am very familiar with this. I don't know whether it is actually serious enough for two agents being sent down here. Anyhow, the weather is nice. You can make a vacation out of it.

"And one never knows what turns up. Just look at the JCS situation you got dragged into. By the way, I have some news of interest to you. Guess who now lives in Orlando? None other than Alicia Gouperz and her sidekick Annette Moez. Alicia found a niche. She has contracts on security policy with some of the military commands down here. Right now she is working on one for us. We are still friends. Annette is an English teacher at an Orlando high school. Isn't it a small world?"

"Al, nothing surprises me anymore. I hope you are right that the James Hunter case can be wrapped up soon. I am anxious to get back to Washington. I talked Bob MacMerial, who took Alicia's spot as our CO, into approving a special assignment for me. It deals with a top secret WWII mission in which my father participated. Until he died, he was struggling to find out the background of this venture. I now want to pursue this where he left off.

"I would not be surprised if somehow his records ended up in the Pentagon. I recall his being there during the year he passed away. When I get back I hope to start cracking on this. Do you have any suggestions as to who may be able to tell me where his papers ended up?"

"Keef, the only thing I can think of is that your former secretary, Eloise, may have some ideas. Through my contacts in my old office I learned that Eloise is doing a terrific job in the Pentagon intelligence bureaucracy. She may be able to steer you to the right place."

"Al, this is an excellent idea. I will call her when I get back. As far as the Hunter case goes, can you brief me on anything to give me a head start?"

"I don't have much information on what the FBI in New York has compiled. I made some confidential inquiries with Camp Blanding where Hunter's unit does its field training. They told me he had a good reputation. This leads me to suggest that you take the bull by the horns. Contact Hunter directly. By emphasizing that Washington has concerns about this, he may be impressed to come clean."

"Thanks, I will follow up and let you know the outcome. I would like to surprise Alicia. What is her phone number?"

After he gave me the number, I ended the call with, "Thanks, Al! It was nice to renew our acquaintance."

I briefed Henry on the gist of my conversation with Al King, explaining how I got to know him.

I asked Henry if he was agreeable to our getting together with Alicia and Annette. Having read my final report on the JCS case, Henry knew something about the roles they played. He told me he was very interested in meeting the two, especially Alicia.

I called Alicia after lunch. She was surprised to hear from me. I explained there was really no enmity between us. Since my partner and I were in Orlando on a case, I thought it would be nice if we could get together for dinner this evening. Annette could also join us, if she was so inclined. Alicia was curious about how I knew they were in Orlando. I related my conversation with Al King, who was connected with this case we were investigating.

She was free that evening. She could join me and my partner for dinner. She would check with Annette. I wanted to try out the motel dining room. Inviting her and Annette to meet us there at 7:00, I rang off. Henry and I spent the rest of the afternoon at the pool.

Just before 7:00, we went down to the lobby to meet Alicia. She showed up on time. She looked pretty much the same, except for the Florida tan. I hugged her and introduced Henry. She looked him over. Apparently she was pleased with what she saw and also gave him a hug. Henry was surprised, but appeared to welcome the gesture. Alicia mentioned that Annette agreed to join us. At that moment Annette walked toward us. She looked more relaxed than the last time we had met. After introducing Henry, we walked into the dining room.

Alicia monopolized the conversation, devoting most of it to Henry. This came about when Henry explained that while in Munich he handled several contracts dealing with security matters. Annette and I were quietly eating our dinners. We were amused to see the interaction between the two. We skipped dessert. Alicia invited us to their place. Speaking for Annette as well as myself, I declined. Alicia turned to Henry, suggesting that he might want to look at some of the problems she had encountered in her contracts.

After Alicia and Henry left us, I chuckled, "Looks like you are stuck with me!"

Annette giggled, "I am tired of Alicia's talking about her workload. Let Henry be the target."

I laughed that on the basis of my experience with Alicia, they wouldn't spend all of their time talking shop.

Annette suggested that we take in a movie she wanted to see. We hopped into her car. The theater was on the outskirts of Orlando. It was an interesting murder mystery. Afterwards we stopped off at a nearby café for dessert.

"Keef, how long do you think Alicia and Henry spent talking contracts?"

"Maybe twenty minutes. As you know, I have had my experience with Alicia. She probably romanced him initially, then she will try to find out what we are actually doing in Orlando. She is naturally nosey. Perhaps she can learn something useful in bidding for another contract."

"You may be right. Alicia has really morphed into a business woman. Also she is getting more heterosexual. Whether this is her conscious motivation or a ploy in her role as a professional business female seeking out male business contacts, I don't know. We are still good friends but less than partners. I have gotten over it and have found other outlets for my needs."

"I suspected you two were no longer as tight as in the past. As they say, 'nothing remains the same in the long run'."

Annette drove me back to the motel. I thanked her for an enjoyable evening. As I expected, Henry had not returned. Maybe Alicia gave him the full works. But that did not materialize. I watched television for a couple of hours and Henry walked in. He gave me a summary of his experience with Alicia. Just as I had anticipated, they initially talked about his work in Munich. Then they had a couple of drinks and Alicia moved in on him. When he got ready to go further, Alicia wanted another drink. While they were imbibing cocktails, their conversation drifted into what we were doing in Orlando.

"I saw no harm in briefly mentioning your trip to New York and the need to tie up some loose ends in the Orlando area. She tried to ferret out what we hoped to accomplish here. I then began to continue our physical contact, but somehow the chemistry between us had declined, as least as far as I was concerned. It seemed to me that she was disappointed that she was unable to squeeze more information out of me. At any rate, I decided to terminate this game, thanked her for her hospitality, and told her we had a busy day tomorrow. She offered to drive me to the motel. I declined, telling her it was too late for her to be running around. I had no trouble finding a cab. They charge outrageous fares here."

After breakfast we discussed our next moves. I was in favor of following Al King's suggestion to establish direct contact with our target, Sgt. James Hunter. I called him and explained how I got to him, mentioning that a girl I ran into was a friend of his sister in Richmond, who worked for the same firm this woman was with. I had told her that I was going to Orlando on business. I thought he might be able to give me some suggestions regarding contacts I wanted to make in Orlando. Hunter said he had expected my call as his sister had alerted him. He said he did not know how he could help me, but would be glad to meet. He also told me that his sister was in Orlando for a couple of days, on temporary duty for her company, which had an office in Orlando.

I suggested that if he had the time we could get together that evening. I would call him in the afternoon to firm it up. I also would like to talk to his sister and thank her for telling him about me. Hunter gave me her work number.

After I hung up, Henry and I made plans for the day. I would try to get ahold of Hunter's sister. Perhaps she knew something I could use in my approach with Hunter. While I was working on this angle, Henry could pursue information about Hunter from various sources. After calling Al King at the Army Central Command to obtain the name and phone number of the CO of Hunter's reserve unit, Henry should contact him. He should also visit the police headquarters to see if they had anything on Hunter and follow up on any leads. I would leave a message for him of my progress, if any. He could use our car. Instead of relying on cabs, I would rent a second car.

Instead of going back to the room, Henry went for a 5-mile run. He said he needed to clear his head after last night's adventure with Alicia. I went ahead with calling Carrie, Hunter's sister.

"This is Kevin Keefer. While in New York on business I ran into a friend of yours, Alice. She mentioned your brother, who she had expected to meet, but he had returned to Orlando before she could. Well, I am down here for a couple of days and I called your brother. He told me that you are here too on business. I want to thank you for telling your brother that I might contact him. Alice said we had lots in common; would like to have lunch with you, if possible."

"Yes, Mr. Keefer, my brother mentioned you. Sure, I'll be glad to get together. The trouble is I don't know how much time I have. I am trying to wind up my work here. However, there is a solution. We have an executive dining room in the building where I will be during the lunch hour. Why don't you stop off here around noon? Can you make it?"

"I will see you there at noon."

"Thank you, see you later."

I had about two hours to kill. So on the spur of the moment, I called Allan Graham, the FBI agent in New York. Fortunately, he was at his desk. I told him I was in Orlando on the James Hunter matter. I had made contact with Hunter and planned to have a so-called social visit this evening. I wanted to check with him on whether there was anything new on this on his end. Allan said he has had some contacts with the Defense Security Service. They advised him that there is something going on with that gang in Brooklyn which has drawn their interest. Two defense industry companies had received some mysterious inquiries regarding contracts from an unknown party. Tracing the calls had met with no success. They were made from a public phone in Brooklyn. The companies were playing along to get an idea about who was behind all of this. I thanked Allan for the update.

I found a parking space in front of Carrie's building. I was in a playful mode. Instead of putting quarters in the meter I attached my "Official" office parking card, with an underlined phrase, "Please waive parking regulations while occupant is on official business." The receptionist escorted me to the inner sanctum where Carrie was supposed to be. A man working on his computer advised me that Carrie had gone to the executive dining room. I walked up and found the place. As I entered, a young woman approached me.

"I am Carrie, you must be Mr. Keefer."

"That's right, but please call me Keef."

"What a coincidence, you are another person who likes to shorten names. Mine is actually Caroline. Thanks for coming up. I wanted to check out whether they had the ingredients for a special salad I like. Sometimes they don't have the time to make it up. Why don't you make yourself comfortable while I go back to the salad chef."

Watching her walk back, I could only approve of what I saw. Carrie looked like she was in her thirties, sporting a nice figure. I would not say she was a beauty, but she had a pleasant face and certainly all her body parts were in the right places.

When Carrie returned, she said we were all set, and recommended the Reuben sandwich on rye with a side of grits for me. During lunch Carrie told me she was almost finished here. I told her of my plans for dinner with her brother and invited her to join us. She seemed pleasantly surprised and said she would love to come. I told her brother I would call him with the details after they were firmed up.

Carrie walked with me out of the building. She wanted to "stretch her legs." As we approached my car I saw a ticket on the windshield. I showed Carrie my "official" parking permit. She laughed. She was not surprised. Half the meter maids were poor in English and the other half didn't know "shit from Shinola."

Telling her to have a nice walk, I gave her a hug and went to my car. At this point I viewed Carrie in a new light. It occurred to me that if somehow I could get closer to her, I might be able to find out more about her brother. Perhaps he had confided in her about his contacts in NY. Also there might have been other recent events in which he had been approached or which he initiated to trade in on any military subjects he knew about.

Although I was never involved in anything like this before, I had heard of other investigators having engaged in affairs with female friends or relatives to uncover information. Inasmuch as Carrie was attractive, I could also have some fun as a side benefit. It was worth exploring.

When I got back to the motel, I started to head to the pool. Henry showed up and joined me. He had been unable to connect with the CO of Hunter's unit. He had a civilian job at Camp Blanding and was out for the day, but Henry made an appointment to see him tomorrow. The police department was cooperative. Other than two traffic tickets there was nothing else on Hunter, except there was an entry that an inquiry had been made a few days ago by the Army. Henry speculated it was someone from the G-2 section from Central Command.

As we passed the front office, I noticed this nice young girl who had checked us in. I approached her and asked whether she could help us out. We had a dinner invitation that evening and I was wondering whether she could join us. I had a date, but my partner did not. It would be much nicer if he could also have one. The girl told me that her name was Annabelle, and she would love to join us. She would be off soon.

As we were starting toward the pool, I received a call from Hunter. His sister had called him and she would pick us up in about an hour. Well, no swim now.

Before going up to the room, I asked Annabelle whether she could join us in about an hour or so. She said her relief would show up in a few minutes. Fortunately, the cleaner had just returned one of her dresses, so she did not have to return home first. I told her no change was necessary, as there was nothing formal about the dinner. We were just going to a neighborhood restaurant. Annabelle insisted on changing. She wanted to get out of what she wore at work.

Henry was delighted when I told him that he had a dinner date. He had not paid attention to the girl at the desk, but now he gave her another look.

He turned to me. "Keef, anything is a plus after my experience last night!"

After introducing Annabelle and Henry to Carrie, we hopped into her rental car. Hunter was downstairs waiting for us. He squeezed into the front seat and directed us to a Tex-Mex place which was one of his favorites. We found a large corner booth. I was fascinated that there also was a good selection of American food, as I was not overly fond of Mexican dishes. For drinks I ordered a bottle of red wine for the girls while the boys went for beers.

The food was excellent. I thanked Hunter for taking us to this place. Hunter apologized that his conversation had been monopolized with Carrie. They had not seen each other for quite a while. Annabelle and Henry seemed to hit it off. Everybody enjoyed themselves, including me just observing the others. Toward the end of the evening, I finally got a word in edgewise with Hunter. I made an appointment with him for breakfast the following morning. On the way home, while Annabelle and Henry were eying each other in the back seat, I finally could chat with Carrie. She told me that first she had to tie up a few odds and ends. If I was free tomorrow afternoon, she would pick me up at her brother's house and take me for a little sight-seeing. I should bring swim trunks along in case it was beach weather. I thanked her for the reminder.

After we dropped off Annabelle we returned to the motel. Henry told Carrie how nice it had been to meet her and went inside. Before I got out, Carrie gave me her card on which she wrote directions to her brother's place so I would not get lost. She also thanked me for the enjoyable meal and leaned over to give me a kiss on the cheek. Before

I could respond she pushed me out, saying she had to get back to her office to line up a few things for tomorrow.

When I wandered into the room, Henry expressed his delight at having met Annabelle. She was off tomorrow. He would drive to Camp Blanding early in the morning. It would probably take him 5 hours for the round trip. As I had returned the second rental, he would drop me off at Hunter's place on the way. He did not anticipate that his business at the base would take too long. He would be back around 1 or so. Then Annabelle would pick him up to take him sight-seeing in the area. I told him not to wait for me for dinner, as I hoped for a nice evening with Carrie. He wished me luck.

Henry dropped me off at Hunter's place early in the morning. I rang the bell and Hunter came down. I asked him whether he had had breakfast. He had not. We went to a nearby place where he said we could talk at leisure. While we were eating I went right to the core of my trip to Orlando.

"Hunter, may I be frank with you as to why I contacted you, other than the referral from your missed date in New York?"

"By all means, do. I suspected your interest in me was not entirely social."

"OK, then, I won't shock you when I relate what brought me here."

I then told him that I was an investigator for the Army. I had been sent to New York to check out his involvement with a group in Brooklyn who had persistently made contact with private companies holding Army contracts. These firms became leery of these inquiries and alerted the Army. An investigation was initiated. He was observed having a relationship with one of the guys in the group. As he was on active duty at the time, the Army had ordered my unit to check him out.

"James, I need to know how you got involved in this."

"Keef, I am surprised how a simple effort by some people to just obtain some information on defense contracts mushroomed into involvement of Army Intelligence all the way in Washington."

"James, just tell me how you became a part of all this."

"My friend in New York knew, of course, of my Army connection. I suspect being sent to New York as an instructor impressed him and his group. They apparently believed I could somehow help them in making connections with these companies. My friend sold me a bill of goods. He convinced me that their scheme, while somewhat insidious, was not really breaking any laws.

"He told me that once they had established contacts with the companies, they could sell the information they were acquiring to what he called 'potential clients.' He was not specific on this."

"Did you, at any time, suspect that foreign governments may be on the receiving end?"

"Keef, this never occurred to me. I thought they would pawn off their acquired data to commercial competitors."

"James, I can see your line of thinking. But the Army has deduced that even if it started out that way, it could evolve into an espionage pattern. That, of course, has to be stopped before it comes to realization."

"I can see what all this could lead to. I really believed it was just a bunch of guys trying cleverly to obtain inside know-how on commercial intelligence which they could sell to other defense industry firms. I speculated they wanted me to tip them off as to who they could offer what they had. My friend knew that I was with Central Command and could steer them to likely customers. As you know, I am looking for a job. This scheme could temporarily help me out. I realize that I did not think much about potential pitfalls. Now I recognize that I exposed myself to trouble."

"You are in trouble. I am sure they will pull your security clearance. I hope they don't kick you out. There is a lot of potential in the Army. I will send my report to New York where they will deal with your friend and his gang. As far as you are concerned, the report will also go to Central Command. They will call you in before they take any action. I strongly urge you to come clean and give them your full cooperation. Informally, I will recommend to my G-2 contact at Central Command to give you a break. Of course, I don't know how they will proceed."

"Keef, I will come clean on this. I will greatly appreciate your efforts to get me back on a straight path. Do you recommend I contact Central Command?"

"No, just keep your nose clean. They will call on you soon. In the meantime, redouble your efforts to get a decent job. Perhaps ask your sister to arrange for an interview with her Orlando office. Tell her you would settle for an internship. I would not say anything about your problem with Central Command. I doubt that this would come up. Anyway, if it does surface, it may not prevent your getting an interview."

"Thanks for the advice."

We walked back to his house. Lo and behold, there was Carrie waiting for me.

After exchanging greetings with her brother, she rolled the top down and patted on the front seat. Then we took off. I asked her whether she had completed her work.

"Of course, otherwise I would not be here on time."

Now I had a chance to look her over. She was dressed like a Florida vacationer. She wore shorts. I looked down and saw that her legs could use a little sun.

"Don't worry, we will get plenty of fresh air. The weather is turning gorgeous this afternoon. Our office manager recommended a nice beach spot about an hour from here. I think we will skip the sight-seeing I had planned if the weather turned out to be cloudy. By the way, what did you two talk about? James looked somewhat withdrawn."

"We had a good talk. It was something that he may or may not discuss with you. But it should turn out to be OK. Don't worry about it. It's all Army business. I actually work for a Pentagon office. I came down here to straighten out something he was mixed up with. I suggest you not press him about it. He is a big boy and will take care of it."

Carrie seemed to have absorbed what I related. She turned to me.

"I instinctively felt that you and my brother were in on something. I learned a long time ago that reticence often is superior to inquisitiveness. I thought there was more to you than a regular business type. At any rate, I am intrigued."

"Carrie, as I said before, don't worry about a thing. I am really a regular guy. I am most grateful for you spending some time with me."

Sure enough, her previous somewhat-worrisome look disappeared. It was replaced by her usual friendly composure which had attracted me when we first met.

I was delighted when we reached the beach. It turned out to be rather small and truly was a hidden spot. There were only a few people besides us. We parked the car near a bunch of trees. Carrie opened the trunk, got a blanket and a picnic basket full of goodies. I was pleasantly surprised. There was a selection of sandwiches and soft drinks, plus the inevitable potato chips. After our fill, we relaxed on the blanket, taking in the warm sun. Naturally, I drifted into a nap, but Carrie shook me.

"I didn't take you to the beach to snore away. Let's hit the water."

We changed into our bathing gear, she grabbed my arm, and we galloped into the water. That really woke me up. It was cold, but after a while I got used to it. We battled the incoming waves for a few hundred feet, and then we finally were in water deep enough to swim. Carrie was an excellent swimmer. She told me she had been a lifeguard at the community pool back home.

I told her, "I sort of feel weak, could you support me?"

She laughed. "Let me try."

Carrie got partially under me and treaded water. I played lifeless. It felt good to have her arms round me.

Suddenly, she said, "Demonstration is over! Let's swim to the pier to our left."

We found a small ladder at the end. I pushed her up. She then pulled me up. Our bodies met as I got onto the pier and I squeezed her. She laughed as our lips touched. We sat down, dangling our feet into the water. I asked her to turn toward me. I wanted to brush her hair from her face. That is when I gave her my first kiss, which had a lot of heat in it. She kissed me back. As we embraced more tightly, my hands wandered to explore.

Carrie got all flushed. "Not here, I see people in that boat are watching us!"

We swam back to the beach. Carrie pointed to the sun, which was westward. She urged that we should start going back as it was at least a two-hour ride.

On the way back I could not take my eyes off her. I blurted out that this was the most pleasant afternoon I had spent in a long time. I felt things stirring up inside me which had been dormant.

"Carrie, I really enjoyed the afternoon. Thank you!"

After a long silence, Carrie chimed in, "I also enjoyed your company!"

"I know we are two different people, each of us have our individual traits. I think we just hit it off."

Then she turned towards me with a lingering smile. "I do hope that maybe this will turn out good for both of us. Instead of going back to your motel, why don't you come with me for supper? I am staying at the house of a woman in the office. She left for a vacation this morning. I am house-sitting for her. There is a veal roast in her fridge which she told me to cook before it goes bad. Are you going to join me?"

"Of course, thanks for the invite."

I helped her unload when we pulled up at the house. She went to the kitchen, telling me she would place the roast into the oven. She was instructed to use a low heat, so it should be done in about two hours. In the meantime, she would take a shower to get rid of the salt water. Telling her I thought the ocean was good for her skin, she laughed. A few minutes later, I decided to play the Good Samaritan by volunteering to wash her back. She did not notice me enter.

"Carrie, I see you have trouble getting the sand off your back. Please give me your wash cloth." Apparently not thinking much about it, she turned half-way and gave me the sponge she had been using. I gently applied it and gradually moved my effort towards her front.

"Keef, that is enough. I can do the rest."

"I know you can, but I have the magic touch which you can't match."

Carrie seemed to acquiesce. I slowly covered most of her body. I noticed that she began breathing hard. I took this as a sign to advance to other parts I had not touched before. When she turned towards me I covered her with kisses. Soon she responded. She helped me remove my wet clothes.

"Now it is your turn. Get into the shower."

As she was applying the sponge, I was getting excited and hugged her tightly. Carrie pulled me out of the shower. We dried each other, she led me to her bed. I played as if I was pooped out and lay on my back. She took the initiative and gently probed all over my body. By the time she got on top of me, I was fully ready and so was she.

I must have fallen asleep. When I woke up I heard the rattling of dishes in the kitchen. I put on the robe she had placed on the foot of the bed. I sneaked in behind her and held her.

"Keef, don't start up with me. Dinner is almost ready. I put your clothes into the washing machine. They are now in the dryer. In the meantime, you may slice the bread and mix the salad."

We had a very good dinner. While drinking the wine she had opened, Carrie suggested I should put on my clothes. She said with a knowing look how tired she was and needed a good sleep. She had to get up early to complete a few things in the office. Then she hoped to catch a flight to Richmond later in the day.

When she noticed my disappointed look, Carrie gave me a hug.

"Keef, I really had a good time. I promise to come up to Washington next month, either on business or for pleasure or for both."

We exchanged phone numbers. After I got dressed, she took me back to the motel.

There was a message for me at the front desk. Henry wrote he would not be back until much later. He finally showed up after midnight, and said he had had a good time with Annabelle.

At breakfast in the morning we took an inventory on where we stood. I told him I had nothing else to do except give MacMerial a call, start working on the report, and call Al King at Central Command. Henry also was about finished with his investigation. He had talked to some people at Camp Blanding, but Hunter's unit commander was not there. He would be there today. Henry believed he could interview him by phone. He doubted whether anything new could come up.

I suggested that Henry brief him on my meeting with Hunter. We might as well read him in as Central Command would undoubtedly contact him when they had decided what to do with Hunter.

I called my office. Amy advised that Col. MacMerial had had to go to the Pentagon. I told her we were just about finished here. I would start composing the trip report while Henry was completing an interview with the suspect's boss. I would also touch base with my contact in Central Command. We would be at the motel until the afternoon. We would possibly take the red-eye tonight.

Then I put in a call to Central Command. Al King was in a meeting, but should be able to get in touch with me within the hour. In the meantime, I made some notes on what I would relate to Central Command. When Al King buzzed me back, I told him we were just about finished. I detailed my conversation with James Hunter. I believed that he had come clean. I recommended that Central Command give him credit for his cooperation. I would write a complete report of what I had uncovered.

The report would go to INSCOM, which had ordered us to come down here. They would promptly forward it to him. I recommended for Central Command to send a copy of my report to Allan Graham of the FBI. The ball was now in the FBI's court. They probably would make a thorough check on that gang in Brooklyn. It will be interesting where this could lead to. Graham would be curious about how Central Command disposed of Hunter's role. I was sure he would bow out of this part of the case.

I decided to phone Allan Graham as a matter of courtesy. I briefly mentioned that we were finished down here. My report would go to Central Command through our headquarters at Fort Belvoir. Central Command would send it on to him for his follow-up. They would handle the James Hunter part.

While I was busy writing the trip report, Henry briefed me on his conversation with Hunter's boss. He had had good experiences with Hunter. He was surprised that Hunter got involved with that gang in New York. The CO was very pleasant, but did not add anything of impact.

We caught the last flight to Washington and arrived there close to midnight. We would brief Bob MacMerial in the morning. Before I hit the hay, I faxed the report I had drafted on the plane to Amy to finalize.

CHAPTER 5

THE GERMAN LIEUTENANT

THE PHONE RANG JUST as I was sitting down for breakfast. It was Amy. She had completed transcribing my report. Colonel MacMerial had just arrived. He would probably read it right away. I should come in at about eleven or so. Henry Kelly would also be there.

Just as I got onto the Beltway, a flash announcement came on the radio about an accident in the north-bound lane of the Baltimore-Washington Parkway, which I usually take when I head for Fort Meade. That would be a mess. So, I diverted to I-95, a four-lane highway which is usually crowded, but I lucked out and arrived at the office shortly after eleven. Amy told me that she had given my report to the boss about an hour ago. Henry was already with him.

"Hello, my commander-in-chief! I am happy to salute your survival while we were in Florida!"

Bob laughed, "Somehow I managed. I read your report and will follow through. In retrospect, I really don't understand why you two had to go down there. But that is water over the dam. It is possible that the FBI will dig up something. In that case, I will file a follow-up on how our MIS people did all the footwork.

"That would please the bureaucrats at Fort Belvoir. Henry will stay in touch with the FBI on this. Now, you are free to follow up on your efforts on your father's World War II exploit. While I was at Fort Belvoir last week, I had lunch with our Commanding General. He was

49

interested in whether he had made a good investment by releasing you to work with Central Command. For him there was no question about it. The Deputy Commander there and he were classmates at West Point.

"I decided to take advantage of his good mood and told him about your father's venture. He became very interested. I casually mentioned it would be a plus for our command if, indeed, the top ranks supported this mission. He asked me to tell you that he fully supports your efforts. You should consider this a special assignment on behalf of MIS.

"Well, needless to say, I was very pleased to get his reaction. First of all, Headquarters has now endorsed your devoting company time on this exclusively. Secondly, at the proper time and place, you may use his personal interest to secure cooperation from the Pentagonites."

"Bob, you are a genius in bringing this up with the General. I am sure this will facilitate my job. Let me outline where I am heading. I would like to go to Europe once more to make sure that I have dug up everything within reach there. Before I go, I want to follow through on Al King's suggestion, which I mentioned in my report, namely touch base with Eloise. Al pointed out that she now knows her way around the Pentagon. She may be able to provide pointers as to when and where I should make contacts there."

Bob endorsed my plans and suggested I get right on it. "While Amy works on your travel papers, you should go over to the Pentagon and see Eloise."

I told Amy to make the necessary arrangements for my leaving the day after tomorrow and to fax me the details. I also asked her to ring up Eloise. I wanted to talk to her. I was in luck; she was at her desk.

"Eloise, long time no see or hear. Are you still calling the tune over there or are just observing the net results of your efforts? I hear you are the coordinator of all coordinators."

"Keef, what a surprise! I was wondering what you were up to, but I had a conversation with Colonel King, and he told me about your job in Orlando. He also mentioned that I may be able to assist you with regard to Pentagon people. When are you coming over?"

"Eloise, if you are free around ten in the morning, I'll see you then. Where should we meet?"

"The weather is nice. Why don't we get together at the snack bar in the center courtyard?"

"See you there. So long!"

On the way home I was thinking - one should never underestimate Bob MacMerial. While he paved the way for my snooping around, he also covered himself by getting Fort Belvoir to become a silent partner. If I should have similar breaks in the future, maybe I can wind this up successfully. Who knows?

It was well beyond the lunch hour. I was getting hungry. When I saw a sign pointing toward Burtonsville, I recalled the diner where I had lunch last summer and the girl who had served me. I think she was a senior in high school, waitressing there in the afternoons. She had told me about her problem with her boyfriend. I sympathized with her. I was able to help her straighten out her love life. She was so grateful that she got me into a Redskins game. Her boyfriend's father had some spare tickets. She was not there today. I inquired about it. I was told that she was in college and now worked part-time for her boyfriend's father. I patted myself on my back. "Keef, sometimes you can help others, even without ulterior motives."

Soon after I got home, Amy's fax arrived. I was all set for my trip. After doing the cleaning, I packed my travel bag. I called my neighbor to say I was going away again. This time I would leave the place in good shape. Then I buzzed my barber friend.

"Hey! I am back from Orlando. No, I don't need a haircut. Have to go to the Pentagon tomorrow. Are you using your parking space? If not, I would like to grace it with my luxurious automobile."

He told me that his wife needed their car. I was welcome to park there.

I had no wait to board a Metro train. In fact, I reached the Pentagon twenty minutes ahead of time. My eyes fell on the shoe shine stand I had patronized last year. It was still run by the same guy. I approached him and saw that the posted prices had gone up. He watched me reading it.

"Costs have gone up, the Pentagon suggested the increase. However, they told me I am no longer a shiner, but a shoe improvement specialist. You see, Colonel, you will get your money's worth."

"You addressed me as Colonel last year. Is there anyone below this rank?"

"Oh, indeed, the poor tippers get down-graded. Had a bird colonel this morning, who pointed at the sign "No Tipping.""

"Told him the sign is correct. You poor privates can ill afford to even pay the listed price. My demoting him did the trick. He forked over a little extra."

"Do you address everybody as Colonel?"

"No, only the ones I recognize. I recall you from the last time."

When I approached the snack bar, there was Eloise walking up to it. I gave her a big kiss. I remembered our "get-together" in her apartment after that last case. After I had bought snacks and drinks, we sat on a shady bench. I looked her over and liked what my eyes conveyed to me.

"Eloise, you look marvelous. You are a picture of health. Maybe I should get a job here."

"Keef, you have not changed at all. I am glad to see you are in good shape. I have lots of news, all good. The work here is tailor-made for me. I enjoy it. On top of this, I have been going steady with a DA civilian. I met him in connection with an inquiry in the Army Inspector General's Office. He is the top civilian there. Somehow we hit it off. We are sort of engaged. I hope I have finally found a partner who will be a father for my boy."

I was not just surprised about what I heard. In fact, I was relieved. I had been wondering how to approach her about cooling off our relationship. All along I had felt that this would not work out for us. She was really looking for a potential husband who would also become a father, and I was not fit for this role. I congratulated her. I told her that I was happy for her. I elaborated on my sensing that our relationship would not have ultimately led to what she really wanted and needed. However, I trusted we would remain the best of friends.

She responded thoughtfully, "I am glad that you are taking it this way. I will never forget you are really responsible for my getting this job, which luckily led me to meeting my husband-to-be. But, what brought you here today?"

I summarized the story of my father's raid towards Prague. She nodded; she remembered it. I explained MIS's approval to make an all-out effort to determine who gave the order. What I needed now was to locate my father's missing files. I suspected they were somewhere in the Pentagon's custody. Giving her a note outlining briefly the May 11, 1945, events, I asked her to check around as to where the files may be.

Eloise was most cooperative. She would do everything possible. She cautioned that, because the raid reflected World War II relations with the Soviets, it could still be highly classified. At least she should be able to ascertain that somebody in the Pentagon had custody. Then how to get to the files would be my problem. I pointed out that I was leaving for Europe the next day. I would call her when I returned. We then departed. All-in-all I believe I got the Pentagon ball rolling.

The flight to Prague was the usual mix of businessmen, tourists, and unruly brats. To my surprise, Colonel John O'Rancher, our Army Attaché, met me at the airport. He had been most helpful to me in the past. I was glad to see him still at the Prague Embassy.

"How did you know I was coming here?"

"Your CO, Bob MacMerial, e-mailed me your plans. He had received MIS's concurrence on your final effort to solve the mystery of your father's World War II venture. He requested my help. I may be able to facilitate your work here. Let's see what we can do."

We drove to the hotel where I had stayed previously. While we had a snack in the coffee shop I told him that some time ago I had talked to the office of the Army's Chief of Military History. They urged me to explore what the Czech military historians had on this. Colonel O'Rancher indicated that he has had some contacts there. He would let me know if they had anything for me.

After lunch I called Uncle Eduard, the Czech Underground operative who had been in contact with my father after the war. I was hoping he may have come across something since I had last visited him.

He answered the phone. I identified myself and asked whether he had more information for me.

"Of course, I remember you. I have thought a lot about what we discussed. I made some calls to the few Partisans still around. None had anything specific. They agreed with me that the Partisans may have played a role in providing the OSS team with information on the German Army encampment near Prague, your father's objective of the raid. Whether the Partisans had any knowledge as to what the Germans had on the Russians is questionable. It is possible the OSS had contacts with one or more German soldiers who were trying to get to the American lines."

I responded, "That is probably the answer. The American Embassy here suggested my checking with the Czech Military History Institute. Do you believe they will have something?"

"I doubt it. As far as I know they are primarily concerned with the activities of the reconstituted Czech Army in the post-World War II period."

"One more thing. I tried your niece Anezka's number. No answer. Is she still with the bank?"

"Oh, Anezka is fine. She was promoted. She is now in charge of establishing new field offices. She does a lot of traveling."

"Next time you see her, please tell her I was in town and tried to contact her."

It was getting late. I was just about ready to go downstairs to the dining room when the phone rang. It was John O'Rancher. He told me he had come across some matters he wanted to discuss with me. He would pick me up in the morning for a meeting with the Czech Military History Institute. He had talked to a major who also suggested I go to the German Army History Office in Potsdam. I told him this was great news. I would fly to Berlin tomorrow afternoon. I would appreciate getting the Embassy's travel coordinator to put me on a plane tomorrow. She had a copy of my travel orders. John picked me up in the morning for a short ride to the Military Institute. We met with a retired major. He graciously invited us to join him for a light breakfast.

I summarized the purpose of my visit to Prague. The major more or less confirmed what I had heard from Anezka's uncle yesterday. The Institute had very little on specific events during the German occupation. From his perspective, in that time frame, he was inclined to give credit to the OSS team for conveying the intelligence on the German headquarters. How, in turn, they scooped this was a matter of guesswork. It is entirely possible they were contacted by individual Germans. However, the Partisans did know about the headquarters which they had surrounded. I assume they were guarding the Germans until the Beneš government could assume custody when it arrived from London, where he had spent the war years. The major reiterated what he had previously conveyed to Colonel O'Rancher. I should, by all means, head for Potsdam. They just might have what I was looking for.

Later I received an e-mail from the Czech Military History Institute.

"This concerns the location of the German Headquarters for the Eastern Front. The main German headquarters which had retreated into Czechoslovakia was Army Group Mitte. The overall headquarters had disintegrated. Army Group Mitte had absorbed several components of the main headquarters. This included the intelligence section.

"Army Group Mitte was captured by the Soviets in Northern Bohemia. The intelligence section, and other units, managed to escape and retreated into Southern Bohemia. They ended up in the area between the towns of Neveklov and Benešov."

This checked out with my father's recollection of the raid. The area he went to during the raid was south of Prague. My father later found out that one member of the Intelligence section of the German headquarters managed to escape while they were retreating south to Neveklov and Benešov. He was a lieutenant who made his way to the American lines. While being interrogated, the officer, Lt. Albrecht Kaufmann, described that his headquarters had extensive files on the Red army. However, this information was already in the hands of the American army which had received it from another source.

We had lunch at the Embassy. John mentioned that his wife, Lucy, could not join us. She was still with her folks in the States. The travel coordinator booked me on a late afternoon flight to Berlin. She would also pay my hotel bill. When John had told her to make sure to charge MIS for this, she laughed. She said she thought we all worked for the same government. John and I then had a leisurely conversation. He said he would fax the German major my arrival time. Perhaps they would meet me at the airport. John, also a World War II history buff, was just as curious as I was about the origin of the raid. He recommended that I contact a recently established unit, the Army Irregular Fusion Cell, part of the Combined Arms Center at Fort Leavenworth. They probably had a historical study section which might have something for me. There was also a newly activated Security Force Assistance organization.

These were new organizations. I believe they are probably under the Defense Department. They might have gathered data from a variety of sources. No harm trying.

He had another tip for me. A friend of his was recently appointed to head of the U.S. Army Heritage and Education Center, a component of the Army War College at Carlisle, PA. John suggested I visit the War College. They had custody of Colonel Koch's papers. Colonel Oscar W. Koch was G-2 of the Third Army and was known as a big-time operator, just like his boss, Patton. Koch may have made some notes regarding the raid.

As we were leaving, the travel coordinator stopped us with a response from Potsdam. They would pick me up at the airport.

The flight to Berlin took only about an hour. This was my first time at Tegel Airport, which had replaced Tempelhof. I knew all about Tempelhof. My father had used it often. I remember it played a key role during the Berlin Airlift. As I entered the concourse I noticed a uniformed man holding a sign "Keef." He took my bag while we walked out of the terminal. It was a 30-minute drive to Potsdam. He would drop me off at a small hotel, picking me up in the morning for a short ride to his headquarters. Major Alters, the Executive Officer, would be at my disposal. I checked in to the hotel for one day. The clerk mentioned that the in-house restaurant would be open in about an hour. He said it had a good reputation. Most of the patrons were local.

Early the next morning, as I was getting dressed, the phone rang. It was Major Alters inviting me for breakfast. A car would be out front in about 20 minutes. I checked out at the front desk, anticipating there would be no need to return.

Major Alters was well beyond his prime. He was not in uniform, telling me that most of the staff was retired military. They still referred to each other by their former ranks. His people had immediately begun extensive research after receiving Colonel O'Rancher's call yesterday. "Most of the historical records on World War II are now located at the German Military Archives in Freiburg. I called a friend on the staff there, and learned that to get information one must go there personally. My friend found out about Lt. Kaufmann having lived with his sister in Oppenheim south of Frankfurt. Major Alters suggested I should see if the sister was still there. If she could find some of his papers, I might not need to travel to Freiburg. He understood that the bureaucracy there was challenging.

Major Alters called the Oppenheim Mayor's office. The Mayor told us about the officer who had lived with his sister, Anna Kaufmann, in Oppenheim. He would give her a ring.

"You ought to talk to her. She probably still has his Army papers. You know we Germans never throw anything away."

I agreed with him. It was certainly worth the effort to check this out.

"Keef, I think I can get you down there quickly. The American Army in Berlin has frequent courier flights to Frankfurt."

I called.

"Army Aviation Center, may I help you?"

"My name is Kevin Keefer. I am a special agent with MIS in Washington, here on a special assignment. I need to see someone in Oppenheim, south of Frankfurt. Major Alters suggested I check with you regarding a ride on the next flight. How does it look?"

"Mr. Keefer, what a surprise. We never met, but I heard about you on when I was assigned with the JCS staff at the Pentagon. We have a flight leaving in about two hours. Just head for the Military Sector at Tegel. I'll tell the pilot to take you on.

"I know where Oppenheim is, it's less than an hour's ride from Frankfurt. If you concur, I'll get a car to take you there. The pilot will direct you. It will wait for you and take you back to Frankfurt. We have a small office at the airport which can assist you with your return flight to the States."

"That sounds great. I sure appreciate your help. When I get back I will call your old boss, General Hepsterall. I understand he is still in his current assignment."

"Mr. Keefer, it is my pleasure. You don't need any paperwork for the courier flight. Just show your ID."

Major Alters had listened in on our conversation. He was pleased that I could get a flight so quickly. He urged me to leave for Tegel right away. A car would take me there. He would call the woman in Oppenheim to inform her that I would come by early in the afternoon.

It took about an hour to get to the airport. It wasn't that far, but traffic was as bad as it is in Washington. Nevertheless, the driver delivered me on time right to the door where the American Military Lounge was located. It was a well-appointed place. There was a lunch counter and, best of all, there was a desk manned by a sergeant. I introduced myself. He said the pilot usually came about 30 minutes before departure. I saw a fax machine. I asked him whether there was a flight to Andrews scheduled after eight tonight. He said there was none, but he could book me on a commercial carrier. I gave him my travel orders and I was able to go business class on the red-eye departing at eleven. Then I faxed a message to Amy, providing the flight number and asking her to request the Fort Meade Motor Pool to send a vehicle to pick me up at BWI.

Just then the pilot showed up. The sergeant pointed him out to me. I went over. He suggested we hit the snack bar so I would not waste any time when we reached Frankfurt. He recommended that I use the car which was available to him in Frankfurt. Furthermore, he was in no hurry to fly back to Berlin. We could return there around 1800 hours. That would give me plenty of time in Oppenheim. The driver of the car assigned to him would wait for me while I was visiting. The pilot would get together with a girlfriend in Frankfurt. She would take care of everything.

Winking his eye, he said, "Of course, we may conduct some other business!"

After we landed in Frankfurt, he escorted me outside where his car was waiting. He instructed the corporal behind the wheel to take me to Oppenheim and to bring me back.

When we reached Oppenheim we stopped at the Mayor's office. He pointed across the street.

Frau Kaufmann was waiting for me. When she opened the door, I smelled the odor of freshly brewed coffee.

Frau Kaufmann was in her eighties. I could see she was not steady on her feet.

"I am pleased to meet you, Mr. Keefer. Major Alters told me all about you. Let's have some coffee and *Bundkuchen*, our local specialty. I have looked through my brother's desk. The only thing of possible interest to you is a diary he had started. I checked the May 1945 entries. There is one item describing how he got separated from his unit during the retreat towards Prague. He had left the headquarters. He did not want to be captured by either the Partisans or the Russians."

"Frau Kaufmann, can you recall anything about what your brother did before he got to the American line? Did he mention that he gave specific information about his old unit directly to the Americans he may have encountered or to Partisans?"

"I don't recall anything specific about that. However, he told me he avoided contact with the Partisans. He knew they would either harm him or make him a prisoner."

I was surprised that she spoke in English until I recalled that Major Alters had mentioned that she was a retired English teacher.

I thanked her for sharing this with me. I had to get back to Frankfurt. We made it there by six. I asked the corporal to drop me off at a decent restaurant near the airport. He should tell the pilot I would meet him at the airport lounge no later than eight. The corporal knew how to get in touch with him.

Everything worked out schedule-wise. I got back to Tegel in good time for the flight home. A car met me at BWI and I finally got home in the wee hours of the morning.

CHAPTER 6

LOVE AND LEAVENWORTH

AS IT HAPPENS, EVERY so often after returning from an overseas trip, I have trouble falling asleep. How should I proceed next? Any dealings with the Pentagon were in abeyance until I heard from Eloise. Then it occurred to me that I should try to get in touch with Lucy. Her landing a job at the State Department might be fortuitous. Perhaps she knew somebody in their historical shop who could dig up some papers relating to events in Czechoslovakia in early 1945. It certainly was worth a try.

I called State. Getting connected to Lucy was a bureaucratic nightmare. Eventually I was referred to the Human Resources Department. They wanted to know why I needed her number. To avoid any lengthy discussions, I told them I was calling from the Pentagon. I was required to talk to her about her stay in Prague. Then the person who wanted to grill me changed her tune. She connected me with Lucy.

"Lucy, this is Keef. Do you remember me from the trip we took together to Strakonice?"

"Of course, Keef, what are you up to?"

"Lucy, I am still with MIS. I was in Prague a few weeks ago. The secretary in the Embassy told me you are now in Washington. I would like to see you. How about lunch today?"

"Sounds great!" She would meet me at the front entrance at about 12:30. I had to wait a few minutes before she appeared. She had her usual serene smile.

"Where are you taking me, Keef?"

"We will go to a nice place on the waterfront. I have been there before. Besides good food, there is parking. When I worked on an assignment for the Pentagon, the FBI was involved. They ate there a lot. In fact, they have reserved parking spaces. As you may know, finding parking downtown is tough. So I will use one of the FBI spots."

"Isn't that the place you met the FBI woman from the Washington Regional Office? Was she the one who bit your ear?"

"Lucy, you have a good memory. I told you about the FBI girl and also the famous ear incident. But those were not directly related. I spent a weekend at an FBI safe house in Virginia. There I went to a dance at a local country club. While I was foxtrotting with one of the locals, this girl took a shine to me and somehow chewed on my left ear. My memory is not what it used to be. When did I relate this to you?"

"On the trip we took to Strakonice you gossiped about that woman involved in the ear incident. I thought that was the funniest thing I had heard in a long time!"

When we arrived at the restaurant, the lot was full. I proceeded to the FBI spots and pulled in. With the weather cooperating, we found an empty table facing the Potomac. I ordered the special for the day while Lucy ordered a salad plate. She seemed to be in a good mood. This prompted me to satisfy my curiosity on the breakup of her marriage.

"Lucy, if I get too personal, stop me. I was surprised about what has been happening to you. The Embassy travel coordinator told me that you and John had separated."

"Keef, I don't mind filling you in. Yes, John and I decided to split. In fact, the divorce papers came through just a few days ago. We sort of drifted apart. He was always busy. His position required lots of travel. I was getting bored sitting in Prague, waiting for him to get back. I went with him on several of his trips, but then I spent lots of time in a hotel room while he was elsewhere conducting his business. So eventually I realized that I had to do something. We decided to split. At first he was opposed, but he finally realized that I had to do something with my life. I had a good education. I wanted to use it, go to work someplace. We parted on good terms. I am much happier nowadays and I doubt whether it has impacted him much."

"John did not say anything about this at all. He only mentioned you were in the States. I am glad that you are doing so well. How did you find this job and what are you doing?"

"Before the Prague assignment, John was with the State Department in Washington for several years. We made many friends there. When I came back here last year, I reconnected with some of them and found this job. It is a temporary position, but they tell me I may get Civil Service status sometime in the future. I work on personnel matters, reviewing files and interviewing people under consideration for overseas assignments. This, of course, keeps me in touch with many different organizations in the State Department."

"This sounds like a great job! I am still doing my MIS chores. They wanted to promote me, but I declined. As my father used to say, 'Let not ambition mock thy useful toil.'"

I noticed Lucy checking her watch. I guessed she had to get back. When I dropped her off, she thanked me and hoped we would do this again. I told her I would call her soon.

While I was doing some household chores in the afternoon, I was contemplating what should be next on my agenda. I started to go over my notes on my last trip to Prague. I had underlined what John O'Rancher told me about Colonel Koch's papers at the Army War College. John thought it was worthwhile to check them out. Koch, who had been Patton's G-2, could well have been involved in the raid. I called the librarian at Carlisle. I gave him some background on the tip I got from Colonel O'Rancher, who was a friend of the colonel running the Carlisle school system. I intended to drive up there in the morning. I wanted to look at Colonel Koch's papers. He said he would have them ready for me.

It took me only a couple of hours to get there. I was fascinated reviewing Koch's files. Apparently, toward the end of the war, Patton gave him plenty of leeway in seeking intelligence on the Germans. For example, on May 8, 1945, Patton received word that an important German general waited to discuss terms of surrender. At the time, Patton had his problems with Bradley and Eisenhower related to his tendency to undertake unauthorized ventures. Patton directed Koch to talk to the German general, because Koch had had previous contact with him. However, I could not find documentation implying that Koch was involved in anything related to the raid. In retrospect, I was not surprised. I believe the order to get the German Army intelligence on the Russians had come directly from an, as yet, undetermined person to the G-2 of the Fourth Armored Division. One must remember that time was of the essence. In those hectic days, by-passing the regular military channels was the way to go. Considering the sensitivity of the raid, the number of people involved had to be kept to an absolute minimum. At any rate, I was glad to explore the possible Patton-Koch involvement.

The following morning I took a mental inventory of what I had researched and what was still ahead. The next thing was a trip to Fort Leavenworth, Kansas. I had kept a note on a newspaper article which covered the recent organizational changes in the Pentagon. There were two items that caught my attention. They concerned two agencies that were in the process of being established with headquarters at Fort Leavenworth. They were to research different aspects of past intelligence actions and how they would possibly have an impact on future military plans. I had kept the clippings, but, in spite of intensive searching in my "to do" folders, I could not find them.

I called Eloise at the Pentagon to ask her to call Fort Leavenworth about making arrangements for interviews.

"Eloise, this is Keef. How are you doing these days?"

"I am hanging in there. You have no idea about all the calls I get from within the Pentagon. They believe I can help them when no one else has a clue as to what they want. What are you up to?"

"Keeping busy with my project on the raid. I think there are two newly established Army units at Fort Leavenworth that may have something for me. I plan to go there tomorrow. Would you please call the post and use your influence to arrange for an overnight stay there? I plan to bring an assistant with me, so we need two rooms."

"Sure, Keef, I will get right on it. Will call you back soon."

She called me back. "Keef, you are in luck. Apparently the field installations are impressed when they get contacted by DOD. I was referred to an aide of the Commanding General. He told me he had arranged VIP quarters for you. Contact Captain Slank at Post

Headquarters when you arrive. The two new agencies are the Army Irregular Warfare Fusion Cell and the Security Force Assistance Proponent."

I needed to take somebody with me to explore around the post to get some hints on approaching the two agencies in case Captain Slank would not get me to see them. Perhaps Lucy would help me out. She could use her State Department cover. Since she is in the personnel game, she could check around Fort Leavenworth to get some dope on the two agencies.

I called Lucy to get her reaction. She was not in. A woman who apparently worked with her mentioned she took the day off. I persuaded her to give me her cell phone number.

"Lucy, how come you are not working today?"

"Hey, Keef, a woman has to do some shopping. I am looking for a birthday gift for a cousin."

"Are you available for dinner tonight?"

"Yes, meet me at the Metro Center at about six."

"OK, I'll be at the street entrance."

I got there a little early. I was surprised she was already there, wearing a jacket I had not seen before.

"Lucy, I thought you were shopping for a gift. I see you are wearing a beautiful new outfit. Did you also get this today?"

"Keef, you are very observant. While looking for a nice present I ran across this jacket. I slipped it on. It fit perfectly, so I splurged. I know a good place to eat not far from here. Let's go, I'm starved!"

She took me to a rotisserie-like place just around the block, well known for its steaks. I asked the receptionist to give us a place where we could talk quietly. She led us to an alcove. Lucy did not desire a cocktail. Instead, she wanted a glass of house wine with the dinner. I declined any alcohol. Instead, I settled for a glass of water with a twist of lemon. Lucy chose their special club steak. She said she had had it before. I ordered the same.

"Lucy, you are not only an expert on food quality, but you have a superior standard for dating."

"Keef, I am glad you think so highly of yourself."

She ordered the Normandy Special for dessert, which she wanted me to try. I decided it was a good time to get into the Leavenworth business.

"Lucy, I have a proposition for you."

"Keef, it is too early in our relationship to go into this already."

I laughed. "Lucy, I am glad to see where your mind is. If I recall correctly, a proposition has several meanings. I meant it as a proposal for your consideration. I want your help with something I have to do. It is related to my current endeavor to discover the origin of the order for my father's venture into Czechoslovakia."

"Keef, I was just kidding. I know you are a gentleman as well as a scholar. What is on your mind?"

I outlined how I had come across the two Army agencies recently established at Leavenworth. I wanted to check them out to see if they had any historical data on events during the last days of the war in Czechoslovakia. I needed her to come with me. While I was dickering at post headquarters to gain access to the information I was after, she could use her State Department position to independently seek access on information on the two agencies. She could cite her need to contact the agencies in order to verify some references an applicant for an overseas position had made.

Lucy listened carefully. She said she would gladly give me a hand, but was leery to do this. I told her I appreciated her concerns, but, first of all, Leavenworth was out in the sticks, and her inquiries there would not trigger any sort of communication between the post and State. Also, if somehow she was questioned at State about having gone to Leavenworth, she could justify her trip, saying she had taken it upon herself to check out references. She had gone there informally to take advantage of accompanying a friend who needed to head for Leavenworth on business. This would provide a justifiable rationale for her trip, if the subject ever came up.

While Lucy was pondering this, I ordered two café lattes. Finally Lucy spoke up.

"Keef, one never knows what you come up with. This reminds me of our trip to Czechoslovakia. I have to give you credit for your vivid imagination. I am inclined to accept your arguments. If you really believe that I can be of assistance, I will tag along. Do you have a time frame in mind?"

I told her how pleased I was that she would come along. I asked her when she could get a couple of days off. She told me she was on leave for the rest of the week. She had planned a visit to her cousin. Well, if that was the case, we could fly there sometime tomorrow and return the following day. I would make all the arrangements. I would call her tomorrow morning.

It was so nice outside, we walked to her apartment. She told me how much she enjoyed having dinner with me. Before she went inside, I told her I had a proposition for her. She laughed. I said, "Here it is." and I gave her a kiss.

When I got home I checked the computer for flights to Kansas City International Airport. I booked two seats for the following day, with departure scheduled at four in afternoon. Then I buzzed Lucy. I told her I had seats on a flight out of National. I would pick her up a little before 2:00. Lucy responded it would be much easier if she took the Metro to National, meeting me between 2:30 and 2:45 at the gate. I should also use the Metro. This would avoid my having to park there, which is a mess.

My last call was to Captain Slank. He told me he was glad I called him. He wanted my flight number so he could send a car. He mentioned that ground transportation from the airport to the post was a pain in the neck during rush hour. He wanted me to stop by his office around nine in the morning.

My neighbor dropped me at the Metro in Silver Spring. In spite of some delays because of track repair work I reached the airport in good time. I waited only ten minutes before Lucy arrived. The plane was half full. We took advantage of this and switched from our seats to the better ones with more leg room.

We had an uneventful flight. When we walked toward the airport exit, we saw a soldier holding a sign "Leavenworth." When I told him my name, he led the way to the car. There was a long line of cars waiting to get through security to enter the post, however our driver whisked us through another gate and dropped us off at the VIP quarters. The Charge-of-Quarters (CQ) was a corporal who took us to the VIP suite.

I ask him whether the club on the post served good food. According to him, we lucked out. Tonight was their monthly special dinner-buffet and there was music starting at eight.

The suite contained a sitting room and two bedrooms. I wanted to take a shower before getting dressed. She suggested I go first. She wanted to take a long bath and soak in the water. I told her to take her time. I would knock on her door about seven.

When I picked her up I noticed she wore a nice dress which, while on the conservative side, definitely accentuated her positives. I said, "You look lovely. You had been well-reared as a young lady."

She told me to cut out this nonsense. She was more interested in checking out the buffet, but she laughed with a twinkle in her eyes.

There was a maître'd at the dining room entrance. He apparently knew most of the people. He stopped us and asked for identification. I showed him my counterintelligence credentials. He mentioned having received a call from Captain Slank. I wondered how Slank knew we were coming here. The CQ of the VIP quarters had probably called him. We were then led to what he said was "the best seat in the house." I could see that Lucy was impressed by the VIP courtesies.

The buffet featured all the usual items, such as sliced ham, roast beef, chicken in various forms, two types of fish, salmon croquets, corn bread, pies and cakes, and, of course, several flavors of ice cream and sherbet. Lucy filled her tray, while I had some room to take some extra chicken nuggets which I knew she liked. When we returned to our table the wine steward showed up. He recommended a bottle of Napa Valley wine. I saw Lucy had consumed all of her chicken dishes. I took a large spoon and ladled over the extra nuggets. She thanked me, noting she shouldn't. She had to watch her weight. I nodded, mentioning there was nothing wrong with either her front or her rear. She did not look matronly to me! She then lectured me that she could do without my observations.

As we were eating I noticed a band was setting up. Tables were moved from the middle to create a dance floor. So that is what the CQ had mentioned about music. For dessert Lucy selected pie a-la-mode while I stuck to raspberry sherbet.

We were just about finished with eating and were sipping on wine when the band got started. It began with several numbers of hot music and most of the below-40 crowd rushed to the floor. We were fascinated by the wild swings they took. Finally, they played a waltz. I told Lucy I was a poor waltzer. She liked to waltz and pulled me along. I could see she was an excellent dancer. Somehow I managed to do better than usual. Then we returned to the table.

After a while they finally struck up with a slow foxtrot. I pulled Lucy up and said now they were playing the way I like it. I think I am pretty good at this. So I was not surprised when Lucy complimented me. They played several numbers. As the band performed one of my favorites, I hugged her a little tighter. She did not seem to mind. Eventually we were cheek-to-cheek. I think she warmed up a bit, but it may have been my imagination. When the band shifted to a faster pace, we left the floor. We had just about finished the bottle. It was time to leave. We had a busy day tomorrow.

When the corporal opened the front door for us, he wanted to know why we came back so soon. I told him we came here to work. Somebody should wake us up no later than seven.

When we entered the suite I asked whether I should turn on the radio for some music. She responded that she was a little tired; she would take a shower and then hit the hay. I was disappointed. The body warmth I had felt at the club lingered on. I would have liked to dance some more. So I wished her pleasant dreams, gave her a close hug, and kissed her. Her reaction appeared somewhat neutral, but she smiled and she headed for her room.

The phone rang promptly at seven. The CQ offered to bring us a light breakfast. They had a small kitchen to accommodate the VIPs. I told him to bring it on, but not before another hour.

After breakfast we made plans for the day. I had made reservations for the flight back at 4:30. Leaving the post around 2:30 should give us enough time, provided we got a car to take us back to the airport. I would see Slank a few minutes before nine. Then I would proceed to the two agencies. I suggested to Lucy that she visit the post library. Librarians usually know plenty about what goes on on the post. Some use the library for a resource or just read magazines. Some also like to gossip with the librarians. She might be able to get more information than I could. If she was asked how she came to visit the post, she could tell them she worked for the State Department and she had to verify some references which had been submitted by individuals applying for jobs. We could meet at the club around noon for lunch. According to a map in the phone directory, the library was not far from here. The CQ would know exactly where it is.

It was a short walk to headquarters. I told the receptionist I had an appointment with Captain Slank. She looked in her log-in register and directed me toward the general's office. His receptionist checked me out again, then motioned me to the door behind her desk, which led to the general's outer office. I went to the desk with Slank's name plate on it. I sat down. Soon he appeared. After we exchanged pleasantries, Captain Slank inquired about the nature of my business.

"As my DOD contact who called you may have mentioned, I am with Army counterintelligence. I am doing some research on World War II for a book I am writing. I started out doing this on my own. My unit at Fort Meade reports to INSCOM, the Army Intelligence and Security Command, at Fort Belvoir. During a meeting between my boss and the Deputy Commanding General of INSCOM, they talked about my application for extended leave to conduct research. The General got very interested. He decided I should not go on leave, but be assigned a special project, namely the research I was already engaged in. I was to report my findings to INSCOM before seeking Pentagon clearance for publishing the book.

"I am digging up all sorts of historical references, but so far have not uncovered everything I am after. It is possible the newly established units at Leavenworth, the Army Irregular Warfare Fusion Cell and the Security Force Assistance Proponent, may have some of the records I seek. I checked with a contact at the Pentagon about the scope of these units. He did not know much, he only knew their mission also required the collection and analysis of data on past conflicts, including World War II. This caught my attention. Workers in those units may have come across records of incidents that are of interest to me. That is the reason for my visit."

"Mr. Keefer, the two organizations are not under our command. They are tenants, along with a number of others on the post. They are under the Combined Arms Center, also located here, which in turn reports to the Army Training and Doctrine Command, TRADOC, located at Fort Eustis, VA. From the little I know about the two units, the Security Force Assistance Proponent deals only with support of overseas allies. Unless your interest is in this functional area, they would not have anything for you. However, the Army Irregular Warfare Fusion Cell is highly compartmentalized and secretive. I heard they have extensive records of the past. Perhaps they have something for you. Let me see who you can see there."

Slank then dialed a number. He talked to someone on the other end, not giving any name. Then he handed me the phone, telling me he would like me to explain my need to talk to them.

"Hello, I am Kevin Keefer with the Intelligence and Security Command at Fort Belvoir. I am doing research on a classified operation at the end of World War II in Czechoslovakia. This has become a full-time job and has the blessings of the brass at Fort Belvoir. Very little data is available in the usual sources, such as the National Archives, the Army's Historical Division, and various other agencies within the DOD. I have evidence that the OSS and SHAEF were directly involved in accord with the general guidelines from the Pentagon and the State Department. However, I have not yet discovered who actually gave the order for the operation. I understand that your unit has extensive historical data. I would like to access it. May I come over and check what you have for the month of May 1945?"

"I regret to advise you that that is not possible. We do not authorize access to what we have to anyone outside our own organization. This is within the guidelines that were given to us when we were established. However, I can help you in one respect. I have spent a good deal of time to assess what we have historical-wise. I do not remember seeing anything which would be of interest to you. I hope this will help. It was nice talking with you, Mr. Keefer."

I turned to Slank and expressed my frustration of hitting another dead end. I have my doubts that I will ever find a definitive answer. Slank then related that he was not surprised. "That unit is a tenant of the post and cannot be made to cooperate with anyone. My Commanding General wanted to inspect their premises when they first opened up, but they had politely denied him that.

I then asked Slank for transportation to the airport. He promised to arrange it. As I still had a few hours on the post until I left, he offered me a car and driver to see some of the facilities on the post, such as the Disciplinary Barracks, which houses the Services' long-term prisoners, and various training centers and schools.

I gladly accepted his offer. I had heard that Leavenworth was a big installation, especially in the training category. I was impressed by how large the post was, as well as the variety of tenant occupancies. I bet the post had a very large budget for logistical support. When I saw a building identified as the 902nd Military Intelligence Group, I went inside and introduced myself to the commanding agent. I told him why I was at the post. He said the Army Irregular Warfare Fusion Cell had a reputation for tight security. There was little contact. When they first came there, they asked the 902nd to provide clearance on the custodial personnel they had hired. Since then there has been no contact with them.

When I got to the club for lunch, Lucy was not there yet. I called Captain Slank to thank him for the tour. He was not in. I left a message with the secretary, who mentioned that transportation to the airport had been set up.

A few minutes later Lucy arrived. She told me she had had an interesting visit to the library. She was hungry. So we got in line for the buffet. I guess to conserve funds the clubs nowadays only rarely have table service.

While we were sipping our coffee, Lucy filled me in. "The librarian was impressed about my story for the reason I was on the post. They had never had a visitor from the State Department. I told her I had talked to the post Personnel Department. I made up a story about two people I was checking on who had provided references to the Army Irregular Warfare Fusion Cell. The head of the personnel office called her Fusion Cell organization counterpart. She was told that several individuals had been transferred, but she did not have any names at her fingertips. The post Personnel Office commented that the Fusion Cell organization had a reputation for not giving out any information. The people I would want to interview were possibly still there. Then the librarian had an idea. There was a patient from the Fusion Cell unit at the hospital who had contacted her for a book. He had called her back and thanked her and chatted with her for a while. She would give him a ring and put me on. Then she left to attend to another customer.

"I introduced myself as a visitor to the post. I told him that when I mentioned to an acquaintance of mine who is into military history that I planned to go to Leavenworth, he told me about having heard of a new organization there, called Fusion Cell. He was wondering whether Fusion Cell had any historical records that might not be available anywhere else in the Pentagon."

He chuckled. "I'm afraid I can't be of much help. Is he after something special?"

"I believe it is something about some action toward the end of World War II in Europe."

"I am sorry you barked up the wrong tree. From what I know we don't have much data on overseas action. Most of the stuff deals with activities in the United States. It is all more recent than World War II. I have been here for a week. Please tell that nice librarian it will be another week before I get discharged. She should send me another book. Also tell her I heard that we will soon move from this post. There are even rumors we may be on the way out. I assume some of our functions would be transferred. This is happening all over. The entire DOD had cuts in funding."

"I thanked him for keeping me abreast and wished him a speedy recovery."

I gave Lucy a brief summary of my endeavors. Captain Slank had been most cooperative, but even he could not get me to see the unit. He did get me into a phone exchange with someone there. He said they were not able to let me do research there, but it would not be helpful to me, anyway. They are pretty sure they do not have much on World War II overseas actions.

Then we went to get our baggage. Soon the car would pick us up.

We arrived at the airport in plenty of time. On the plane I thanked Lucy for her efforts. She said she was glad to help me. She had rather enjoyed it. We took the Metro back to Metro Center. Before catching a short cab ride to her place, Lucy invited me to join her for dinner at her place on Saturday around six. I asked what the occasion was. She replied, "To let you experience some good cooking."

I responded, "Indeed, if your culinary expertise is on the level of your information gathering skills and attractive appearance, I absolutely cannot refuse this." She told me to cut this out.

Saturday came pretty quickly. I decided to drive to downtown Silver Spring and park at my barber's spot, which would be vacant by the time I get there, and go the rest of the way by Metro. I went down to my wine storage and picked a bottle of rosé, which would go with anything. Before I boarded the train I went to my favorite bakery and bought a couple of fancy French specialties for dessert. I arrived a little early at Metro Center. Since the weather was nice, I decided to take the 20-minute walk to Lucy's place.

When Lucy opened the door I gave her a brief kiss. The dining area of the living room was all decked out, as if for a royal visitor. I looked around. I inquired whether her apartment-mate was in. She was out of town for the weekend, visiting her folks. I gave Lucy the bottle to put into the fridge, as well as the dessert. She came up with a thank-you speech, but I stopped her. Then we sat on the couch. She spelled out the menu, consisting of salmon fillets, asparagus, a mashed potato placed inside some dough, a mixed salad, and some home baked rolls. I exclaimed that it sounded great! I was getting hungry!

Lucy asked me to take care of the wine, while she attended to the oven. We had an excellent dinner. She told me how happy she was that her move to Washington has worked out so well. Running into me was a super plus. It provided a spark in her life to lift her out of the routine pattern she had fallen into. I replied I also felt much perkier since we reconnected. I realized what I was missing was a true friendship. Her coming with me to Leavenworth converted a dull business trip into a pleasure cruise.

"Keef, this is enough baloney! Help me put things away before we indulge in the dessert."

After we cleared the table, I told her I was all filled up. I needed a break before the dessert. She indicated that I took the words right out of her mouth. She also would rather wait a while. We sat on the couch, sipping from what was left in the bottle. There was small talk, but I could not take my eyes off her. What were we going to do, just sit and idly talk until we were ready for dessert?

"Lucy, while you were in the kitchen, I noticed there is a nice record collection in the cabinet near the window. Are they yours or your roommate's?"

"They belong to her, Keef. She has all sorts of records. If you want to hear some, I can play them. I'll get the record player out of the closet."

She brought out an old-fashioned one which, originally, you had to manually wind up. Lucy set it up, explaining that her roommate had inherited it from an aunt. She had it updated. It now runs on electricity.

"Keef, why don't you pick out a few?"

I selected several, one waltz and the rest foxtrots. She placed the waltz on first and started to sit down. I took her by the hand and asked her whether she wanted to dance. She nodded and suggested I should help her move the rug. Then she kicked off her high heels. She told me I picked up readily from my slow beginnings at the Leavenworth club. I responded, "Thanks to a good teacher."

When we switched to foxtrots, I felt more at home. Soon we were closer. I kissed her on her cheeks and moved my right hand slightly up and down her back. I felt her breathing more noticeably. I found her lips and pressed her against me.

Lucy then said, "I have to take a break. Let's just listen to the next one." When we sat down on the couch, I took her in my arms and bent over, running my fingers through her hair. Now she finally reacted. She kissed me and grabbed my left hand, guiding it toward her breasts. This really got to me. I bent over and start to unbutton her blouse.

At that point she also seemed like she was ready for my advances. She stood up, bent over me and pulled off my sweater. I then also got off the couch, removed her blouse and gently kissed the nipples of her breasts. Without saying anything, Lucy pulled me with her to her bedroom. She was breathing heavily, but never said a word. She quickly took my pants off while I removed her skirt. I am sure she could feel how ready I was.

She pulled me onto the bed on top of her. Her moves became more rapid while I had a tough time controlling my urge to climax.

Finally, she whispered in my ear, "Now!" After she eventually calmed down, she leaned in to me. "Keef, I am sorry if I was a bit on the wild side, but I have not done anything for two years. I have dreamed about sex. Now that it became a reality, I lost all control!"

She started to fondle me, but I knew my limitations. "Lucy, you are dealing with a soon-to-be senior citizen. Let's have dessert."

She laughed and put on a robe. She gave me another one.

The dessert was indeed delicious. Lucy put on some good music and we sat on the sofa. I laid my hand in her lap. I needed a rest. I may have dozed off. Soon I became aware of Lucy's gently moving her hands all over me. After I while, she said, "Keef, it is a miracle! The old man has come alive again!" She dragged me to the bed and wanted me to lie on my back.

"Lucy, I can't do this. I have some problems lying down this way."

"I think I can fix this. My ex used to have pain there, and he went to physical therapy. I went with him several times and observed how it is done. My ex said I was better than the pro. Let me give it a try."

She was at it for about 15 minutes. I really was quite comfortable when she turned me over. But by this time my sexual appetite had gone to zero. We both went to sleep.

About six in the morning I had to go to the bathroom. As I was heading back to bed, Lucy came by me, telling me she felt like taking a shower. I followed her in, announcing I would soap up her back. "After all, you took care of my back and now I will pay back!" While she was washing her hair, I took a soft sponge, soaped it and went to work. I could tell she liked it. Then she took the sponge and gently covered my body. As we were showering the soap off us, I kissed her breast and fondled her rear. That got her going on me. She must have felt that my penis became alive. We hastily dried each other off and headed for the bed.

This time we did not debate my back issue. I complied with her wish; she sort of kneeled on top of me, inserting my organ into her and came to a speedy climax. I was not quite ready. So I turned her over and got on top of her. Soon she cried out and hugged me tightly. We stayed in bed for a couple of hours, napping and talking. After a while, she pulled me out of bed, announcing that I should help her with getting the breakfast ready.

After we were finished, I told Lucy I had to get back to my place. My neighbor had arranged for a cleaning service to take care of both our homes. I hoped they were still there. I want to make sure they did a good job.

Lucy then told me she also had things to do and had to get dressed. One of her girlfriends at State had invited her to go with her to the Kennedy Center.

Giving her a long hug, I thanked her for the delicious meals and her charming company. She responded, "Keef, don't be silly. You gave me a new lease on life!"

CHAPTER 7

GERMAN ARCHIVES

I DID NOT SLEEP well that night. All this searching for the origin of the order took something out of me. Perhaps the time had come to make a concerted effort to locate the steel cabinet in which my father stored his records. I was not looking forward to this. I could picture all the hoops I had to jump through at the Pentagon to get somebody to steer me to where I might find it. I decided to make one last attempt to see, if by any chance, Dad had left something pertinent in those old desks and one file cabinet I had retrieved from his house. While he spent a good deal of time at the Pentagon, he had also worked at home. The only places I might come across something useful would be in the nooks and crannies in those drawers. I had not perused all of them before, thinking they would be full of stuff he did not need, but had not dumped.

After a light breakfast I placed the dishes into the sink. I went downstairs. I headed straight to what could charitably be called a desk. I emptied the drawers onto the floor. As I had suspected, there were plenty of as old bills, correspondence with various companies, and a few old letters. At the bottom of the pile was a surprise. There was a relatively neat Pentagon manila folder containing notes. Apparently he had removed it from his files at the Pentagon and brought it home for a reason.

I was curious what this was all about.

I knew Dad had a one-track mind when he was interested in one specific goal, namely the origin of the order for the raid. However, the answer was not in the folder. Instead, it covered another subject.

I began to read.

"Sometime in early May, while the Division was at its assigned sector at the Line of Demarcation, I was called one morning to report to the G-2. He came right to the point. He explained that the Division's main checkpoint at the Line was overwhelmed with refugees and others trying to get into the American Zone. He had requested the Czech Liaison Officer to assist our personnel with the flood of individuals clamoring to gain admittance.

"In compliance with SHAEF policy, the checkpoint automatically turned back Russians who had been with the German Army (so-called Vlasov Army), German military, and Czech collaborators. Exceptions were only to be made for those who had valuable intelligence data. The checkpoint had particular difficulties with Czech nationals. The expertise of the Czech Liaison Officer was needed to see who should be granted permission to enter the American Zone. The number of people trying to do this was increasing daily. The Czech Liaison Officer had appealed to the G-2 to give him help. The G-2 knew I was aware of the Germans' use of Czech collaborators. He told me to check in with the Liaison Officer. I was to work with him until the flood of people had ebbed.

"I had previously met the Liaison Officer. He was pleased to see me. My job was to interrogate those Czech nationals, and those who looked suspicious would be referred to the Liaison Officer. I was able to find at least a dozen whose backgrounds were questionable. One thing they all had in common; they spoke German fluently. I identified several Czechs who had had connections with the German occupiers. Some were informants for the Gestapo. I took their personnel data and gave them to the Liaison Officer. I suggested that he provide this information to the appropriate Czech authority, once the Czech government was reconstituted.

"The Czech Liaison Officer told me he was amazed at how many collaborators were trying to escape, but he was convinced these people knew they would face retribution once the Czech government began to function. Apparently, being questioned by an American gave them an incentive to admit their cooperation with the Germans. They probably believed the American would find them useful for their knowledge of the German occupation forces. He thanked me. He would recommend me for appropriate recognition to the Czech Defense Department."

Thanks to many conversations with my father through the years, I had become familiar with numerous unusual activities he had been engaged in. Nevertheless, I was startled reading about his G-2's assignment to assist the Czech Liaison officer. In the past, the G-2 had kept him out of many activities. This took me completely by surprise because he had never discussed with me this relationship with the G-2. Reading about my father's work with the Czech Liaison Officer might provide another lead in my search for who ordered the raid.

To clear my mind after this new information, I decided to clean up the dishes I had left in the sink, go into the back yard to trim some of the bushes and mull over my new discovery. A few tree limbs were hanging down, keeping the grass and flowers below the trees from growing, so I gave the trees a haircut.

All these activities pooped me out. After a light supper I watched a couple TV programs. Then I hit the hay. Thanks to all the physical activity I slept well. I had one dream. It covered travel in Europe. When I woke up it occurred to me that the dream pointed the way for my next endeavor; still another trip to Europe to tie up some loose ends.

After breakfast I rang Lucy. "Oh, it's you again. No I can't take time off for another trip."

"Lucy, that is not why I called you."

"I know, I was just pulling your leg."

"Lucy, can you meet me for lunch today? I have to go to Europe again. I want to run some ideas by you."

"Okay, Keef, meet me around twelve at the front entrance."

I drove downtown. Lucy was waiting for me. I told her the restaurant was on M Street, just a few blocks from here. Could I park anywhere here? We approached the security guard. Lucy mentioned to him that she had an important meeting with this gentleman from the DOD. Could he park in one of the VIP Visitors spots? He asked for my credentials.

"I figured you are here on a security basis. I will call my office to have someone park the car for you. Just leave the key."

While we were walking along the street, I told Lucy, "You really look *saftig* today. When she asked me the meaning of this word, I said, "I have to practice my German. I plan to spend several days there on my trip. The literal translation of *saftig* is juicy, but actually it is an expression for 'well rounded.'"

"I told you before, Keef, I don't appreciate remarks like that. Cut it out!"

"Lucy, I only meant that you are so appealing!"

We soon reached the restaurant. It had received high marks in several reviews I had come across. There were several available tables. I asked the maître'd for one where we could talk undisturbed. While we were looking at the menu, the waiter recommended their most popular entry. The waiter could not remember its right name. He said the head cook knew its name, but he was not here today. The dish was soup-based, featuring various delicacies and potatoes, cream, fresh dill, butter and eggs. We both gave it a try and loved it. While indeed rich, it was smooth, tasting terrific.

After lunch, we talked for a while.

"Lucy, yesterday I was rummaging through an ancient desk my father used once in a while. Most of the drawers were full of miscellaneous papers, of no interest to me. In the bottom drawer was a file marked 'Pentagon.' I guess it was part of the documents he worked on over there. He must have taken it home for some reason. The folder dealt with an assignment he had at the Line of Demarcation. His task was helping the Czech Liaison Officer screen people trying to escape to the American Zone. The Liaison Officer was grateful for his assistance, and said he would recommend him for an award. My father attached a note to check on this. I doubt that he ever got around to looking into it. On my trip over there, I plan to stop off at Prague to see whether this award was made, but somehow never reached him. My question is whether I should approach your ex to help me out?"

"Keef, if I were you I would touch base with the American Embassy. You have had contact with the Embassy before. They will be able to approach the top side of the department directly, rather than the contacts my ex deals with."

"Good, I will do this. The number-two guy there has helped me in the past. Lucy, I need a favor. Among the papers in the old desk I found a note my father had written to the State Department for their records covering May 1945. He had contacted the library there. Would you check with the library to see whether they have anything on this? I can't give you even an approximate date he talked to the librarian. It must have been several years ago."

"I will be glad to do that, Keef. When are you leaving?"

"Probably in a couple of days."

"I may have an answer for you before you leave. I'll give you a call."

On the way back, I suggested that Lucy take the afternoon off. I wanted to show her some of my etchings.

She laughed. "Your mind is nowhere near the art. I will take a rain check."

Lucy called me the next day.

"Good news! I talked to the head librarian this morning. He remembered your father's request. He had sent some Xerox copies of pertinent papers extracted from the 1945 historical documents, "Foreign Relations of the United States, Diplomatic Papers, Volume IV, Europe" to your father. I asked him if he could give me another set. He explained that the records experts went through all of their files. They retired everything dated before the twenty-first century. He does not know where these papers are stored. It would be more than just a tedious process to get to the 1945 files. Surely your father kept them."

"Lucy, thanks a lot for your detective work! This gives me additional incentive to find his files at the Pentagon.

"I expect to leave for Europe tomorrow. I'm trying to get everything lined up this afternoon. I will fill you in on what, if anything, I've accomplished when I get back. Maybe I'll eat some delicious meals that will make your mouth water."

"Keef, you are incorrigible. There are two things always on your mind; food and love! Have a pleasant journey and stay away from your old flames!"

Then she sang to me a ditty, "I love coffee, I love tea, I love you and you love me!"

I needed a car in Europe. My best option was to fly to Frankfurt. I booked an evening flight out of BWI on Lufthansa. I picked Lufthansa, hoping that Hannah Merkla, the flight attendant with whom I had become friendly, would be on duty. Then I e-mailed the American Army Aviation Center in Berlin. They had helped me with a flight from Berlin to Frankfurt and provided a car with driver for my trip to Oppenheim. I identified myself and told them that they had made travel arrangements for me previously. I was engaged in an important investigation for the Pentagon. I required a car in Frankfurt for approximately two weeks. I would arrive there early in the morning on the following day.

Within an hour I had a response. "Mr. Keefer, we checked our records. You contacted us a couple of months ago. The sergeant who scheduled your previous trip is back in the States. He put a note on his report regarding the arrangements he had made about your working for the JCS. Of course, we will be glad to accommodate you. Please respond whether you need a driver and where you plan to go."

I answered that I did not want a driver. I would first head for Prague, then from there to a number of locations within Germany. Soon, another e-mail arrived. The car reserved for me was licensed for use throughout the European Union. I should please check in at the American Military Lounge when I arrived in Frankfurt.

I called the Uber office in Washington to send a car to pick me up early in the evening. They told me I could not use Uber if I was not registered with them. I would have to install the Uber program on a smart phone first. I ended up taking a regular cab. When I checked in, I asked the counter clerk whether Hannah Merkla was on this flight. She said she did not know. I should ask when I boarded. A crew member told me he knew Hannah. She was on a leave of absence to take care of some family problems.

Upon arrival I went straight to the lounge. The desk sergeant told me he had received the papers from Berlin. A car was ready, a mid-sized Opel. He also gave me an official certificate identifying me. It would facilitate my business at Army posts in Germany, including accommodations and car maintenance. A map was in the glove compartment. He had marked the best route to Prague. I would pass through Kulmbach. There was a Quartermaster Depot there if I needed to find some food or lodging.

After lunch at the Kulmbach facility, I topped the gas tank. Reaching Prague early in the afternoon, I drove directly to the hotel where I had stayed before. I called the Military Attaché's office. Colonel O'Rancher was not in. He was on a field trip. I talked to the travel coordinator, and I told her I had been hoping to have dinner with Colonel O'Rancher at the executive dining room at Charles University. I was wondering if she could make a reservation for me like when I was here a couple of years ago. She remembered me. At that time she had called the club for the Colonel and me, even though he also was not available then. He was a Club member. They would only admit those who belonged and their guests. She was glad to make the arrangements. After I was seated, she would call the Club to advise them that the Colonel was delayed. I should not wait for him as it might be some time later. I thanked her and said I would be at the Club around seven.

The sun was shining brightly. It was warm enough to relax on a lounge poolside. I checked the water; a bit on the cool side. As I had mentioned to Lucy, I was getting impacted by middle-age. This was borne out that afternoon. After reading only a few pages of a book, my eyes closed.

While I was getting ready to go, I remembered that the Club had a dress code at dinner time. I put on the only suit I had brought with me. I took a cab to the university just in case I felt like having a couple of cocktails. The maître'd checked the reservation list. He had just received a call that Colonel O'Rancher had been delayed. After he had seated me, a waiter showed up with a bottle of wine, explaining that O'Rancher's office had called, requesting his favorite selection. As I tasted it, I glanced around.

I was surprised to recognize a familiar face. A few tables to my right sat Carla, the movie producer whom I had assisted a few months ago. I walked over to her.

"Carla, do you remember me?"

"Of course I do. The movie is in the final stages. Are you waiting for someone? If not, why not join me?"

"Thanks, Carla." I moved over, bringing the wine with me. I poured her a glass and started to look at the menu. Carla recommended her choice. It was a French dish consisting of broiled cubed steak combined with a sauce of sautéed leek, bacon and mustard, which were then cooked together. Carla's selection was delicious. While we were enjoying after-dinner drinks, Carla confided to me that she had broken up with her long-time boyfriend. After they had separated, she had moved into an apartment. As we were leaving, she invited me to stop over at her place. She wanted my advice on some decorating problems.

Ordinarily, I would have been happy to accept. While no spring chicken, I had been attracted somewhat when we first met. But Lucy's parting words rang through my ears as a reminder that I had other commitments. I regretfully declined, saying that I had to prepare myself for a meeting at the embassy early in the morning. She responded that she understood, and even provided me a ride back to my hotel.

The following morning I called the American Embassy. They connected me with the Deputy Chief of the Mission. After I explained how I came across my father's note on working with the Czech Liaison Officer, I asked for his help in reaching the Czech Defense Department. I gave him more details and he agreed to call his contact there. He left a message and was told the contact would return his call soon. While we were waiting, I gave him a rundown on my current trip. He was surprised that I had been unable to pin down the source of the order. Finally, we got the call back. We laid out to him what I was seeking. The Defense Department guy responded, "Even though this is quite out of the ordinary, I understand Mr. Keefer's efforts to discover what, if anything, had happened on this. It will take quite a bit of digging into old records to see if there is any reference there. I have my doubts, but we will try. I'll put someone on this. It will take quite a bit of time. I will get back to you. It may take a few weeks."

I thanked the Deputy Chief for his efforts on my behalf. I would call him in a few days to see what he found out.

Upon returning to my hotel I contemplated on what to do next. I was finished here in Prague. I still wanted to know how the German Lt. Kaufmann, the Order of Battle Specialist in the German Army Headquarters for the Eastern Front, was involved in getting the intelligence information to the U.S. Army. Had he conveyed this to the OSS team operating near Prague? Was he involved at all with anyone? If not, this puzzle might never be resolved. I believe the lieutenant must have left some records. I had my doubts that the alleged memorandum at Frau Kaufmann's in Oppenheim was the whole story.

I needed to get my hands on the historical files at the Freiburg German Military archives. My previous effort to persuade Freiburg to do the research was unsuccessful. I had to convince somebody in Germany to push Freiburg on this. I had written to the German Embassy in Washington some weeks ago for assistance. The embassy's reply was that they would try to get me an answer. I had no way of knowing whether they followed up. I decided an unorthodox approach was worth a try. I would contact Müller, the police detective in Passau, who had provided valuable input in my Pentagon-ordered investigation a couple of years ago. Müller was the kind of person who knew how to tackle all sorts of problems.

I checked out of the hotel. There was no bill. They would send it to the Embassy. I took off. I drove to the Quartermaster Depot at Kulmbach to stop overnight. I asked the guy in the office at the gas station where the mess hall was. He laughed. "Don't go there, the food is lousy. There is a small hotel in Kulmbach. I think it is called *Kulmbacher Hof.* We eat there lots of times."

He also had a road map on the wall. The best way to Passau was to take a secondary road to Weiden. From there a major highway let to Regensburg and continued to Passau. By the time I was ready to roll I would hit Regensburg around noon. There was an Army gas station at the center of town.

The road to Weiden was not in good shape. I did not reach Regensburg until well after noon. Gassing up at the GI station, I saw a snack bar next door, apparently run by the PX. I was hungry and took advantage of their special; sandwich, French fries, and a drink. All for the grand sum of $2.50!

The highway to Passau was in excellent shape. I set the cruise control on 130 kph. I kept passing cars and the weather was good. Why were so many others slow-poking? I soon found out. Pulling over when I heard a siren, I expected an ambulance. Wishful imagination. It was the *Schutzpolizei*, the German highway patrol. I gave him my registration and my CIC identification. He was courteous in the beginning. Then he became friendly.

"I was in an exchange program with the Virginia State Police a couple of years ago. It was only a few weeks. Among the places they took me was Fort Belvoir. I see that is where you are located. Is that I-95 still a traffic nightmare?"

"I am actually stationed at Fort Meade, but I do go to Belvoir every so often. 95 is now worse. I heard they are going to add another lane. By the way, why did you stop me? I was going only 130. Isn't that the limit speed limit?"

"It is 130 on the Autobahn. On this road the limit is 120."

"So you stopped me for a few kilometers? In the States we usually have a leeway of 5 or 10 miles per hour."

"You know the German mentality, a rule is a rule. Fortunately, I have learned to be flexible. I seldom hand out tickets. By the way, where are you heading to?"

"To Passau, to visit with Inspector Müller, an old friend."

"Oh, yes, Müller is well known around here. I hear he may get a promotion, and transfer to Munich."

"I hope Müller will take me again to his family restaurant. It is in a small village on the edge of a forest. Besides excellent food, their waitresses wear *Dirndls*."

"I know this place. I eat there when I am in the area. I am acquainted with the owner. Give her my best."

After lowering the cruise control to 120, I was on my way. I made good time and reached Passau in the late afternoon. Elfriede, in whose house I had stayed on my previous visit to Passau, welcomed me with open arms. She invited me to have dinner at her friend's bar down the street.

She said, "I'll tell him to prepare his specialty, *Weisswurscht mit Kartoffelsalat*."

I thanked her, but I had to see Hans Müller right away. I really regretted having to decline. The dish was made with boiled white-meat sausage and potato salad, and was hard to pass up. I walked to Müller's office. Just as I approached the police station, I saw Hans leaving the building. I shouted. He turned around. His face lit up when he recognized me.

"I came to Passau specifically to seek your advice. Can we talk?"

"I was leaving early because it has been such a quiet day. Why not join me by having dinner at my favorite inn? I'll pick you up at Elfriede's in about half an hour. You don't have to change. It's very informal."

Müller showed up with a new car. "Your previous one was only 2-3 years old. Did you wreck it?"

He laughed. "No, I got a promotion. With it my transportation was upgraded."

When we got underway, I described my encounter on the highway. "I learned you may be heading for Munich."

He said, "Rumors travel fast. Thus far, nothing is official."

Soon we reached the inn. There were two waitresses in *Dirndls*. The owner greeted us as we entered. Hans introduced me. She remembered me. "You came with Hans a few years ago."

I commented that she had new waitresses. Did they wear the same old *Dirndls*?

She laughed as she led us to Hans' favorite table. I also gave her greetings from the *Schutzpolizei* officer. She said he was a good customer.

"I don't know whether he comes here for the beer, the food, or the *Dirndls*."

While we examined the menu, the waitress brought us a couple bottles of Hans' *Stamm Bier*. We started out with what we declined the last time; the house soup, cream of mushroom with locally grown vegetables. The main course consisted of venison steak with *Spätzle*, a noodle dish special to the area. As the food arrived fairly quickly, Hans suggested we put a hold on serious matters until after dinner. The venison was well-done, mild in taste. The *Spätzle* was served with a thick brown gravy. The side dish of the locally grown mushrooms was meaty and tasty. After we had ordered coffee and the in-house baked cheesecake, we settled down.

"Hans, do you remember what I told you about my father's venture in May 1945 in what was then Czechoslovakia?"

"I do. I also recall you had planned to discover who gave him the order."

"Well, I have been working on this for several months. I dug up a lot of circumstantial material, but nothing definite. I am now running down something which may provide at least a part of how it came about.

"A German intelligence officer, a Lt. Albrecht Kaufmann, reported to the Americans, when he surrendered, that there was extensive intelligence on the Russian Army at the remnants of a German headquarters near Prague. We already knew about this. My father's raid on that headquarters took place about a week or so before this lieutenant's arrival at the Line of Demarcation. I am trying to unearth whether Lt. Kaufmann had previously contacted somebody, possibly OSS officers. If so, where and who were they? Was he the original source of the information which prompted the raid?

"The Lt. Kaufmann is, of course, now deceased, but he may have left some memoranda on this. His records are at the German Armed Forces Archives, the *Bundesarchiv*, at Freiburg. I contacted Freiburg via e-mail. They responded by providing an application form for me to fill out before they would schedule a visit. It would take several weeks before I could be accommodated. I don't have the time or inclination to spend several weeks waiting for something which may or may not pan out.

"I was wondering if you have any ideas of how I may gain access to Freiburg on this trip."

"Keef, I can't promise anything. A colleague of mine is with the *Kripo*, the criminal police, at Freiburg. He may know somebody at the *Bundesarchiv* who can cut the red tape. I'll call him early tomorrow. Drop by the station to check what I have found out."

I tried to grab the bill, but, like the last time we were here, he insisted that this was against his office's rules. Again, we split it. Before we left the inn, I took a picture of the *Dirndl* girls. I was not surprised that Elfriede was still up, waiting for me. She always wanted to know "everything," but I declined to gossip, telling her that I had to hit the hay to dream about my new love. That got her even more curious. I showed her the picture I had taken.

"Keef, you are pulling my leg. This girl is pretty. She is probably married or has a dozen admirers."

In the morning, after having breakfast with Elfriede, I walked over to the station where Hans told me I was in luck. His colleague in Freiburg has a friend who heads one of the divisions of the *Bundesarchiv*.

"You should go. He will go to bat for you. One of his researchers will pull the May 1945 files on Czechoslovakia. See him tomorrow morning. His name is Franz Eppenstein. He has a Ph.D. You should address him as *Doktor*. I also asked to have the records checked for any data on survivors of Lt. Kaufmann. The *Doktor* recommended that you stay at a small guest house near the *Bundesarchiv*. Its name was *Zum Höllental*. He will make a reservation for you.

"I have already searched for the best route for you." He took me to a map mounted on the wall. I was to go back up to Deggendorf, turn left on A-92 leading to Munich, take the Munich Beltway until A-96, continue on A-96 to Bodensee, just north of Switzerland, turn right on Route E-54 which runs through the Black Forest to Freiburg. He also indicated he would call his friend in Freiburg to notify the guest house. He would tell them I might not arrive there until late in the afternoon or evening. I thanked Hans for his assistance and said I would reciprocate when he became chief of the *Kripo* in Munich and came to Washington on an exchange visit. He chuckled, saying he would rather skip this and go for Chief of Police. Now it was my turn to laugh. "Dream some more," I said.

Thanks to Hans' directions I reached an Army depot he had mentioned to me shortly after noon. It was a major installation. I gassed up. The Officer's Club was nearby. Food was served buffet-style. There was a good selection. There also was a table with sandwiches and fruit. I took some along for the road.

I reached Bodensee in the mid-afternoon. Stopping at a gas station I obtained an estimate on how long it would take to reach Freiburg. I was told the road was in good shape. I should be there between six and seven.

When I reached the outskirts of Freiburg, I saw a parked police car. I went over and asked the officer for directions to the *Bundesarchiv*. He indicated it was complicated. It was on the other side of the city. I asked him to lead me there. He replied that he was not permitted to do this. He gave me directions and I proceeded.

The guest house recommended by Eppenstein was a relatively new building. I offered my credit card, but the desk clerk declined. He had been instructed to send the bill to the *Kripo*. The room was spacious. I took a shower and changed clothes. Going downstairs, I asked the clerk where I could get something to eat. He recommended a cafeteria. *Kripo* personnel use it all the time. "Tell them you are guest of the chief. Maybe they will send the bill to them. They do it all the time." I requested him to look up the home phone number of Franz Eppenstein, call him, and tell him I would like him to join me for breakfast.

The cafeteria was crowded. They must have a good reputation. I observed that most customers had chosen the meatloaf. I also took it with selected Brussels sprouts and mashed potatoes. I topped it off with pie à-la-mode. Upon reaching the cashier, I pulled out my identification card, mentioning I had an appointment to see the Chief of the *Kripo*. She Xeroxed my I.D. card, did not accept my payment, and told me it will go on the *Kripo* account. When I returned to the guest house, the clerk advised he had reached Dr. Eppenstein. He would be there at nine and join me for breakfast. I asked him for a wake-up call at 7:30.

Franz Eppenstein was already seated when I entered the dining room. He stood up. We shook hands.

"It is a pleasure to meet you, *Herr Doktor*, please call me Keef."

"So, please call me Franz. Keef, my chief filled me in on your connection with Hans Müller. I met him last year at a convention. You know, in Germany, we go for titles. Here a Ph.D. is addressed as *Doktor*. Foreigners with a Ph.D. are not so addressed. The reason is that many in other countries, particularly in the United States, obtain the degree on a wholesale basis. In Germany it is much more difficult."

"In the States many people like to flaunt their Ph.D., even if it is honorary or obtained by mail-order courses. That is really a shame. Even at U.S. universities it takes a lot of time and work to obtain advanced degrees."

After we finished breakfast, Franz brought me up-to-date. The only pertinent remark in the lieutenant's file was a note about having become separated from his unit, the intelligence section of his headquarters. To the lieutenant this was unfortunate because they had lots of data on the Russians which he intended to turn over to the Americans. There was also an entry about his having notified the Americans of this when he surrendered. There was nothing in the files on whether he was involved in getting his information to the Americans before he reached their lines.

"Well," I said, "I am not surprised. If he had communicated with Americans prior to his surrender he might have saved it for later use. Perhaps he wanted to write a book. Or he may have wanted it as a plus factor if he tried to work for the U.S. Army."

"You may be right. Like many in the German military, he foresaw the approach of the Cold War. I thoroughly checked his personnel file. He had a sister in Oppenheim who may still be alive. I also found an address in Heilbronn for his only son. Yesterday, I called the police in Heilbronn to check whether he was still there and to get me his phone number. He died last year. His wife has remarried and still lives in the same house.

"So I called her. She agreed to gather his papers. I told her you would stop by within a couple of days. Her name is Ingeborg Hassel. Here are her telephone number and address. She told me that it is easy to find. Her place is right off the *Marktplatz*, in the center of the town."

"Thanks a lot for all your efforts! Franz, you have saved me a lot of time. I will tell your boss how much I appreciate his making you available to do all this research. Now I don't even have to go to the archives. I will leave shortly for Heilbronn. From there I will make a stop at the Army Headquarters, USAREUR, in Heidelberg. Then I will head for Frankfurt to fly back home. What is the best way to Heilbronn?"

"I suggest you backtrack the way you came until you hit A–81 going north through Stuttgart to Heilbronn. It should take about five to six hours or so."

"Thanks, *Herr Doktor* Franz, *auf wiedersehen!*"

When I was on the outskirts of Stuttgart, an MP on a motorcycle passed me. I honked the horn. He pulled over and stopped. I got out of the car and showed him my identification. I told him I was not lost, but was low on gas. He told me there was an Army station a few miles down the road. There is a sign there. "You can't miss it."

I thanked him. He estimated that I would reach Heilbronn in one to two hours. I asked him whether there was an Army facility there where I could stay overnight. He mentioned a small depot on the north side of Heilbronn where they did heavy maintenance on military vehicles. They didn't have a good snack bar there, though. I should check with the CO for a good restaurant.

After I had gassed up, I put a heavy foot on the pedal. I was getting tired. I stayed on the main road through Heilbronn. The Army depot was just outside the city limit. I followed the sign pointing to the headquarters. It was just a room in a small office building. There was a CQ watching TV. I showed him my identification, telling him I was on a special mission for the Pentagon. That startled him. He called the CO at home, saying he had a VIP visitor from the Pentagon. The captain wanted to see me, so the CQ got in my car and guided me there. He explained the captain had a rented house just a couple of blocks outside the depot gate. The captain came out and greeted us, inviting me in. He introduced me to his wife. They were just about to have dinner. I was most welcome to join them. The captain had come to this post just a few months ago. His previous assignment was as an instructor at the Ordnance School at Aberdeen.

The meal was broiled chicken with baked potatoes and string beans. The captain suggested we could talk in the living room while we were drinking coffee.

I gave him a brief rundown of my trip. He was surprised that there was nothing in the National Archives on my father's venture near Prague. While we were chatting I noticed there were a number of financial publications on a nearby table. I asked him whether he found them useful or merely entertaining.

He told me his father had subscribed to them for him, trying to get him interested in financial investments. His father had retired from his job as an auditor for a large enterprise. Having been a busy man all his life, he became bored quickly. A friend steered him into buying stock in several companies. This was several years ago. Since then, having had some success, he decided to be an investment advisor. At one time, he looked into starting a mutual fund, but two things persuaded him not to get into this. First of all there were too many funds. Secondly, after investigating how they worked, he became convinced that this was not for him. They were tightly regulated, generated numerous required reports, and, above all, the fund customers were obliged to pay income taxes when the fund sold stocks. They had to pay even if the fund retained the capital gains for further investments.

His father felt it was much better for serious investors, as opposed to the practice of in-and-out traders, to make long-term commitments. His method of operation was for individuals, whose portfolios he managed, who would commit themselves not to make any sales unless his father gave them the word to do so. His father did not require a specific initial amount to be invested. He did not take on anyone who did not have substantial assets. "He told me he wants to withdraw from active management in a few years. He wants me to take an early retirement from the Army and take over. That will be at least five years hence. In the meantime, I plan to make some investments myself to see whether I have a knack for it. My wife brags I will be the future Warren Buffett!"

I started to yawn. It had been a long day and I was ready to leave. The captain persuaded me to stay overnight, if I did not mind bedding down on the sofa in the living room. I should not have to go back to the depot. The CQ could properly come up with something, but it would be more comfortable here. I gladly accepted his offer.

I woke up late. The captain had already gone to the depot. His wife insisted I have some breakfast. I drove to the depot to thank him for his courtesy and hospitality. I asked him to call Heidelberg for me. I wanted to talk to the CO of the CIC Detachment. When we were connected, I introduced myself and explained that I was on a field trip authorized by the Pentagon. I requested him to check with the Historian's Office on whether there were any old records dating back to 1945. I told him there was a chance that some Army records of SHAEF had ended up at USAREUR instead of being shipped to the National Archives. "Specifically, I am looking for data on an Army raid in Czechoslovakia in May 1945." I told him I would stop by that office later in the day to see whether anything was found.

I drove back into the town center of Heilbronn. There was plenty of parking there. I asked a pedestrian to direct me to Mrs. Hassel's residence.

She had been expecting me. She had searched through all the documents still in her deceased husband's desk. The only pertinent paper was a note that his father had left; his memoranda on the war was at his sister's at Oppenheim. Well, here it was -- another dead end!

There was a major highway from Heilbronn to Heidelberg. It took me a little more than an hour to get there. At the gate of the USAREUR, I asked the MP how to get to the Historical Office. He was puzzled. He had never heard that there was one. He looked it up on the post directory. He pointed out the building. I was able to park in front by using one of the spaces reserved for general officers. Let them sue me!

The receptionist was a German woman. I greeted her, "*Wie geht's mein Fräulein?*"

"Thanks for the compliment. It's been twenty years. Now I am a *Frau!*"

"That doesn't matter, you look like a *Fräulein!*"

She laughed and asked how she could help me.

"I am from the Pentagon. I want to see the historian."

She took me back to the next room. There was another *Frau* sitting there. I introduced myself. She told me the boss was in a meeting, but she explained that he had conducted a search. One box was left from the stuff the office had inherited from SHAEF. Most had been shipped to Washington years ago. However, there was this one box. She didn't know why it was kept. Her boss had looked through it. There was nothing in there on Czechoslovakia. Another dead end!

I took the Autobahn to Frankfurt. I managed to get there within an hour. It took me about 30 minutes to battle my way to the airport. Traffic was worse than downtown Washington. I left the car in a 30 minute spot and headed for the American military lounge. I showed my identification and travel orders to the desk sergeant. I told him the Army car I had used was parked out front and gave him the keys. He checked a file folder and found the Berlin office's request to provide me with transportation. I had to sign a paper to certify that there was no damage to the car.

Then I told the Desk Sergeant I wanted to return to Washington immediately. I told him I wanted to take the next available commercial flight. He booked me in business class on a flight leaving early in the evening. As I was heading toward the snack bar, he advised not eating too much since they served dinner on my flight.

I arrived at BWI early the next morning. It was not a particularly smooth flight. The plane was crowded. I did not fall asleep until we were halfway home. Instead of going through the hassle of a shuttle bus, I opted for a cab home. It was not long before I was in bed catching up on sleep.

CHAPTER 8

MISSILE CRISIS

AFTER A GOOD NIGHT'S sleep, I woke up late the next morning. Even though I had nothing specific planned, I decided to get up rather than linger in bed. I knew there was a pile of mail waiting for me. When I was sitting at the edge of the bed, I became uncomfortably aware of a sharp throbbing pain in my left leg. Maybe I twisted something. I thought I would rest for a while. As soon as I laid down flat on my back, the ache ceased. I was sort of daydreaming for a while. Whenever I sat up the pain reappeared. Standing up to put on my pants, there was no cramp. I went to the kitchen for breakfast. As soon as I sat at the table, it started again. In order to eat, I had to stand. What in the world was wrong? I hoped it was something temporary. I would take it easy for the rest of the day. After picking up the newspaper, I plunked into my favorite chair, a recliner. As soon as I sat down the soreness was activated. I tilted back, but there was no change. When I stood up I felt fine. While I was walking there was no problem. This pattern was with me all day long. I went to bed early, hoping after a good night's sleep I would be completely normal again.

But not so, I felt exactly like yesterday. I took it slow in the morning. After lunch my patience had reached its limit. I called my doc at his Silver Spring office. His nurse told me he was with a patient. He would buzz me after he was finished with her. About half an hour passed before the phone rang. Before I mentioned my problem I engaged in small talk.

This guy was my father's physician, and I took his place after he died. I became very friendly with the doc. He loved to gossip with me. I asked if he got the card I had sent him from Freiburg a couple of weeks ago. He said he did and thanked me. Then he changed the subject.

"Keef, I know you well enough. You must have something on your mind. Spell it out."

"Doc, I have a puzzling problem."

After I gave him a summary, he wanted me to come in that afternoon. While I was waiting at his office, the nurse took my temperature and drew some blood. Then she wrote down what had occurred. When I finally got in, the doc told me he had gone over the nurse's notes. He was unable to pinpoint what ailed me.

"Keef, this is a serious condition. I am very concerned. I suggest you see an arthritis and rheumatism specialist. He is the best in the area. His office is on Georgia Avenue. He has a very busy practice. I will call him to see you as soon as possible. Here is his card, call him also. Your problem is serious, but not life-threatening. Don't let them divert you to one of his partners. If necessary, wait while he has time for you. I will send him the data my nurse has compiled."

It was getting late in the afternoon. Since I could not sit down for dinner, going to a restaurant was out. I went out and picked up some Chinese food for a stand-up meal at home. It was too late to contact the arthritis guy. I would do it in the morning. I was going to check in with Lucy, but I changed my mind. What was I going to tell her at this point?

The next morning I called the specialist. The receptionist said the doctor was on vacation. She could connect me with one of the partners. I declined. I asked her to connect me with his nurse.

"This is Kevin Keefer. I need to see the doctor as soon as he returns. Did you receive the e-mail my GP sent you yesterday?"

"Yes, Mr. Keefer. I placed it on his desk."

"When do you expect him back?"

"He will be gone for a week, possibly a couple of days longer. I see you have a serious condition. I suggest taking one or two aspirins a day and seeing if massaging the leg will help. Just avoid being in a sitting position as much as possible. I will call and tell you when to come in."

"Thanks. I hope it will be soon." I didn't take any aspirin, because I'm allergic to it.

My next call was to Bob MacMerial. Amy picked up. He was at the Pentagon. Amy started to yak. I interrupted, telling her I had some serious health problems. I would be out of action for at least two weeks. I didn't want any calls referred. I had seen the doctor. I was getting treated. I would touch base with the colonel as soon as I knew what was what. Then I hung up.

Standing up at the kitchen counter, I started to write my trip report. It took a little over an hour. I kept it succinct, just covering the highlights. Then I faxed it to Amy.

I went into the kitchen to clean up. I suspected that Lucy would do some cooking. I washed the dishes, and set up the self-cleaning oven. Everything looked pretty neat, except the floor. How to attend to this without kneeling down? I tried but the pain appeared quickly. I got a bucket full of soapy water and placed some clean rags around the broom. I followed up with clear water. It looked fairly good after spending an hour at it.

Around six Lucy showed up. She had a shopping bag full of stuff. After she dropped it off on the kitchen table, I gave her a bear hug. She looked around, pleased to see how everything looked so neat.

"Your neighbor's maid did a good job. Hope you paid her well."

"Lucy, what you observed is actually attributed to me. I had made such a mess yesterday, I cleaned it up this afternoon."

"You should have gotten somebody else to do this, Keef, she said. I reckon you couldn't find help on such short notice. But give me your support, mostly moral, on what I may be able to put on the table."

"I learned from my mother, when someone does not feel well, you give him homemade soup. Watch me. I hope the result will be worth the effort."

Lucy explained she would cook up something similar to what I had described to her on our trip to Czechoslovakia a couple of years ago. "Someone took you to a hidden jewel of a restaurant in the woods of Bavaria. You mentioned their favorite *Tagesuppe* (soup of the day) was a goulash concoction. You liked it. Then the main course was beef rolls, they called it *rindsrouladen*, accompanied by the inevitable *spätzles* (small dumplings)."

My only contributions were to hand her the pots and pans and set the table. She was well prepared. All the different food items were cut to size and placed into separate bags. It took only about an hour to get the finished product on the table. I must say that, while it did not exactly match what was served in Bavaria, it was delicious. The fact that I was mighty hungry may have had something to do with it. For dessert she had bought my favorite, cherry pie. We also finished the rest of the coffee I had made in the morning. Lucy wanted to clean up the kitchen, but I nixed it. It would give me something to do in the morning after checking the mail.

We went into the living room to relax and gossip. I had consumed the meal while standing, but now I would try sitting in my recliner. The pain shot up with a vengeance. I went over to the sofa which I often use to nap on. Lucy had enough room to sit next to me. She asked me if I had tried to massage the leg. No, the doc had prodded the area, but did not say anything about rubbing or kneading. Lucy was not deterred. She helped me take off my pants. After getting some cream out of her handbag, she gently moved her hand up and down. As she used a light touch, the pain was more bearable, although it did not disappear. A few moments later I grabbed her hand, suggesting going further upwards. She pulled off my shorts. As she gently massaged me in the area where the leg joined the body, I noticed that while the pain persisted, I became aware there was another effect. My penis reacted even without receiving direct attention. Lucy also noticed the swelling. She stopped her handiwork. She bent down and kissed my organ. She unbuttoned my shirt. After pulling it off, her hands worked all over me while we kissed deeply.

Lucy got up and removed her clothes and slid beside me. It did not take long before I pulled her onto me. I was immobile. She engaged in all the moves. I felt good after the climax. I told her she knew better than the doc about what I really needed.

I felt it was time for a good rest. Muttering to Lucy, I said I was getting somnolent. She asked where I picked up this word. I told her that my father sometimes was a show-off. He used "somnolent" occasionally to impress people with his sophistication.

I must have fallen asleep. I was not aware of Lucy getting off the sofa. When I woke up a couple of hours later, she was gone. She left me a note, hoping I would feel better, and she would call me in the morning.

While I was busy in the kitchen cleaning up, the following morning, Lucy called. I told her there was no change in my condition. I was grateful to receive a relief last night. I asked her to come again soon. I needed to take a shower and needed help. She chortled and thanked me for the invite, which reminded her of the shower assistance that Carla, the movie producer, rendered in Prague. I told her she got this confused. My relationship with the movie gal was strictly platonic. Lucy then speculated that she got the story mixed up. I had mentioned the experience to her. It must have been someone else. I chuckled. "Yes, this did happen but it was not her. How do you know about this?"

According to Lucy, I had mentioned the episode when we had lunch weeks ago at this place near the State Department. She said I must have been thinking of us becoming involved and wanted to clean the slate. Lucy was correct. I believed she and I were in love and we would see what the future would bring.

"Lucy, I understand one confesses to a priest. When were you ordained? But all this is beside the point. When are you coming over? Can you make it tonight?"

"Keef, you have to fend for yourself. I found out this morning I have to attend a week-long Department Seminar. They hold it once a year at some resort, usually in Pennsylvania. I will check in with you from there."

"I am disappointed. I really need to take a shower. Your massaging gave me some relief. I'll go out and buy one of those vibrator gimmicks and think of you while I use it."

"Cut out all this nonsense. Don't let Bob MacMerial send you some help. You don't need it."

The week passed quickly. Bob and Henry Kelly came by on different days. They took me out for dinner. I picked places where there was counter service. This way I could stand while we ate, while they could sit. Henry observed he had been stood up on dinner dates, but never this way.

At the end of the week I received a call from the orthopedic doctor's nurse. He would see me on Monday.

I arrived there early, anxious to get this over with. I had a two-hour wait. The nurse confided that he had shown up late. Then they had had a lengthy staff meeting.

The doctor was past middle age. He did not apologize for seeing me so late. After he examined both legs and my lower back, I had to take three x-rays. He could not identify the problem, and wrote an order for an MRI.

When I saw him a few days later, he reported that there was nothing in the MRI he was able to pinpoint as the cause of the pain. He made an appointment for me the following day with an orthopedic surgery practice. The surgeon was young, courteous, and made me feel at ease. He examined me and went over the MRI with me. He believed the cause was pressure of the spine on the ribs. He did not recommend surgery. He thought that eventually there would be a shift, taking off the pressure. In the meantime I should take full strength aspirin daily.

After returning home, I called my regular doc. I related my experience with the two physicians. He thought this was encouraging. He had heard of similar cases. They were all resolved without surgery. As I was allergic to aspirin, he suggested a substitute, acetaminophen. To my surprise there was immediate relief after taking the first pill. The pain eased when I was sitting. I went out in the yard to do some trimming. Then I read the paper sitting in the lounge chair. The sun was beating down on me. My eyes closed. I must have napped for about an hour. When I sat up the pain was almost gone. I called my doctor. He was happy to hear this. He believed the combination of the pill and my shifting around while doing yard work might have affected whatever caused the pressure on the spine. He recommended I get back to my normal activities.

That was good news! I was tired of standing while eating, doing yard work, cleaning house, and, above all, sleeping. I called Lucy at work, looking forward to celebrating that night. Her phone rang quite a while. Finally a colleague picked it up. Lucy was out of town. Her boss took her with him to New York. They had to run up there, some problem at the UN. She had no idea when they would be back. If this was an emergency, I could notify her secretary. She knew how to reach her. I asked her just to leave a note that I called.

Next, I phoned Bob MacMerial. Amy got him on the line. I gave him a rundown of my doctors' visits.

"I knew you would snap out of it. I spent two days at the Pentagon. You have no idea what is going on over there. It is busier than a beehive. This is all related to the budget battles in Congress. It is referred to as sequestration, Federal spending cuts. The Pentagon has demanded the departments earmark the cuts. The Army will be severely affected. I don't know why Ft. Belvoir designated me. I imagine they didn't want to send a higher-up whom they could press for commitments. I did a lot of nodding, very little speaking.

"I just finished talking to the Chief of Staff of INSCOM. He said the CG (Commanding General) had wanted him to go. He convinced the CG to let me represent us.

"'You've spent a lot of time there, know lots of people, and know how to pass the buck to us, if necessary.'

"The Chief requested me to come over tomorrow morning. Something has come up that the CG wants me to handle. 'Bring Keef along, if he is not gallivanting in Europe.'

"I'll pick you up tomorrow around eight. Don't bother with breakfast, let INSCOM treat us."

The next morning, while we were heading for Virginia, I expressed my surprise that instead of Bob's own car, we were in an Army mid-size automobile with a soldier at the wheel. "Well, he said, "since my promotion I take advantage of all the privileges. Not only that, the Fort Meade staff has suddenly become more cooperative. They are faced with downsizing, part of the Pentagon's upcoming moves. They don't want to see us leave the post. They want to keep their motor pool busy."

We arrived shortly after nine. There was not much traffic. Most of it was cars, buses, and vans heading the other way, towards Washington. The driver dropped us off at INSCOM Headquarters. When we entered the Chief of Staff's office, his secretary explained that he was with the General. As Bob anticipated, there was coffee, toast, and other goodies on a serving table. We were both hungry and dug in. We were just about finished when the Chief showed up. He growled that the General had had a call from the Pentagon that we were not exempt from that damn sequestration business. The General instructed him to offer some token cuts here, none in the field offices, except empty slots.

"Keef, are you now finished with touring Europe?"

"Sir, I thought I was. My visit to the German Army record center at Freiburg did not yield anything on the German Lt. Kaufmann. You may recall, I believe he is the key link in the chain of events on the origin of the information on the German records on the Red Army. Eppenstein, my contact at Freiburg, sent me a note recommending that I go to France, where a younger cousin to the lieutenant resides with his French spouse. He believes that this cousin may have some of the lieutenant's records. I thought I had finally eliminated Europe in my search. Now that this has come to light, I feel have to follow it up. Sir, you may rest assured running around empty over there is not something I enjoy."

"Well, Keef, you may forget about Europe for the time being. The reason we called Bob MacMerial to come here today is to assume responsibility for an investigation of the mysterious absence of a member of the anti-missile defense headquarters in Nebraska. With all the bad publicity the Air Force has been getting lately, the Pentagon elite wants us to determine just what is going on out there. They don't want the Air Force to be in charge in this check-up. One rumor going around is that this absent individual may be sympathetic with one of the groups fighting in Syria. Who knows?"

"I heard that Sec/Def was notified. He has been after the Air Force to clear up the personnel problems at the missile sites. Now he wants another arm of DOD to look into this. That is how we were picked.

"Bob, contact the G-2 of the missile command and send Keef out there. With the budget tightening up, see if you can book Keef on a MATS flight out of Andrews. Keep me abreast of anything significant Keef may uncover. I am trying to impress the Pentagonites about how busy we are. I will try to get additional funding. This may ease some of the cuts they will try to impose on us."

On the way back Bob told me he would get right on this. "I'll have Amy take care of the travel orders and make the Andrews reservation. You should go on this trip in uniform. I will phone you tomorrow afternoon."

"You have read all the news about the lackadaisical working atmosphere of the crews manning some of the sites. DOD cracked down. They are probably very touchy when dealing with people from Washington."

As I was eating lunch, the phone rang. It was Lucy.

"Keef, how are you feeling?"

"The problem has been resolved."

"Keef, I am still at a meeting. I will buzz you tonight."

I spent the afternoon preparing for the trip. The uniform was clean, but needed pressing. I made a quick trip to the cleaners. When I returned, my neighbor knocked on the door. She invited me for dinner. A niece was visiting them. I accepted, but cautioned that I expected an important phone call, so I could not linger. I went over around six with a bottle of white wine. The food was excellent, as was the company. The niece was a little younger than I was. She was very pleasant. She was a special education teacher. In response to my questions, she related various problems which cropped up almost daily.

Around eight I finally was able to cut myself loose, apologizing for leaving such enjoyable company. Just as I walked into the door, the phone rang. It was Lucy.

"Keef, I called before. Where were you?"

"I was next door. They invited me for dinner. Her niece was visiting from Chicago. She is a teacher, not bad looking. I was tempted!"

"You are pulling my leg again. So tell me, what was your problem?"

"Something to do with the spine. Went to two orthopedic specialists. They last guy put my MRI on the screen, explaining he hopes it is temporary. He was right, gave me a pill. The day afterwards I was on the mend.

"I asked him whether I could resume my sex life. He chuckled and told me, 'The more the better.'"

"Keef, cut it out! I will be out for another week. We've been at a conference in Canada. To my surprise my boss took his secretary along.

He explained this was such a sensitive subject, he needed her to take extensive notes. We have had many discussions for the past two days. She was at the meetings. I did not see her keeping a detailed record. I suspect there is more to it. They have adjoining rooms. Maybe she is taking notes all night!"

"Lucy, you are a prude. Let them have fun. You are just jealous that I'm not in the room next to yours!"

"You men are so tolerant. I would be, too, except this guy has a lovely family. I was at their home once. Besides, this woman has poor manners. While we were having cocktails before dinner, she sat with us, but was on her phone, tweeting."

"Lucy, I may not be here when you come back. INSCOM is sending me out west to check on a problem at the missile command. Why the DOD doesn't want the Air Force to clean it up, I don't know. Maybe DOD thinks I am the best investigator for the job. What do you think?"

"Keef, you are always trying to take credit where none is due. The DOD just wants someone not directly involved. Call me when you are back in town."

"I wasn't serious, Lucy; just wanted to hear your reaction. *Au revoir.*"

The travel order was faxed by the afternoon. Amy called me a little while later. She could not get me on a flight from Andrews tomorrow. "They could put you on one the day after. Colonel MacMerial did not want a delay. So I booked you commercial. Your flight departs at 10:00 in the morning. I will fax the details."

CHAPTER 9

NEBRASKA

MY NEIGHBOR GAVE ME a ride to the Metro. I reached Reagan National in time. The flight was uneventful. I took a cab to the headquarters. I was surprised that I was not questioned at the gate. At the headquarters a guard stopped me. He checked my orders. Then he called someone. A few minutes later a middle-aged woman greeted me. She introduced herself as Maria O'Neal.

She explained the G-2 had asked her to be my contact here. I asked her why she was not in uniform. She was a civilian, the administrative officer for the G-2 section. As it was about lunch time, she took me to the cafeteria. I asked her whether she knew why I had come here. Yes, she had read the messages the Air Force had sent. There was turmoil caused by the irregularities uncovered at some of the missile sites. But the organizational and manpower irregularities were doomed, in part, by failures at the command level.

Why had the Air Force in Washington agreed to have an outsider conduct the investigation? I explained that the DOD was getting heat from Congress. This is how I, of the Army's Intelligence and Security Command, INSCOM, got the assignment. When I had been briefed on this I had been advised that the recently appointed Secretary of Defense was fuming that the Department of the Air Force had apparently failed to recognize all the ramifications of what had occurred at one of its key Air Force field commands.

According to Maria, the G-2 became quite concerned when he read the Department's message about the involvement of an investigation from INSCOM. He was also ordered by someone in the Air Force Chief of Staff's office to give the Army his full cooperation. I pointed out that I was curious that the Missile Command's counterintelligence unit was not already involved. She told me that counterintelligence was ordered to get busy on this when the situation finally came to the Command's notice. Maria believed the CG and the G-2 wanted to keep control at this level.

"Tomorrow a member of the G-2 staff, who does special investigations for the CG, will meet with you. George will be your guide and bring you up to speed on his investigation. He is not here today."

After lunch we went up to her office. She took me to the G-2, a Brigadier General, who welcomed me and assured me that I would get full cooperation. Maria was to be my contact here. Tomorrow I would meet his special investigator, who would be at my disposal. I asked Maria later about this special investigator. She elaborated that he was a former FBI agent who lives nearby. He had contacted the G-2 after retirement. He had been in counterintelligence and wondered whether they had a requirement for someone with his qualifications. The G-2 asked Personnel whether they could hire him directly. There was an obscure provision permitting the direct appointment of someone with special qualifications to meet urgent needs.

He was appointed as a warrant officer last year. He seems very capable and well-liked at the headquarters. "You two will get along splendidly."

"I would like to spend the rest of this afternoon getting some background information. First, I want details on the Command's organization as well as those of the subordinate units. Second, I want to see what actions the counterintelligence team might have taken thus far, including how this all began."

"I can easily provide the organizational part. But we haven't received a preliminary report from counterintelligence. The practice had been that no report is made to headquarters until all the work has been completed."

I said we had an unusual situation. "You now have an outsider sent in who has been charged exclusively to get all the facts and resolve the problem. I want counterintelligence to fax the G-2 a summary about how this got started and what has been accomplished to date."

We then walked back to the G-2's office. I explained to him what I required. I must have the complete background of the problem. He agreed and faxed an order to the unit to provide me a detailed summary. He expected them to comply within the hour and fax him the report. He also pointed out that George Mizells, the Warrant Officer who would work with me, could fill me in on what he had been able to extract from counterintelligence.

Maria invited me to use a desk in her office. She brought me a folder on the organization. She needed a copy of my travel orders, which included my security clearance. Because the folder included extremely sensitive data, a special authorization from the G-2 was needed. So we went back to see him once more. I told him it I needed a full background on this. He was tempted to check with the Department of the Air Force on this, but finally he gave Maria the OK on his own authority.

I spent more than an hour on this folder. I wanted to get a broad outline on how the command operated. The organizational structure of the active missile units was too complicated to really delve into. I was impressed at the sensitivity and details of the operational orders.

Maria brought me the data she had received from the investigating unit. They had called her when the G-2's orders arrived. Why was the usual SOP by-passed? She told them this was essential in compliance with the DOD decision to have an outsider pursue his own investigation. Full cooperation was in order. Maria had glanced over the submission. It was sketchy in spots, but the description of how this case arose appeared to have sufficient details for an uninitiated person's edification.

For the next two hours I reviewed the report very carefully. I began to comprehend why the DOD called for an external independent investigation. I jotted down a list of the key elements on a memo pad. What started all this was the mysterious disappearance of a trusted member of the G-2 staff, namely Technical Sergeant Paul Kerriko. He had the highest security clearance. His main function was to assure that all important events were properly summarized in the daily "Key Events Report" submitted to the CG. He was familiar with all the locations of the missile batteries, their states of readiness, and problems which arose.

I discussed what I had read with Maria. Why couldn't this be readily explained? She related there was much more to it, not covered in the report. The G-2 has had George Mizells spend all his time on this. She had seen most of his reports. He believed that Kerriko's unexplained absence required an in-depth review. The counterintelligence unit was checking on field activities about what connections might have taken place between Kerriko and the field commands. Of course, some of the contacts might be part of his normal duties. Maria suggested that I wait until tomorrow. George would undoubtedly give me a thorough briefing.

I wondered aloud why and how DOD got into this. Maria speculated that George had convinced the G-2 that this might be a serious security matter. He urged the G-2 to report it to Washington in light of the FBI's uncovering a number of attempts and actions against military facilities in the United States. The Air Force probably included it in their reports to DOD on matters of significant security interest. That might have caused the DOD's insistence on a vigorous look-see by an outside party. Maria was not really involved in all this. George would fill me in.

It was getting late. I had had enough for the time being. Maria had made reservations for me at the BOQ (Bachelor Officers Quarters) for me. It was nearby. As I was leaving the office Maria casually mentioned something about a special barbecue tonight. Would I like to come? I told her it was too hot outside. I liked creature comforts. She laughed. "No, it's inside." This was agreeable to me. She would pick me up after seven. It was in a nice setting a few miles from here. She said it was informal. No need to dress up.

I checked in at the BOQ. The receptionist revealed that Ms. O'Neal from G-2 had asked to make sure I would receive nice quarters. There were only a few rooms with adjacent bathrooms. He said I was the first visitor from Washington since he had been manning the desk. He would make a wake-up call at 0700 tomorrow. They had a small kitchen in the building. There would be a light breakfast between eight and nine. They had modernized. Instead of a key, I received a punch-in code.

After showering, I put on the only civilian outfit I had brought with me. I did not have a tie, but doubted it was required. I was sitting in the reception area when Maria showed up. I was stunned. She was no longer the middle-aged plain Jane. She wore a skirt and light sweater which was low cut enough to reveal enticing features underneath. She must have gone to the beauty parlor to get her hair done. I told her I hardly recognized her. How did she take the ten years off from this afternoon? She laughed and led me out to her car. It was pretty beat up. She apologized. She was in the process of getting rid of it.

The clubhouse was what one usually finds on a post. Nothing fancy about it, very functional. The maître'd greeted her. "I reserved a nice table in the rear. I trust you will like the barbecue, Mrs. O'Neal."

When he addressed her this way, I must have shown my surprise. Maria noticed it. She remarked, "Let's get some food. I am starved, but don't worry, an angry husband won't show up. I'll explain later."

After we were seated I opened a bottle of white wine. I inquired how Maria knew I would like this. "After I dropped you off at the BOQ, there was a call on my cell phone to return to headquarters. I was to call a Colonel MacMerial at Fort Meade. When I got him on the line, he asked me to get you. He had not been able to reach you on your cell phone. When I told him that you had just left, he asked me to take some notes and convey the info to you.

MacMerial said, "'Tell him that the Chief of Staff of INSCOM buzzed me. He had called the National Missile Command Center at the Pentagon. He wants to ascertain that they had ordered Offutt to assure that Mr. Keefer will get maximum cooperation and assistance. Mr. Keefer is to touch base with me if this arrangement is not working out to his satisfaction.'

"I responded that I would give Mr. Keefer the message tonight. He would accompany me to dinner later at the club. Colonel MacMerial commented that he thought that this was a good idea. 'Don't let him drink too much. Make him stick to white wine.'"

We then proceeded to join the buffet line. The barbeque looked enticing. I took a generous portion. Maria urged me to sample the

Brussels sprouts which were locally grown. She concentrated on filling most of her plate with the offerings of the salad bar. For dessert we picked a selection of cookies. While sipping coffee, Maria turned to me and impulsively covered my hand.

"I know you are curious about having dinner with Mrs. O'Neal. Actually, it is the former Mrs. O'Neal. My divorce was finalized last month. My ex works for an engineering firm in Omaha. We were married for over ten years. We drifted apart a couple of years ago.

"I can't put my finger on exactly how it happened. We have two kids, both boys, ages seven and nine. They are with me. My mother lives with us, taking good care of them. My ex gets them two weekends a month.

"While the legal proceedings were not exactly friendly, we decided to be agreeable. Make the inevitable as peaceful as possible, especially in consideration of the boys. My ex now lives with a woman who used to work in his office. I have never met her. Whether anything was going on between them before all this, I don't know. I won't dwell on that. I don't feel exactly liberated, but I accept what has happened."

I expressed my regret. I was glad to see how well she has gotten over this. She looked absolutely stunning to me tonight. She responded that thanks to her determination, she turned over a new leaf in her life. Unlike in the past, she now goes regularly to the beauty parlor, shops for more outfits and is in a yoga class. This evening was actually the first time since the divorce that she had gone out for dinner with someone. She was so glad I appeared out of nowhere. Then she leaned over and kissed me on the cheek. That was a surprise!

While talking we had not noticed that the band had started to play. Some couples were already swinging it. I asked her if she would like to join me on the floor as soon as a slow foxtrot was played. Maria said she would love to. I led her to the floor. She was a little rusty and had not danced for over two years. That was great! It would bring her up to my level.

Soon the band struck up something to my liking. I took Maria by the arm as we moved toward the floor. She turned out to be an excellent dancer. We were soon cheek-to-cheek. She moved closer to me. I couldn't help myself. I started kissing her, which she returned.

While we danced the next number Maria became flushed in her face and kept moving her arm around me. My body reacted with a gradual erection. As we sat down at our table, Maria turned to me, kissing me heartily. Apparently she wanted more. She claimed it was getting too stuffy in here. She suggested we leave to go to a nice place in Omaha.

This posed a dilemma for me. How could I politely turn her down? I decided to be straight forward.

"Maria, I don't think this is a good idea. You see, a couple of years ago I was on duty in Prague as part of running down events which happened at the end of World War II. I worked with the American military attaché to follow up on one clue. I had to proceed to a smaller town. The attaché suggested I let his wife drive me there as she was familiar with that area. She proved to be very helpful. To cut a long story short, I had to return to Prague a few months ago. I wanted to take the attaché and his spouse out for dinner, but he told me that she was back in the States. Before I left, one of the secretaries who had helped me with travel orders told me that the attaché and his wife were separated. She returned to the State Department where she had met her husband a number of years ago.

"I am a nosy guy. Those two seemed to me a happily married couple. When I was back in Washington I ran her down at State. She was surprised to hear from me. We had lunch a few days later. She told me there were irreconcilable differences between them. They mutually agreed she would file for a divorce. She was very appreciative that I had contacted her. She had no family in the area and most of her former co-workers had moved elsewhere. We had several dinners together. I gradually found myself in love."

Maria had listened intently. She thanked me for laying out the facts for her. "You are one in a million. On one hand most of the guys I have known would not have acted like you. On the other hand, I probably was too playful. As I told you, I have been without a man for some time now. I was lucky to have run into you. I am attracted to you and just followed my feelings. I do want to thank you for making this evening so pleasant."

After Maria dropped me off, I took another shower to cool off and get to my normal self. I had come close to breaking my goal to stick only with Lucy. But I also learned that while I possibly could get into similar dilemmas in the future, I would be able to stick to my guns.

The following morning, after breakfast, I rambled over to headquarters. Maria was expecting me. She introduced me to George Mizells, who was in uniform. We went to his desk and started to chat. He briefly ran down his career with the FBI and how he obtained his position here. He said that I did not need to detail my background. When he had been informed about his working with me, he had touched base with his connections in Washington. He laughed when he said that I was practically a colleague, having worked with a guy he knew and by being a regular user of the FBI parking facilities at the restaurant at the Potomac.

"You know a lot about me, but I bet you did not know I was a movie advisor in Prague."

That aroused his curiosity, so I briefly related my contacts with Carla, the producer of a movie on the last days of World War II. This chit-chat created a friendly atmosphere. George began to give me a complete rundown of what he knew about the case in his organization.

He started out with what he knew about T/Sgt. Paul Kerriko. "I have run into him from time to time. He occasionally approached me when he covered something I was familiar with in the Key Events Report. From this limited contact I deduced him to be a bright fellow. He had been doing his job in G-2 for over a year. His report covers events command-wide, thus he was well versed with what was going on.

"About three weeks ago he went on a one-week leave. He asked for it, telling the G-2 that he needed to take care of some personal matters. He has not been back since. We checked his apartment. There was no clue where he may have gone. As Maria briefed you, our counterintelligence unit has been checking the subordinate commands in case he made contact with them. He knew a bunch of people there who fed him data for his daily report. Thus far, they have not come up with anything.

"The G-2, after we came up with nothing, became quite concerned. We checked with the State Police and hospitals in the area. We came up with zilch. Because of Kerriko's sensitive position, the G-2 alerted Washington that we might have a problem. I have handled calls from our bosses at the Pentagon. They did not seem to be greatly disturbed. However, to cover themselves, they notified the Department of the Air Force, which, in turn, passed it on to DOD. That is how your outfit became eventually involved.

"I found a loose-leaf phone listing in Kerriko's apartment. I ignored all the basic numbers, such as restaurants, cleaner, etc. A few individuals were listed. I assumed they were friends or bridge partners. I knew he played regularly. There was a female listed who was not included with those he played bridge with. Her name is Carolyn Smithfield. I called this number and a woman answered. I asked for Carolyn and found that I was talking to her mother. I explained I was with the Offutt Air Force Base and was looking for T/Sgt. Paul Kerriko. She then explained that Paul was Carolyn's boyfriend. They were on a camping trip. I told her I wanted to come over that afternoon, and she agreed to see me.

"She seemed like a pleasant enough woman. Her husband is in the Navy. He would be gone for several weeks. He was on board a carrier in the Pacific. Carolyn was her only child. When I informed her that Kerriko was two weeks overdue from a one-week leave and he was now considered to be technically AWOL, she was surprised. Carolyn told her they would be away for at least a month. They left with a trailer attached to Kerriko's car, full of canned food, a tent, and camping equipment.

"When I asked her whether I could see Carolyn's bedroom, she readily agreed. I was immediately puzzled when I saw a large map of the Middle East posted above her desk. There were several places in Syria underlined. I asked her mother if she know what Carolyn was doing with the map. She had asked her. Carolyn's response was that she was writing a paper on medical problems in Syria. Carolyn was taking a nursing course twice a week at the local community college. She also had a full time job in a doctor's office.

"I asked her how long she had been with Paul. She estimated that it was at least six months. I asked her what else she could tell me about Carolyn. She was a computer nut, on the Internet all the time. She took the computer with her on this trip. The only other unusual event was that recently Carolyn had become friendly with a woman who picked her up several times. This woman never came into the house but waited

117

in her car. Once she got out of the car to help Carolyn carry something. She looked like she may have been of Middle Eastern origin.

"I requested a good picture of Carolyn. She came up with a photo taken recently. I was surprised that she was a well-built, attractive girl. I told her mother she must be proud of her. Mom was. Carolyn was a popular girl, both in high school and in the two years she went to college. Before I left I asked her for directions to the doctor's office where Carolyn works. It was not far. I got there before closing time.

"The doctor was just finished with his last patient. I showed him my credentials. He waved me into his office. I asked him how long Carolyn Smithfield had worked in his practice. It was about two years. It was after she left college. He was concerned about her not sticking with it to get a degree. Carolyn claimed she left college for financial reasons. She is an excellent employee, very helpful, especially as an assistant when he performed minor surgery in his office. Why did he grant her four to five weeks leave? She had not had a vacation for two years. He thought she deserved a break.

"I mentioned Paul Kerriko. The doctor had met him several times when he had picked her up at the end of the day. He seemed like a nice fellow. As far as Carolyn's attending a nursing course at the community college, he acted very surprised. It was the first time he had heard of it. Then I told him her mom pointed out to me that her daughter was very ambitious. The mom thought that Carolyn had been taking a special nursing course at the local community college every Tuesday and Thursday. The doctor responded that he could see the street from his office window and Carolyn was picked up by the same woman on those days. When I asked him to describe the woman, he said she was not dressed like most local women. He agreed when I mentioned that she probably was Middle Eastern.

"He then offered to check this out. He called the registrar of the college, who had been his patient last year. She responded that they did not offer nursing courses in the evening. Then she checked the registry, in case Carolyn was enrolled in another course, but could not find anything. Carolyn was not a student there. I noted her mom's description of her preoccupation with Syria. He had not realized that she was involved in any way in political aspects."

I thanked George for his briefing. He had done lots of digging. I could understand why he had alerted the G-2 of his suspicions.

It was getting late. George wanted to know if I had any plans for the evening. When I shook my head, he invited me to accompany him for dinner at his house. He called his wife to put out an extra plate. He had invited an out-of-town colleague. She protested that they were only having leftovers. He laughed, telling her she was a genius in the kitchen and would come up with something.

George's house was in a typical middle class section of Omaha. George thought he had overpaid, but his wife insisted upon it. She had checked out the quality of the schools, and this proved to be the determining factor.

His wife came out of the kitchen. Her name was Abigail, but she went by the name "Abby." He also introduced his two youngsters. They said "Hello" but went back to the TV. Abby explained that they were actually watching an educational series. She strictly limited their TV time. Abby exclaimed she was happy to meet me. I apologized for barging in without any due notice.

She smiled. "You are no trouble. We were going to have leftovers. Fortunately, I took advantage of a grocery sale this morning. I bought some veggies and a chicken. I had put it in the freezer this afternoon but I took it out when George called. I hope you like chicken."

I replied that I actually preferred it to barbeque. Abby had a puzzled look.

"The food is cooking; we'll eat in an hour or so. Let's go to the living room. Do you care for a cocktail?"

I responded, "Will you split a beer with me?" I pointed at his belly. "I want to keep you in shape." While we were sipping our drinks, I turned to Abby.

"Let me explain about the barbeque. Last night the woman in the G-2's office who briefed me invited me to try the special buffet at the club. They featured barbeque. It was OK. I would rather have had something else. Maria, my companion, liked it a lot. We had a good time. She opened up about her divorce. I found her very personable and rather attractive. She seemed to be drawn to me. We almost got to the point of becoming more intimate, but I recently got involved with a steady girlfriend. We love each other. A future may develop for us. I related this to Maria. She seemed to understand my situation."

Abby piped in. "I know Maria. She has had dinner with us a few times. She was deep in the dumps. After college I worked for several years as a marriage counselor. I felt I needed to do something for her. Although she is no youngster and does not fall into the millennial category, she had to get rid of the "I am too old for change" feeling. We talked at length when she was here. I took her shopping for what the younger women wear these days. My beauty parlor changed her hair-do. Also, I invited her to my weekly yoga class. Of course, this was done to restart her social life. At work, George tells me, she dresses conservatively and is very business-like. Last week I ran into a guy, a friend of a friend, whom I want to introduce to her. I hope it works out."

Abby turned out to be a well-qualified hostess. The food was delicious. She joined us in the living room after putting stuff in the fridge. She said the dishes could wait until tomorrow. They would shop for a dishwasher as soon as they had finished paying off the new furniture. The old one was *kaput*."

Before I left, Abby gave me a small package for Maria. It contained a necklace still in the original wrapping. Abby had bought it to give to Maria on her last visit, as a present, but she had forgotten it. On top was an envelope with a typed note. "Thanks for a wonderful evening. Wear it well."

It was almost midnight when George dropped me off at the BOQ. I told him I would show up later in the morning. He had an appointment at 0900 to brief the G-2 on where we stood.

The following morning, before checking in with George, I stopped off at Maria's desk. She was not there. I dropped the package on her desk.

George had just returned from his meeting. He said, "The G-2 has received nothing further from the counterintelligence unit. I summarized how we would proceed. He hoped we would come up with an answer. Yesterday he had another communication from his boss at the Pentagon. They are anxious to bring this to a conclusion."

We decided to visit Carolyn's mother again. We had to find a clue as to where the couple had gone. George closely examined Maria's phone listings. He saw one number he had overlooked. It was preceded by XYZ. We dialed it and heard an answering machine with a woman's voice. "I am not home right now. Leave your name and number after the beep." George recorded that he was calling from the Offutt Air Force Base and left his number.

By questioning Carolyn's mother once more, she told us that she had urged Carolyn, before they left, to call home once they had reached their destination. She did receive that call a few days ago. They found a nice campground near a small lake. When her mother pressed her as to where she was calling from, Carolyn complained that her phone was going dead, but she was calling from a small town where they went to purchase supplies. We asked what date Carolyn had phoned. She did not remember, but the call came in the morning on the day an e-mail arrived from her husband. She had kept that and went to look for it. She found it and told us Carolyn had called a few days ago.

Upon return to Offutt, we went to the snack bar for a bite. Maria was sitting there, at a table, with another woman. I said hello to her. She got up and thanked me profusely for bringing her the necklace. In turn I hugged her. "Think nothing of it."

After lunch, George took me to the contracting office. He briefly explained our investigation to the person in charge. We wanted to establish the identity of the owner of the phone whose answering machine we had called in the course of our investigation. We also needed the location from where Carolyn Smithfield had phoned her mother. He would request all this from his contact at the phone company in Omaha. He would check in with us as soon as he assembled the data.

About an hour later, the contracting officer came to George's office. He had had quite a time to move the phone company on this. They claimed they needed first to contact their main office. He was able to forego this. He advised them that this case was being pursued by direct order from the Pentagon. They could verify this with the G-2 at Offutt. As far as the woman was concerned, he gave us her name and address. The phone company went through their records and found that she made frequent calls to Turkey and Syria.

The other item took some time to pin down. The call was from a pay phone in a food market in Winnebago, Nebraska. He gave us the name and location.

It was only 1400 hours. George thought we should go there. It was less than two hours away. Last summer he had taken his family to visit an Indian reservation not far from there. Before leaving, we stopped by Maria's to notify her where we were heading. George asked her to call and tell his wife that he would be home late.

We reached Winnebago before 1600 hours. Talking to the food store manager, we explained our mission. After mentioning the picnic grounds near small lakes, he knew where it was. It would take less than half an hour to get there.

We had no trouble finding the lake. There was a shack at a place where a sign advertised rental boats of all sorts. We approached a man sitting on a bench near the door. We asked him whether a young couple who was camping nearby had rented a boat from him. He noted this was not the prime season, but most of his rentals were to young couples. When we showed him the photographs of Kerriko and Carolyn, he recognized them. They had taken a canoe for an afternoon last week. He checked his log. They had a reservation for a couple of weeks at one of the campgrounds nearby. As far as he knew, they were still there. He had seen Kerriko driving by yesterday.

We found Kerriko sitting in front of a tent, cleaning his fishing gear. He immediately recognized George, who introduced me. Kerriko was surprised. He wanted to know how we knew about this place, assuming we had come for a couple of days' leave.

"You are AWOL Sergeant, and the G-2 ordered us to find you and bring you back. Where is your girlfriend? Why didn't you come back to Offutt when your leave was up?"

"Let me tell you exactly what happened and why I am still here. First of all, Carolyn planned our trip. I was madly in love with her. At that point, I would have gone with her anywhere she chose. We had a good time; she spoiled me to no end. Toward the end of the two weeks, Carolyn told me she wanted to stay longer. She couldn't get enough of me. Her mother knew lots of people at the base and Carolyn had phoned her mom to get an extension of my leave from the G-2. She said her mother had called back and we had another two weeks for our vacation.

"I was amazed that the G-2 would extend my leave, but I did not mind her manipulating this at all. I learned long ago that women can get things done, better than we can. Now that you're here, though, I guess all that was a lie.

"Later that same day, a car drove up and dropped off a middle-aged lady. Carolyn introduced her as an old friend who she had casually told to come and visit us, if she had the time. She was very nice and went on hikes with is.

"A couple of days after she arrived, the two took a long walk. When they got back, Carolyn announced a surprise to me. Her friend, and I don't remember her name, but it was foreign to me and I had never before heard it, anyway, her friend has a very wealthy cousin in Turkey who commutes to her place in Syria when the political situation permits it. Carolyn's friend thought it would be a break for Carolyn to go with her and bring her boyfriend along. Carolyn urged me to join them. When I said I would love to have more time with Carolyn, but I had to be at Offutt in another week, Carolyn claimed this should not be a problem. I could fly back here by myself in case she wanted to stay there longer.

"I told her that I didn't believe this would work out. I could not take a chance on not getting back to Offutt before my leave expired. Besides, I did not have my passport with me. It might also have expired. Carolyn believed I could still accompany them. Her friend was a sophisticated world traveler and would take care of this somehow. This did not change my mind. Carolyn and her friend left the same morning. The same car that brought this woman here picked them up.

"My feelings for Carolyn have changed. She obviously did not care as deeply for me. Her enthusiasm for constantly nagging me and initiating love had been new to me. In my mind, at the time, those were demonstrations of deep feelings for me. I now suspect her pursuing me was prompted by an ulterior motive. Her friendship with the middle-aged lady seems to bear this out. When I look back at our relationship, I recall how often she told me she admired me for holding such a responsible job. She followed this up wondering how I had reached this level. Once in a while she wanted to know what I was actually doing. One time when she visited me I had to run some errands. She stayed. She wanted to cook dinner. The following day I was doing some work on my desk and I noticed a pile of papers I had brought home from the office seemed to have been disturbed.

"They were not classified papers which could not be removed from the office. I had brought them home to meet a request from the G-2 for a summary on the complaints about irregularities at the missile sites. I had asked if she had touched the papers on top of my desk. She responded that she had gone into my office while I was running around yesterday to bring some order into all that stuff lying around. She had to do this because I had not cleaned anything for a while. There was dust all over. She had moved everything on top of the desk in order to wipe it clean. So when she moved the stuff back, it probably did not end up exactly where it had been. I thanked her and told her that, in the future, she was not to touch anything in my office.

Kerriko continued. "Now I am, of course, upset about all this. When I get back to Offutt, I will ask counterintelligence to see if they can find out anything about Carolyn's friend."

"Don't do that." I said. "When we return, I will initiate action by my home office, INSCOM, who will get the FBI involved. Incidentally, why didn't you return home after Carolyn departed?"

"See the next camp site? There is a nice couple from Seattle who stopped off for a few days after visiting a friend in Winnebago. They invited me for dinner last night. They have a nice-looking daughter who eyed me all the time while we were eating. Afterwards she asked me to walk with her to a little food store on the other side of the lake. On the way, we stopped at an overlook. We sat on a bench. She snuggled up and we smooched a bit. She asked me to go hiking with her the next day. I nixed this as I had to return to Omaha."

On the way back to Offutt, since Kerriko was technically in custody, I rode back with Kerriko in his car and George followed us. After we had escorted Kerriko to the Duty Officer at the G-2, George suggested that I get right on this with my office and the Pentagon. I told him that I smelled trouble as soon as I had heard about the Carolyn's Mideastern friend. But first we have to brief the G-2.

It was close to 2000 hours after we dropped off Kerriko. We stopped at a fast food place to get a bite. George called his wife and told her not to wait up for him. He dropped me off at the BOQ. I asked him not to see the G-2 until I had arrived there in the morning.

George phoned me while I was having breakfast. The G-2 was not available until around ten. That was fine with me. I went there early and waited for Maria to arrive. I ran down for her what happened yesterday. She said she would write a memo for the record, if this was OK with me. I concurred. I advised her to notify counterintelligence to terminate their investigation. I would be departing for Washington soon. DOD and the FBI would now be carrying the ball. I requested that Maria fax a detailed message to my boss in Fort Meade. I recommended that he immediately pass this on to INSCOM.

Meanwhile, George came over to us. I outlined what Maria and I had cooked up before his arrival. I emphasized that my doing this was exercising the responsibility assigned to me by DOD. I gave him equal credit in running this down. He agreed. He had been instructed to assist me, not to run the show. In that vein, I briefed the G-2.

He was most pleased in what I had accomplished. I reiterated George's valuable input. He showed us a report he had just received from the counterintelligence unit. They found interesting details. They had uncovered the relationship between Carolyn Smithfield and that mysterious Middle Eastern woman. They were able to get more data on Carolyn than on her patron, whom she met twice a week. By questioning people in her office and some others she had been at school with, they developed a good profile of her. Carolyn apparently was restless in her job. After she became friends with the Middle Eastern gal, she let it out that this woman had convinced her that she was wasting her time and she should get into international politics. Carolyn thought she should go back to school where she had been successful before. Before she left school, her professors had advised her to stick with it. They considered her a candidate for magna cum laude. But this woman exercised control over her. She talked about first getting some practical experience by visiting the Middle East with her.

As far as the mysterious lady was concerned, the counterintelligence operatives could not get much. She was an American citizen, had travelled to the Middle East frequently, had had unidentified visitors every so often. She had no intimate friends and kept pretty much to herself. How, and exactly when, she first encountered Carolyn is unknown. At one time there was a young girl working in the doctor's office whose parents emigrated from Syria. Perhaps this girl's parents were acquainted with the mysterious lady. The investigators had been trying to locate this girl.

I restated to the G-2 that Kerriko was not a guilty party for some of this. I was certain about that woman taking advantage of Kerriko's relationship with Carolyn, and convincing Carolyn to take this overseas trip with her. But he had smelled a rat and declined. Of course, his part in this play would be essential for the record. I believed that George was best qualified to interview him for the official report. It might be wise to withdraw Kerriko's security clearance temporarily until his role has been clarified beyond doubt. I realized he was a valuable employee. I personally believed he was roped into all this without having an idea what it could lead to.

I suggested to the G-2 that he notify his supervisors in Washington that the investigator sent by DOD had completed his work. A thorough report would be forthcoming from INSCOM to the Secretary of Defense, through regular channels.

If he had not alerted Washington, this might have become a serious national security problem. Who knows how long it would have been before it would have been looked into. With a smile I commented that perhaps I would have dealings with him when he got a promotion and ended up in the Pentagon. He grinned and thanked me again.

George and I had a quick lunch. I asked Maria to make a reservation for this evening on a return flight to Washington.

Then we made another visit to Carolyn's mother. We caught her just as she was getting ready to leave her house. When we related what we had uncovered on our visit to the campgrounds near Winnebago, she was shocked. We emphasized that Carolyn's friend was deep trouble. The FBI was after her. Carolyn was also in peril because of her association with her. When Carolyn called her from Turkey, she should stress that Carolyn must return home immediately. She should get away from that woman and go to the American Consulate in Istanbul or the embassy in

Ankara, whichever is closer. The FBI agents in Turkey would arrange a return flight. She should tell her that no matter how deeply she was involved, she must not make her situation worse by remaining with her friend. She should think about her future. By cooperating she would make points with the investigating authorities. She must get away at once. Her mother should convey to her that a Washington investigator had assembled her history. He talked to the dean of the community college she had attended. It would become a four-year institution next year. The dean believed that on the basis of her record she would qualify for a scholarship. She shouldn't miss out on this.

As I spoke, the mother gradually relaxed. She believed she would be able to persuade her daughter to come home.

It was getting late when we left. I suggested that George draft a detailed report for the G-2. He would find it indispensable in any communication he will have with Washington. When he dropped me off at the BOQ, I told him I was very grateful to have met him and his family. Of course, his input was invaluable in resolving the case.

My travel details were at the BOQ when I checked in. Maria had the foresight to give me sufficient time for dinner at the airport.

On the flight I took advantage of the time to draft a report, emphasizing the key points. After glancing at the mail when I got home, I faxed my draft to Amy to edit and to put in on MacMerial's desk. I woke up late in the morning, soaked in the bathtub for thirty minutes, threw out the junk mail and made up a grocery list. I had a light lunch at a fast food place.

As soon as I returned, the phone rang. It was Bob MacMerial.

"Keef, I just finished reading your report. It is very detailed. Amy mentioned your draft was atrocious in places. She cleaned it up. I am happy she is finally getting into the groove filling Eloise's place. I am going to fax it to INSCOM. I will include a cover note about the urgency to stop the two suspects from getting into Syria from Turkey. I will suggest that the Army attaché in Ankara ask his contacts in the Turkish military to find these two and turn them over to the American Embassy. Of course, in case the mother has been contacted by her daughter, and succeeded in getting her home, she won't need embassy assistance for this.

"I will also ask INSCOM to get DOD to authorize us to contact the FBI at once. They have personnel at the embassy who can work with our attaché. I will be in touch with you. No need to come in now."

"Bob, after you have dispatched the fax, you may want to call INSCOM. Ask them to get DOD concurrence on my contacting the FBI. Also, I would like to give them a copy of my report."

About an hour later, Bob was on the phone. The Chief of Staff of INSCOM had called him. "The General was most pleased with your report. He had faxed it to the Department of the Army for getting it to DOD. They called him back and authorized you to get the FBI involved. They should get all the information we have. You should touch base with your FBI contacts on this immediately. Amy has just faxed a copy of my report to you." I had asked for a second copy for the FBI.

Looking through my little booklet where I had listed work contacts, I found the phone number of the Counterintelligence Office of the Washington FBI Field Office. A secretary picked up the phone. I explained that I was on a special assignment for the Secretary of Defense. I needed to speak to the head of her office. She connected me.

I summarized my trip to Offutt. I told him I was in the process of getting a copy of my report, which I would send him. To complete this project, I needed FBI assistance, both here and in Turkey. I gave him my address. He would have two agents come to see me within the hour.

I called Bob. He would get over to my house to participate in the meeting, bringing another copy of my report. Soon the two guys showed up. I started to introduce myself, but they conveyed knowing all about me. I was in their office's data file, covering my previous contacts with Barbara Sheralds, with whom I had worked some time ago. They also found coverage of my meeting with their New York office a few weeks ago. They expressed their pleasure at working with me.

At that point, Bob MacMerial was knocking on my door. After explaining who he was, they glanced at the report he had brought. They were pleased to get the details. Yesterday their boss had a lengthy phone conversation with the FBI office at Omaha. Somebody in FBI headquarters, a friend of George Mizells, a retired FBI agent, had had a conversation with him. He mentioned that George just completed assisting a DOD investigator on a suspected espionage situation. He related it to his boss who then alerted the Washington office that there was an urgent matter for the FBI to aid the DOD. That prompted the Washington office to call Omaha which then contacted George, whom they subsequently interviewed. FBI headquarters instructed them to wait until they heard from DOD before doing anything.

Bob then told them there was nothing to do here now, but the FBI in Ankara should assist the Military Attaché in getting hold of the two women before they absconded to Syria. They agreed that they would talk to the FBI in Ankara immediately. For further orientation they should peruse the report the DOD agent had compiled. The Army attaché had a copy. The two then left. Bob got on the phone to INSCOM. He wanted to brief the CG on the current situation. He was ordered to come at once, as the CG was anxious to be updated.

It was late in the afternoon; the rush hour had begun. Bob had come in an MP vehicle. It was the only one available. That was fortunate. If the driver had not put on his emergency lights and moved around the traffic blockages, it would have taken almost two hours. Bob had figured out we needed to brief INSCOM. It was especially important that they were updated by us. Then INSCOM could orient the Pentagonites on the latest, before they got it from someone else.

The Chief of Staff took us to the General right away. He made us wait while he read my report and Bob's comments. He would have it faxed to the Department. In accordance with the arrangement he had made with the Pentagon, it would also go directly to his contact in the Sec/Def's office. Army would probably send a copy to Air Force.

I then briefed the General about my contacts with the FBI to attempt to block the two women from getting into Syria. He instructed me to stay on the case until it was wrapped up. I would inform the Pentagon about having involved the FBI in Turkey. Bob was ordered to notify his Chief of Staff of any new developments.

Bob dropped me off. I invited him to join me for dinner at one of my favorite restaurants. He declined. They were expecting company at home. He suggested that I not come to Fort Meade in the morning. I should deal with the FBI from home. Also hire someone to clean my house. It must need attention after my lengthy sojourn to Nebraska. He was right. Besides, I needed to relax for a day or so.

I was still asleep when my cell phone rang. It was Carolyn's mother. Finally, Carolyn had called her. She was at a place called Suruc near the Turkish border with Syria. Her friend had stepped out to run an errand, but she inadvertently left her cell phone on the table. There was another person in the house, a man who spoke no English, who had met them in Istanbul. He flew with them on a Turkish commuter flight to eastern Turkey. From there they had gone by car to Suruc. He was asleep in another room. He was going to get them into Syria as soon as he had received the word from a contact.

Her mother had listened patiently. Then she asked her daughter to pay careful attention to what she was going to say. She repeated what George and I had instructed her. At first Carolyn was not deterred, but when her mother stressed the fact that the Turks and the FBI were going after them, she finally saw the dangerous situation she was in and agreed to try to get out of the house and hide someplace until the FBI would find her.

I immediately contacted the FBI. They would dispatch agents from Ankara immediately. They would also contact the Turks to have their people in Suruc search for Carolyn. I was just about ready to update Bob MacMerial when another call from Carolyn's mother came in. Her daughter had just phoned her. She had lucked out. She found a refugee encampment not far from the house. Spotting an American car there, she saw a man starting the motor. She went over and introduced herself. The guy was the local representative of an American company who worked for the U.S. Government supervising U.S. food distribution in the camp. He invited Carolyn to his office where she told him the predicament she was in. He urged her to leave with him at once. They were now on the way to Incirlik Air Force Base where they expected to get on a flight out of Turkey. Upon my reaching the FBI again, I was assured that they would have an agent at Incirlik to escort Carolyn back here. Other agents would proceed to Suruc to take Carolyn's friend and the man with her into custody. The Turks had been alerted to look for them.

Just after I had completed these arrangements, a fax from George arrived. "Keef, I made some further inquiries after you left here. Carolyn's female friend's plans were based upon her control of Carolyn. She was interested in getting her into Syria primarily to make her available to work in a hospital. Also, she could be persuaded to reveal whatever she knew about the missile sites. Of course, if they had succeeded in getting Kerriko to go with her, he would have received intensive "persuasion" to provide data on the missile sites. That, in a nutshell, is what this was all about. Hopefully, the FBI will uncover the organization this woman worked for."

For the next couple of days I was badgering the FBI for information on the woman who was a U.S. citizen and who was an undercover agent for her associates both in the United States as well as in Syria. Finally, we had an answer. Turkish intelligence had their local contacts search for Carolyn. Unable to find her, the woman and the unknown male had quickly disappeared. The house they had used was known to the police as one of several locations used by smugglers and Syrian agents. Thus, unless the FBI could persuade their contacts in Syria to look for this woman, we would have to write her off for the time being. Hopefully, the FBI would be able to get something from Carolyn when they questioned her.

The INSCOM role had now played out. I drafted a final report for INSCOM and faxed it to Bob. He called me. He had heard that DOD was also most pleased to draw the curtain on this. Bob had also ferreted out that the expected personnel cuts for INSCOM had been suspended. Bob had me put on leave status for a few days. I could get in touch with Amy to work out that pending trip to Europe.

CHAPTER 10

OLD NOTES

THE PHONE RANG EARLY in the morning. It was Jennifer, in Atlanta.

"Dad, I tried to contact you several times during the past few weeks. I finally called Bob MacMerial, who told me you were in the field most of the time. Headquarters at Fort Belvoir had you tied up with all sorts of projects. Are you staying home now?"

"I hope so, but I have to make one more trip to Europe to tie up loose ends. What is new with you and Larry?"

"Larry was at the local library and read an article on Operation Paperclip. He wondered whether your father had anything to do with it."

"Jennifer, no, but I am familiar with 'Paperclip.' Did Larry tell you what it was all about? Briefly, it was a top secret program under the auspices of the Joint Chiefs of Staff. It was initiated sometime early in 1945. The U.S. Army collared Nazi scientists, their research data, and hardware on biological and chemical weapons. This was done to prevent it from falling into Soviet hands. Initially, the Pentagon designated this program 'Operation Overcast.' Later, it became 'Operation Paperclip.' About 1,600 Germans were recruited. They included hard core Nazis, SS officers, and war criminals. Their involvement in the German weapons program was the key for their selection. Their Nazi activities were ignored.

"Later, the U.S. attitude changed. Congress and the American public became aware of the personal histories of many 'Paperclip' recruits. In

1998, President Clinton signed the 'Nazi War Crimes Disclosure Act' which ordered the declassification of American intelligence records on the program, including FBI, Pentagon, and CIA files. A majority of the Germans involved were in the U.S. to work here on the development of biological and chemical weapons, as well as rocketry.

"While I had some interest in this program, I was not really concerned about it. When checking out some of my father's notes on the raid, I found among them a memo to himself. In it he wrote of what a contact in Czechoslovakia had told him about the German military facilities in the Benešov-Neveklov area. It really had nothing to do with his mission to seize the German intelligence on the Red Army. The information dealt with an underground facility run, by the SS, which had something to do with the development of secret weapons. This operation was run by an SS general who later had probably been recruited for 'Operation Paperclip.'

"My father made a note to himself to pursue this later. He thought it was possible that the instructions he had received on the raid had been incomplete. Perhaps they included that he was to look into what was going on in that underground facility. This was something he would check out when he uncovered the source of the order to conduct the raid.

"Jennifer, you can tell Larry of your grandfather's indirect connection with 'Operation Paperclip.' As far as I am concerned, these circumstances do not help me in determining the source of the order for the raid."

"Dad, I will tell Larry. We were hoping you would come down here for a visit. Perhaps, when you finally wind up the raid business, you will find the time."

"Jennifer, believe me, I want to close the book on this. I am sure I will eventually. Then I will visit you and introduce you to my new lady friend."

"Dad, tell me, who is she?"

"Not now. It's a long story."

"Dad, one more thing. I recently dwelled on what Grandma told me before she passed away. She had finished typing Grandpa's notes on his World War II record. She told me where they were. I retrieved them and gave them to Grandpa. I don't know what he did with the manuscript. He must have put it in his files. You never mentioned that you knew about it. You should check this out."

"Jennifer, I vaguely remember that Grandma had told me something about that. I plan to go through his old desk in the basement. It may be in there or else is among the stuff he worked on in the Pentagon. Thanks for telling me."

I thought about what Jennifer had just discussed. It was most timely. If I found his diary it could help me schedule our sojourn in France. Although, of course, it had nothing to do with my express purpose of going to Europe once more, it could certainly be an added element to the trip. I have never really known the details of his WWII experiences except for the raid.

I had previously rummaged through the old desk in the basement. After I had found the papers on his screening activities with the Czech Liaison Officer, I had not thoroughly examined the last drawer. I had opened it. It was full of papers. I had glanced at some of them. They were just notes to himself on future projects.

Going downstairs, I emptied that last drawer. At first, there seemed to be only a bunch of his memos. But, lo and behold, on the very bottom of the pile there was a neatly typed manuscript. It was titled, "The Diary of my World War II Experiences in Europe." This was the paper my mother had typed! In addition to what my mother had compiled, there was my father's original diary. It was pretty shop-worn, but still legible.

I took the material upstairs and started to look through it. It drew my interest. It dawned on me that this was an excellent guide, if I could find the time, to follow in his footprints. Perhaps I would incorporate it into my plans. I really became excited.

I decided to give Lucy a call. "Lucy, what are you up to?"

"I'm so glad you called, it is about time we get together. Are you available this afternoon?"

"I am also anxious to touch base with you."

"There you go again. Your mind is always on that."

"Lucy, it is your mind, not mine. I just thought about seeing you. Do you want to come up here for an early dinner? My neighbor recommended a terrific dish. I have most of the ingredients for it."

"Keef, you know I would love to. However, my roommate got tickets for a show this evening. Let's meet for an early dinner at your favorite place on Maine Avenue. We should go there. I read in the paper that whole area will undergo major changes soon. All fish markets and restaurants will disappear. I'll meet you there around five."

"Okay, don't forget to park in the spaces reserved for the FBI. They are toward the back."

Lucy was already seated when I got there. It was a warm afternoon. She had picked an outside table near the waterfront. She was sipping on a glass of white wine when I sneaked up on her. I pulled her up and have her a tight hug. She had already ordered for us. Lucy gave me a rundown of what she had been up to. After a leisurely dinner, I told her about my plans for the final trip to Europe. I described Jennifer's call in which she had mentioned my father's diary. I told Lucy that I want to expand the trip to more or less follow my dad's itinerary. I had always wanted to learn more about his WWII ventures. This provided a great opportunity.

I told her my thoughts about this trip. As we now have a future together, I would love for her to accompany me. I turned to her and stroked her face and hair. "I don't want to do this alone. I am hoping you will take some leave and join me."

Lucy had listened intently. She leaned over and kissed me. "Thanks for inviting me. I am intrigued. I agree the trip together would be *wunderbar!* I am getting so attached to you. I missed you when I was in Canada. When I came back you were out in Colorado. I will do what I can to get away. How long would the trip take?"

I suggested she should try to take off about three weeks. If possible, I would like to leave as soon as possible. Lucy promised to have an answer for me sometime tomorrow. I walked her to the car and kissed her goodbye.

I was on pins-and-needles the next day. She finally called in the afternoon. She sounded very excited. When she saw her boss, he seemed very friendly. Before she even asked for leave, he said he had been about ready to call her.

Something had come up at the Paris embassy. There was a problem with the secretarial help. The chargé d'affaires had called the European desk for guidelines. He had asked whoever he spoke with to send somebody over there to straighten it out. From what her boss knew, he believed that one of the clerks might have to be brought back to Washington. It would be up to Lucy to determine what should be done.

Lucy then told him that she had come to seek an extended leave for a trip she had planned. Coincidentally, her destination was France. After she resolved the embassy business, she wanted to stay in France for a tour. If he was agreeable, she would need about three weeks.

He approved her leave. He also suggested she should make all her travel arrangements to assure they were compatible with her leave. She should go home and start to work on her travel plans. He would give her a ring tomorrow.

I spent the rest of the day planning details and an outline of the trip. I had, for a long time, wanted to visit Iceland. A friend had told me that he had had a good experience with Icelandic Airlines. They flew into Luxemburg with a stopover in Iceland. I called them. They are now known as Icelandair. They no longer went to Luxemburg. They fly directly from Reykjavik to Paris.

The main reason I wanted to include Iceland on the trip was because of what my father had described about his experience there. That was in the 1960s. A problem had come up among personnel manning the DEW (Distant Early Warning) line. He had been sent there to check it out.

I had to do one more chore. Freiburg had sent me a message that the Lt. Kaufmann's nephew, who had married a French woman, now lives in France. That, after all, was my reason to head for Europe one more time. I thought about e-mailing Freiburg to obtain their address. Then I had a better idea. I dialed the phone number of the Frau Kaufmann in Oppenheim. She had told me of keeping up-to-date with her family. She remembered my visit with her. I summarized my experience at Freiburg. They had suggested I should to go France to see the lieutenant's nephew. They did not give me an address.

She apologized for not having suggested to me, during my visit, to check with the nephew. It had just slipped her mind. She was getting so forgetful nowadays. At any rate, the nephew's main residence is in Bayeux in Normandy. She hears from him once in a while. She had no phone number. As my inquiry pertained to events long ago, it would be best for me to talk with him in person.

Then she said that her nephew's wife was financially well fixed. She has a summer home in southern France. I may end up going there. I thanked her. I would tell her nephew about my nice visit to Oppenheim.

When I called Lucy in the morning, she told me that she had already initiated the necessary paperwork. I explained to her about a stopover in Iceland. She thought it was a good idea. She had never been there. I would make the travel arrangements for both of us. She could fax the details to the embassy in Paris. We may be able to depart the day after tomorrow. As we both had official passports, there should be no problem getting entry clearance for Iceland and France. I suggested that she should keep her baggage to a minimum. We might have to do quite a bit of travelling in France.

Lucy agreed. She would complete the forms right away. Then she would go home, head for the beauty parlor, and start packing. She would check her passport to make sure it was still valid. I should come tomorrow for a home-cooked meal. Her roommate was away. I could stay over and we could leave for the airport together.

I thanked her for the invite. I suggested we have an early dinner. I told her about Jennifer's call and of my locating my father's World War II diary and the annotated write-up prepared by him and edited by my mother. I would bring it with me and we could read it together. Lucy was surprised. She said she would look forward to going through it with me.

Next I buzzed Amy. I asked her to obtain my travel orders for four weeks, including a stopover in Iceland. She should fax them to me as soon as she got them from the Ft. Meade travel office. I wanted to talk to Bob MacMerial, but he was out for few days. Amy would leave a copy of my orders on his desk.

Then I rang Icelandair. I requested to be transferred to whoever handled U.S. government reservations. A woman came on the line. She was most courteous and offered to assist me. I gave her my name and rank, told her that I had an official passport, and wanted reservations for me and an individual from the State Department who would travel with me. I spelled out Lucy's full name, and her rank as a special assistant. We desired to depart the day after tomorrow for a flight to Paris, with a 24 hour stopover in Iceland. I was put on hold for several minutes. She came back and said we were on a flight from Dulles airport. Upon arrival, we should check in at the desk where the flight to Paris would be arranged. She would notify Reykjavik of our arrival and the planned stopover.

I spent the rest of the day preparing for the trip. I managed to place all the clothing, extra shoes and socks, two dress shirts and toilet articles into my carry-on. I had recently bought it at the PX in order to meet the new dimension limitations of the airlines. My new spinner luggage was somewhat smaller than what I had had before. It was also lighter and more flexible. There were exterior pockets to be used for what could not be put inside.

To get a good night's sleep, I bedded down early.

The next morning, I cleaned the kitchen. I washed all the dishes and put them away. I called my neighbor about my 4-week absence. As usual, she was very inquisitive. I did not mention Lucy, but told her I was following up some leads picked up on my last European trip. I told her I had to go downtown in the afternoon.

Around lunchtime, Amy called. She had faxed the travel orders. She wondered why I was going on such a long trip. I responded that I had to go to a town in northern Normandy and possibly also to head for southern France. Additionally, I planned to spend some time in Paris. In case Colonel MacMerial wanted to get ahold of me, he should contact the Military Attaché at the U.S. Embassy. I would check in with him every so often.

Now I could relax. But not for long. Lucy called. The State Department travel people wanted to make reservations at a hotel which the embassy uses. She told them it was not necessary. She would be staying with friends. Otherwise, she was all packed and ready to roll. She said I could come in the early afternoon.

The next day, I was just about ready to call a cab when my neighbor's husband called. He was home to change clothes. He had been invited for a meeting downtown. If I needed a ride, he would take me. I told him I was planning to meet a friend and stay downtown. I would like for him to drop me off not far from the State Department.

My neighbor was all dressed up when he knocked on my door. After putting my luggage into the trunk, I asked him why he was wearing his best Sunday suit. What was the occasion? He related that an acquaintance had invited him to meet somebody he knew in a hotel in Georgetown. This guy had an important job with a national company and they were opening a Washington office. So this was an opportunity for him to finally land a good job. I wished luck. He said he needed it. He would give me as a reference, if things moved along.

CHAPTER 11

RENEWAL

I FOLLOWED SOMEBODY INTO the entrance who apparently lived in Lucy's building. He held the door while I brought in the luggage. I knocked on Lucy's door. She wanted to know how I got in without buzzing her. I told her I used my skeleton key. She laughed. I hugged her tightly.

"No, no, I am not sleepy," she said. "I told you to come early because I was anxious to go through that diary of your dad's with you."

We settled down on the couch. I placed the typed manuscript and the diary on the coffee table.

Sometimes Dad used subheadings, sometimes not. Perhaps when my mother was typing it, she also did some editing. One of the things I had noticed when I was glancing through the typed diary earlier was that some sections were detailed while others were sketchier. This led me to believe that he may have originally wanted to write a historical document, but never followed through. Thus, we have a mixture. I explained this speculation to Lucy. She did not think it would distract from the authenticity or value of the document. I pointed out that most of the diary entries were probably made while he was either in the jeep or in a foxhole. This would account for grammatical errors and incomplete sentences.

We started to review my mother's manuscript from the beginning. Lucy wanted to go through it all in one stretch. We stopped for a short time when the timer bell rang in the kitchen. Lucy had put a casserole into the oven.

What follows is mainly from my mother's typed version. We only referred to the diary itself to clarify some of my mother's entries.

The title she gave it was:

<u>Notes on the Background before D-day.</u>

"Preparations for the invasion were detailed and extensive. In marshalling yards in southern England over 2,800,000 soldiers in 39 divisions were assembled, including 160,000 in the D-Day force. Eisenhower's command, the Supreme Headquarters Allied Expeditionary Force (SHAEF) had promoted Project Fortitude, disseminating, for German consumption, false information that the invasion would occur in the Pas-de-Calais area, the shortest distance from Dover. This project proved to be successful. Hitler apparently believed it and concentrated his best troops, especially Panzer divisions, there. Convinced that the Normandy assault on June 6, 1944, was not the major thrust, the elite German forces in the Pas-de-Calais area were not shifted to Normandy until several weeks after June 6.

"Eisenhower visited the 101st Airborne Division in the evening of June 5 as they were boarding planes headed for points behind the German coastal fortifications. The mission of the two airborne divisions, the 82nd and 101st, was to prevent the Germans from bringing in reinforcements for the coastal forts.

"Besides convincing Hitler that the Pas-de-Calais area was the place for the actual invasion, SHAEF used further ruses to draw attention away from Normandy. They included spreading rumors about a non-existing army under Patton in southwestern England preparing to lead the main invasion. This misled the German's thinking that Normandy was merely a sideshow. Another factor that contributed to the success in Normandy was the German command structure. There were actually three separate commands: Commander in Chief West (von Rundstedt), Army Group B (Rommel), and Hitler himself. Von Rundstedt had no authority over the German Air Force and the naval units in France. In the final analysis, Hitler directed the overall defense strategy.

"German preparations for the fortification of French coastal areas facing England had been accelerated in the fall of 1942. To do the heavy work, Hitler assigned responsibility to *Organisation Todt*, a quasi-military construction entity that conscripted foreign nationals.

"Another SHAEF deception was a fake invasion force supposedly to be assembled in Scotland to invade Norway. Proof that this also was convincing is that the Germans kept large forces in Norway, instead of shifting the best units from there to France.

"One cannot over-emphasize the contributions of the FFI (French Forces of the Interior), the British SOE (Special Operations Executive), and the American Office of Strategic Services (OSS). The SOE and OSS operatives parachuted regularly into France to work closely with the FFI in intelligence and supporting missions. The OSS had agents in France since 1943.

"I crossed the Atlantic in April 1944 on the Queen Mary, converted into a troop carrier with a capacity for 35,000 men. We all disembarked at the Firth of Forth near Glasgow, Scotland. The Queen Elizabeth preceded us in December 1943. Among its passengers were a group of OSS agents selected for the Jedburgh units, which were parachuted into Normandy on the eve of D-Day. The 3-man teams consisted of an American (OSS) or a British (SOE), a Free French Army Officer, and a radio operator. Their mission was to cause turmoil behind the lines to facilitate the onslaught of the landing forces beyond the beaches. The teams became known as Jedburghs. They were named after the locality of Jedburgh in Scotland where they were trained and organized.

"At Glasgow I boarded a sealed troop carrier train to London. All windows were covered and the car doors were barred. On reporting to Eisenhower's headquarters (SHAEF), I was ordered to attend a SHAEF advanced intelligence course taught at a British army facility in London. Upon completion I was assigned to a 3-man intelligence team. Our equipment included a jeep, side arms, a carbine and hand grenades. On the last day of the course, I was given a blank 1944 diary to chronicle my team's day-to-day activities and movements.

"The team was attached to the G-2 of the Fourth Armored Division with headquarters in Chippenham near Bristol. Our mission was to seize German Order of Battle data by all possible means. The primary assignment was to assist the division G-2 in analyzing information acquired by other division intelligence teams who were responsible for counterintelligence, interrogation of prisoners of war (POWs), and photo intelligence. We also reviewed S-2 reports from subordinate division components. While direct collection of intelligence was not our primary function, I spent most of my time doing this in the field. The other members of my team became essentially part of the G-2's entourage.

"In late May, the 4th Armored Division moved to a marshalling area near Winchester in southwest England for final preparations, including waterproofing the Jeep, which in armored divisions was called "peep." We departed from Southampton in mid-June, on an LST (landing ship-tank), crossed the channel and moved under our own power onto Utah Beach. While most of the underwater obstacles and fortifications along the cliffs facing the channel had been cleared, there were still many remnants testifying to the severe fighting on June 6 and the days after. The invasion beaches were not finally cleared until June 11. As there were only a few exits from the beach, our tanks' move inland was delayed for several days. Proceeding through the German fortifications was also hindered by the condition of the roads. Additionally, there was reverse traffic of returning airborne troops and Special Forces descending from the hills as well as disabled equipment. I took advantage of the division's delay in moving inland by surveying the German fortifications on Utah and Omaha.

"The impact of the invasion on a 50-mile expanse of the Normandy coast was in evidence everywhere. On D-Day, 5000 ships of all kinds were involved. Around midnight on June 6, U.S. parachutists and glider-borne troops landed behind Utah, near Saint-Mère-Église. The small town became well known. One of the paratroopers, John Steele, got tangled up on the steeple of the Sancte Marie Ecclesia church in the town center. The trooper played dead until he was rescued later when the town was taken.

"At dawn on June 6, landings took place at five invasion sites. All of them became locales of intense fighting. The landing infantry became the target of terrific firepower from the German fortifications on the cliffs. Despite pounding by Allied aircraft and from ships offshore, the well-placed and protected forts were damaged but were still functioning when the first troops came ashore.

"As I walked from Utah to the adjoining Omaha Beach, I stopped to examine Pointe-du-Hoc, the key installation at Omaha. Dug deep into the ground on top of a cliff and crowned by massive concrete, it had not been destroyed despite relentless bombardments from the air and the sea. It was finally eliminated when

225 men of the 2nd Ranger Battalion climbed up the steep cliff and routed the defenders with grenades and flamethrowers aimed through the air openings facing the rear. The Rangers took heavy casualties, including 81 dead. I learned that the Rangers had a favorite motto; *audentes fortuna invat* (fortune favors the daring).

"Pointe-du-Hoc was only one of numerous well-defended positions. These had to be taken out before Allied beaches could be linked together to provide both length and depth for the main debarking forces. These units had to mark time in landing craft offshore while the initial assault units cleared the beaches.

"I was particularly interested in Pointe-du-Hoc, the first major action by Army Rangers in Normandy. In the winter of 1943, I had participated in Ranger-type combat training at Camp Sharpe, a former National Guard site near Gettysburg. The training there was conducted by the Military Intelligence Service to prepare a small number of intelligence personnel for potential behind-the-lines operations.

"By June 12, the beaches and the immediate hinterland in Allied hands varied from 5 to 16 miles. Until early July, there wasn't sufficient room for the armored divisions to move into the inland battle areas. Before checking whether the Fourth Armored could finally get into action, I saw a POW cage guarded by Military Police. Among the prisoners, I noticed a wounded major. I walked over to interrogate him seeking to learn about German reserves we might encounter in the days ahead. He had blood dripping down his shoulder. As I approached him, with *"Wie geht's, Herr Major?"* he looked surprised and pointed to his shoulder. I found a nearby medic and got him to attend to the prisoner's bleeding.

"When I returned, the major seemed more relaxed and said both in German and English, *"Danke schön*, thank you," and he asked me where I learned German. I told him my grandparents had immigrated to Milwaukee. They brought me up and taught me German. He told me an uncle of his lives in Milwaukee, Did I ever meet him? His name was Müller. I laughed. "There are thousands of Millers there. He probably anglicized his name to Miller." The major then related he had studied English at Heidelberg University and also spent a year in England as an exchange student.

"At this point I felt there was sufficient rapport between us, so I casually mentioned that his division, the 352nd Infantry, gave us a lot of trouble, He seemed surprised that I knew about his division. I explained that I was with Military Intelligence and had a good idea about the German outfits facing us. That inspired him to tell me how long his unit had been manning the line near Pointe-du-Hoc. Relating the thinness of the German forces at the beaches, he mentioned that his commander could not understand why they had not shifted the Panzer divisions of the Fifteenth Army idling at the Dover Strait to Normandy. When I told him that SHAEF had persuaded the German high command to expect the major Allied effort to take place along the coast closest to England in the Dunkirk area, his face lit up. "You really fooled the *Wehrmacht!*" He also told me that this had a far greater impact, such as committing available reserves to the invasion front. I then departed, wishing him speedy recovery and urging him to cooperate with us in consideration of his post-war future.

"While we waited on the beach, the infantry had a tough time fighting through the hedgerows in the *bocage,* (Norman term for woodland and grass pastures). An ordnance unit developed a solution. They attached *tetrahedran*, a Greek word for a device, to the bows of tanks, enabling them to slice through the hedgerows.

Subsequently, I learned that the idea for this contrivance is credited to an American soldier, Sgt. Culin.

"The Fourth Armored Division moved steadily inland, passing through the territories previously liberated by the First Army's infantry divisions, By July 20 we reached the front line and dug in.

"Our jeep window was kept down to avoid reflections inviting air attacks. The Germans took advantage of this by stringing wires across the road which cut off the heads of the jeep occupants. In response to this tactic, our motor pools welded steel posts on the jeep bumpers to cut the wires. To do this, our ordnance people utilized the steel obstacles the Germans had placed in the water and on the beach.

"Through visits with our counterparts in the adjacent 83rd and 90th Infantry Divisions, we exchanged intelligence information. On July 25, General Bradley became commander of the 12th Army Group, which was activated on August 1. It consisted of the First Army and the Third Army under Generals Courtney H. Hodges and George S. Patton, Jr., respectively. The Fourth Armored was one of two tank divisions of the Third Army; the other was the Sixth Armored. July 25 was also the date Operation Cobra began, namely the breakthrough by the American Army through the German lines established behind the Normandy areas seized and expanded in the initial assault. Watching from a foxhole I saw an unending stream of aircraft bombarding the roads leading from Normandy into Brittany. Cobra ended July 28 when the Fourth Armored captured the key town of Coutances.

"July 25 was a key date. I was in a foxhole. We were about 20 miles from the invasion beaches. Soon I became intimately acquainted with foxholes. Depending upon the soil, it took a lot of effort. It wore me out. But soon the situation improved. I realized that the area we were in had previously been occupied by an infantry unit. When they had pulled out, they left a lot of foxholes, some quite elaborate. Instead of digging my own hole I always looked for an existing one. But soon this foxhole business was over. Once we broke out on July 27, our division kept moving. When we halted, we frequently bedded down in vacant houses. Most were damaged. Many just had walls; no roofs.

"We used the main highway from St. Mère-Église to Coutances. I was by myself in the jeep. The other two team members were in a half-track with the G-2. He wanted them near him to quickly identify the enemy units encountered. I was hailed by a farmer who asked me to come with him. He took me to a barn in which around 80 or so dead Germans were stored. They were neatly stacked like cords of wood. I asked how they got there. He told me he had brought them in from his fields, where he needed to plow. He wanted to know how to get rid of them. I told him that our combat troops could not remove them. The rear echelons had grave registration details that could take care of it.

"On July 29, I made my way to the first large town after St.-Mère-Église. It was Perriers, almost completely destroyed. The following day I passed through Coutances. It also suffered a lot of damage. On July 30, the column I was travelling with reached la Haye Pesnel, another key town. Bumped into the French Interpreters Team (Military Intelligence Interpreters - MII) attached to the Fourth Armored. This town did not suffer much damage, a credit to our fast-moving division against only scattered resistance. The population was very enthusiastic. They plied us with food and drinks.

"The following day, July 31, I joined another column. After we passed through the town of Ducey, on

August 1, I left the detachment to check on a Mercedes which had been ditched on the side of the road.

"On August 1, when in my jeep on the road near Avranches, I noticed a large German army staff car ditched on the side. I stopped and scrambled down an embankment to examine the Mercedes and found the occupants, the driver and a passenger whose uniform identified him as a General Staff colonel, dead. A briefcase was attached to the officer's belt. I cut it loose to examine its contents. Lo and behold I hit a goldmine! It was a treasure trove of high-level combat intelligence information on the enemy, including detailed data on a German Army Corps held in reserve: units under its control, their armaments, personnel data and other order of battle material. While I was checking all this out, several German fighter planes strafed the road. The windshield of the Mercedes was hit and glass splinters were embedded my face. Ignoring my wounds, I stopped an MP on a motorcycle and told him to take the briefcase immediately to the G-2 of the corps headquarters because it contained important data, Then a medic attended to me.

"The contents of the briefcase proved to be extremely valuable, providing the American forces with important information. Later, some if it proved useful in our efforts to relieve the trapped units of the 30th Infantry Division on Hill 314 in the Falaise Gap. These units were surrounded by German forces, which had been ordered to cut through the American lines all the way to Avranches. Some of the attacking German units were those whose vital data had been contained in the briefcase. Patton's forces, including Fourth Armored Division units, were able to reach the Falaise Gap by August 13. On their drive to the Gap, the Fourth Armored Division units encountered a river, but they had no means to get the tanks and armored personnel carriers across. Fortunately there was an OSS operative in the area who was able to guide them to a bridge, which had not been destroyed.

"With the Canadian forces attacking from the north, the Allies were able to stop the drive toward Avranches and force the Germans to retreat. To avoid firing on each other, Canadian units and Patton's forces were ordered by SHAEF to stop some distance from the area where they were to meet to completely close the Gap. Thus, substantial German forces were able to avoid complete encirclement. However, they had to abandon much of their armaments. With the elimination of the German effort to cut the American lines across southern Normandy, the American offensive, which began on July 25, could continue.

"On August 3, the column I had rejoined stopped near Rennes, a city in Brittany. I found the division headquarters. Wrote a formal report on the documents in the Mercedes. Briefed the Assistant G-2 and the head of the CIC Detachment.

"On August 6, we passed through Rennes. Apparently, there had been not much fighting there. I did not notice much damage.

"On August 7, I was with the first column to reach Vannes, a port city on the Atlantic coast. There was no opposition. The facial wound I had received when I examined the ditched Mercedes started to bleed. I drove to the field hospital attached to the division. A French civilian stopped me after I left the hospital. He pointed to an area where he had seen a German soldier. I drove there, pointed my pistol and he came out of a ditch with his hands up. I put him on the hood of the jeep and took him to an MP checkpoint.

"On August 8, I stopped at the main marketplace to talk to some armed FFI men there. They had been on a sabotage mission in the area. I took some photos of them. They suggested that I go to the prefecture, the seat of the county. I participated in a ceremony raising the French flag.

"My wound started to bleed again on the next day. The Assistant G-2 got a driver to take me to the hospital. This time, they spent more time with me. I was assured that it would not reopen.

"We remained in Vannes until August 14. Those were "free" days. Went swimming several times. Also found an excellent restaurant; went there for dinners with G-2 personnel. Had good meals. Paid for the food with rations and cartons of cigarettes.

"Left Vannes on August 14. Moved on a major highway through the towns of Redon, Châteaubriant, La Flèche, Saint-Calais, and through Orléans. We traveled rapidly, including through some of the nights until we reached the town of Courtenay on August 22. We encountered no resistance. Our advance elements had to clear out of Courtenay, where the Germans had set up roadblocks to slow us down. Shortly before reaching Courtenay, we lost our third team member. He had an accident while driving one of the G-2 jeeps. He was evacuated.

"On August 23, we reached Troyes, the first city after Orléans. The residents celebrated; gave us food and drinks. We could not linger. The division moved on. Two days later we were slowed down. Drew some artillery fire. Crossed the Marne River at Joinville. Bridge was intact.

"Stopped at Gondrecourt on September 2. Bivouacked there. The supply train, especially gasoline, had to catch up with us. Had a toothache. The dental officer sent me to a mobile dental clinic in the rear. Had the tooth pulled. Met mayor of Gondrecourt. He arranged for a seven-course dinner for the Division Civil Affairs Officer and myself. What a break from a steady diet of K-rations! CIC Team returned from Paris. They brought back goodies, which they shared with me.

"On September 10 we finally moved out. Stopped at Domremy and stayed for two days. The next town, Neufchâteau, seven miles down the road, was still in German hands. While waiting to get the road cleared, we got a surprise. Bing Crosby, accompanied by a group of entertainers, set up a show near Domremy. I spent a couple of hours there.

"Moved out on September 13. Finally got through Neufchâteau. Used a secondary road. Bivouacked for two days near Bayon. On August 16 stopped outside of Lunéville which was still occupied by a sizable German unit. We finally cleared the town after severe fighting. Went into Lunéville. Searched the German headquarters.

"On September 18, a German tank battle group counterattacked, trying to retake Lunéville. They were repulsed. Lots of French civilians were fleeing from the combat area, clogging the roads. Moved toward Nancy. Stopped at Dombasle, where one of our tank units relieved the 42nd Cavalry which had been trapped there.

"The following day, changed directions toward Arracourt. Encountered strong German resistance. Our column was periodically shelled. We stopped in a forest. There was a threat of German tanks heading our way. The headquarters company manned the perimeter with bazookas. Several Germans were captured. Some of the interrogation reports had important information. We sent it up to Corps.

"Stayed in the bivouac area until September 25. Weather was cold and rainy. Moved the division headquarters setup near a village, Réméréville. The division was placed into reserve status. Many tanks needed repairs and infantry replacements had to be integrated into the units. Our CG wants to move beyond Lunéville toward the Rhine in two weeks. PWs said the Germans had only limited resources in that area. One big problem, however. The Third Army was out of gasoline. It had been diverted to Montgomery and his divisions to try and cut through Holland to the Rhine; "Operation Market Garden". They failed. If we had gotten the gas, we could have made it to the Lower Rhine.

"We remained there until November 12. Went into Nancy several times. Visited a quartermaster shower unit. They issued new fatigues, underwear and socks. One morning I saw a jeep approaching with flashing lights. Out stepped Patton, about twenty feet from my foxhole. He came to visit our general, John Wood. I was perplexed about his ostentatious arrival. I figured it would invite an artillery barrage, as we not far from the front line. Apparently, our general became concerned; convinced Patton to leave. Sure enough, as he was departing, we received several rounds of artillery.

"I had been fighting a cold. After I had a bad night, I went to see the medics. I had high fever and was shaking. They wanted me to go to the field hospital. I declined. I got permission from the Assistant G-2 to stay in the house of a farmer with whom I had become acquainted. He was glad to put me up. I brought plenty of rations and several cartons of cigarettes in exchange for room and board. After about a week there, I recovered.

"We moved out on November 12. Headed north to Château Salins, which still had the German signs, i.e., Salzburgen. The town was completely deserted. Partially destroyed. Found a German hiding in one of the buildings. He wore civilian clothes. He may have gotten rid of his uniform. I turned him over to the CIC. One night the town was strafed by the Luftwaffe.

One plane was shot down. Stayed in Château Salins for several days.

"After departing from Château Salins, we went through several villages. We by-passed the town of Dieuze which was flooded. Some had French names, other were German-sounding, such as Lauterfingen. This reflects the history of the area which was sometimes a part of Germany, sometimes of France. Finally stopped at Fénétrange, a small town, on November 28. Stayed there until December 6.

"Moved westward toward the Nancy area. Stopped in Domfessel until December 19. We stayed in unoccupied houses in the villages and small towns. Only a few civilians had remained there, reflecting the considerable fighting in this area.

"On December 19, we left early in the morning, using the major highway to Metz and Luxembourg. Went through Pont-à-Mousson, southwest of Metz. Entered the Luxembourg area through the town of Longwy, by-passed Luxembourg City, got to Arlon in Belgium late in the evening. The movement from France to Belgium was in response to the unexpected German invasion of Northern Luxembourg and Belgium on December 18."

I turned to Lucy and said, "Lucy, I believe that this was the beginning of the Battle of the Bulge. Let's continue." So we went on.

"There was lots of traffic on the highway. At this point in time we did not know that the division had been ordered northward due to the German attacks. It took several days before we realized that we were the leading force heading north, ordered by Patton. Other Third Army elements were also going in the same direction. Due to heavy traffic, we got stuck when we entered Belgium. I saw a hospital near the road, told my driver I would go there and catch up with him later. It was a Catholic hospital. When I entered I asked a nurse if I could take a bath. She did not understand me, took me to a sister who spoke good English. While I was in the tub, they took my clothes and washed them. Then they fed me a good meal. I needed all that. Our rapid movement provided little time for personal hygiene.

"After leaving the hospital, I hailed a jeep on the highway. Got to the city of Arlon. I found our division headquarters. We remained in Arlon for several days. Our combat units (CC A, CC B, and CC R) were all moving north. They frequently had to change direction until their final objective, the relief of the beleaguered city Bastogne, became their designated goal.

"The icy roads hindered all Third Army reinforcements heading north. We stayed in Arlon until December 27. The division's combat commands were often out of touch with both division and Corps headquarters. Finally, the first units of Combat Command B entered Bastogne on December 29.

"December 31, Fourth Armored Division Headquarters was mistakenly bombed by American aircraft. *C'est la guerre.*

"Division headquarters returned to Arlon on January 2. Moved to Assenois on January 9. From there entered Luxembourg. Rumors floated around that we would stay in Luxembourg in reserve status. Many of the units needed rehab. Tanks and artillery pieces needed overhaul.

"Headquarters took over a high school in Dudelange. We were assigned quarters with Dudelange residents. I ended up at the house of the town's mayor. Moved in on the 16th. Stayed in Dudelage until February 24.

"Division was reactivated on February 25. Got a five-day pass to Paris. Division had moved forward toward Germany. When I returned from Paris on March 2, headquarters was at Oberweis, near the border. March

4 was the last day we were in Luxembourg. Entered Germany on the road toward Bitburg."

At this point we stopped reviewing the manuscript. It was way beyond midnight. It took us that long because Lucy was asking numerous questions.

Those hours of reading and the discussion of the contents had worn me out. When we hit the hay we both fell sound asleep in no time. When the alarm rang in the morning, I did not hear it. Lucy had. When she pulled me out of bed, she was already dressed. She urged me to take a cold shower to get me to shape up. We had a quick breakfast. I told her I would call a cab. She nixed it. The travel agent at State had requested transportation for Lucy when she cut the orders. There, I saved the Army some money!

We had an easy time at Dulles. They looked at our official passports and whisked us through the security desks. The plane was not crowded. The third seat in our row remained vacant. We were already over the Atlantic when a severe pain hit me in my left leg. Lucy was concerned. I told her the orthopedic guy I had seen weeks ago had cautioned me that my problem could reoccur without warning. I had almost forgotten what I had gone through. I had placed a bag of acetaminophen pills in my suitcase as a routine procedure when I was packing. Unfortunately, we had requested our luggage to be placed in the hold.

I stopped the flight attendant to ask him if there were any acetaminophen in the medical kit. He knew what it was, but they only had the regular aspirin. I related my problem. He suggested that I utilize the empty seat. This helped somewhat. I also got up every so often to walk the aisle.

Upon arrival at Reykjavik we checked with the desk to confirm the trip to Paris. The young man who took care of us was very friendly. I mentioned that my father had preceded me in the Army. In the 1960s he had been to Iceland in connection with some equipment problems with the DEW Line. He enjoyed his visit to Reykjavik. Stayed at a nice hotel and swam in a pool with geothermal water. I was wondering whether any of the DEW Line sites were kept as tourist attractions.

"I don't think so. When the Cold War finally ended in the 1990s, the American Army left. The facilities were dismantled." He recommended a hotel which also had an excellent dining room. A shuttle bus would take us there. In the evening he suggested that we go to a musical performance at the Harpa Auditorium, not far from the hotel. I thanked him for his advice. As we were on the way out to catch the bus, he called us back. He had checked on our flight and saw that the first class compartment was almost empty. He upgraded us. I thanked him profusely.

When we checked in at the hotel, the desk clerk told us that the airport had called to make sure to accommodate us. We were given a room which looked out towards the bay. There also was a bottle of wine, accompanied by an assortment of nuts at a table next to a desk. I immediately took out the pills and started to feel better after I popped one. Lucy suggested a hot bath while she went downstairs to check out the shops in the hotel. After the bath, the lack of enough sleep caught up with me. Lucy must have been gone for a couple of hours. When she woke me up I tried to pull her towards me. She laughed. She would take a shower now. She gave me a beautiful tie she had bought. I should wear it when I got dressed. Then it was time for dinner. She was starved.

The dining room was not very large, but it was attractively furnished. Lucy ordered a cocktail, while I stuck to water, which had an unusual, but pleasant, taste. I asked the waitress about it. She laughed. She emphasized that the hotel did not serve plain tap water as it was somewhat bitter. We suggested that she select local dishes for us. After a leisurely meal, we proceeded to the front desk and inquired about the Harpa music place. We were told the performance was about to start. It was only a ten-minute walk to get there. We enjoyed the concert.

When we got back to the hotel, the desk clerk told us there was a small dance floor in the back. An ensemble from a local high school was performing. There were only a few couples on the floor. We joined them. After a few numbers we went to our room. I took ahold of Lucy and made up for all the time we had lost.

We got up early in the morning and had breakfast at the hotel. Then we went on a sightseeing tour of Reykjavik and environs. It was well conducted. Among the many interesting sights were the pipes along the sidewalks which carried steam from hot geysers to keep the sidewalks free of snow and ice. The homes were all heated the same way. We also enjoyed watching people swim in an open air pool also heated by the geysers. The tour took us to see the homes that had been restored and preserved to show how the people had lived many years ago. We met a young couple from Pittsburgh who told us this was their second trip to Iceland, as they loved the beauty of the area and found the people to be friendly.

We were then bussed back to the airport. Checking in went smoothly. Soon we were on the plane.

The flight to Paris was very smooth. The hostess sat with us. She was curious how we got the upgrade. I told her that somehow the Reykjavik desk had found out I had a connection, namely I played lots of tennis in Washington with an Icelander. She grinned. She told me that that was a good story. She apologized for being so nosey. To make up for it, she served us a delicious meal. For a change I settled for a beer while Lucy stuck to her cocktail. Time went fast. Before we anticipated, we saw the lights of Paris below us.

CHAPTER 12

IN SEARCH OF RELATIVES

WE CLEARED CUSTOMS IN no time. Cabs were lined up outside the terminal. I went up to the first one in line. We spoke in a mixture of English and French. I mentioned that my father was one of the liberators of Paris during World War II. I wanted to visit some of the places he had been through from Normandy to Lorraine. It appeared I had stimulated his interest. He told me that his father had been active in the FFI.

I asked him about a good hotel which did not charge outrageous prices and was located near the American Embassy. He said he knew of such a place and would take me there. Then I signaled to Lucy to join us. I introduced her. We loaded our baggage into the trunk and were on the way. I noticed he had not activated the meter. I thought that was a requirement. I asked him about that. He laughed. He was treating us as friends. He would charge us half of the cost.

When we arrived at the hotel, he had an animated conversation with the doorman. He helped us register and gave me his card. I should call him if I needed his help. The desk clerk assured us our room would be very pleasant. The rate was fairly reasonable. We got a discount as they wanted to attract customers from diplomatic missions.

Lucy sank into a chair. Apparently all the traveling had worn her out. She looked pale. I suggested we stay put for the rest of the day. Contact with the embassy could wait. She agreed.

I thought some good nourishment would pick her up. I ordered room service for a light lunch. We lucked out. Instead of the usual elaborate dishes, there was a bowl of chicken soup and a bunch of small sandwiches. I reckon the hotel was acquainted with the tastes of American clientele.

Lucy was beginning to look better. Color had returned to her face. Then she surprised me. She was going to change into something comfortable. She wanted me to dig the diary out of my suitcase to go over the rest of my dad's entries from where we had previously stopped.

We sat on the couch and started to read from the point I had marked in the entry of March 4. That was the day the Fourth Armored had left Luxembourg to enter Germany.

> "On March 5 we were still near Bitburg. The G-2 told me that one our advance units, while clearing the roads, had captured a German Lt. General. He had sent him up to Corps for interrogation. Had to drop off our jeep at Ordnance. The transmission had ceased to function.
>
> "Moved to Darscheid on March 6. Jeep still at Ordnance.
>
> "Crossed the Moselle River on March 16 near the village of Karden."

I told Lucy that I remembered my father's friend, Robert Calvert, who was in his division. He had been with the 51st Armored Infantry Battalion. His platoon was ordered to seize a bridge on the Moselle. They ran into a German ambush. Robert was severely wounded and had to be evacuated. This must have been be around the same time.

> "Moved slowly in general western direction until March 20 when we reached the Rhine at Worms.
>
> "Between March 21 and 24 moved alongside the Rhine.

"By March 24 the Engineers had constructed a pontoon bridge. We crossed over around 1100 hours in vicinity of Leeheim.

"Between March 25 and March 27 went north-westward.

"On March 26 got startling news. Patton had ordered a 4th Armored Division Task Force to liberate a German PW camp at Hammelburg, located outside the Third Amy operation area. The information was tightly controlled. Later I learned that Patton's son-in-law was a prisoner at Hammelburg.

"Crossed Main River at Münzenberg on March 28.

"Division captured another German general March 29.

"On March 30, Division received the Presidential Unit Citation.

"Between March 31 and April 4 moved rapidly through various towns in which the population had displayed white sheets.

"On April 4 we entered the city of Gotha. There was no resistance. The citizens appeared happy.

"On April 5 Combat Command A had liberated a concentration camp at Ohrdruf which was part of the Buchenwald Camp complex. I had heard there was also an administrative headquarters at Ohrdruf. I took the jeep and drove there. I checked a large building on the grounds. It was completely empty. Later I was told there had been a weapons research center in the basement. When I left the building I saw a large number of bodies on the ground. They were dozens of inmates who had been killed. Apparently, they were left there because the guards fled before they could dispose of the bodies. I read in the "Stars and Stripes" that Generals Eisenhower, Bradley, and Patton later visited this site. Eisenhower was very angry when he saw the piles of bodies.

"Between April 6 and April 23 moved southeastward.

"Stopped April 24 at Bayreuth. For the next several days worked with CIC detachment at request of Capt. Flynn, the CO.

"Moved southward, arriving at Deggendorf, near the frontier of Germany-Czechoslovakia, on May 2.

"May 3 and 4, German forces surrendered in Italy, Austria, Holland, Denmark, and Northern Germany.

"Rumors on May 5 about moving into Czechoslovakia.

"May 6 entered Czech city of Susice. All German forces in the west had surrendered.

"May 8 - War is over. Attended party at Hotel Krone.

"May 10 Met Russian Army units.

"May 10 moved to Strakonice which was on the Line of Demarcation, which had been negotiated by Eisenhower and Zhukov.

"May 11 received orders, through G-2, to go beyond the Line of Demarcation to investigate the German Army Headquarters elements which had retreated near Prague and had surrendered to Czech partisans. In spite of heavy fighting in the territory we had to go through between Germans, Czechs, and Vlasov Russians, we were able to seize a truckload of documents and return with them to our headquarters.

"After several days at Strakonice, division moved to Bavaria for occupation duty."

"Well," I said to Lucy, "this is the end of the diary. I thought we should get dressed and go out for dinner."

Lucy reminded me that many French still have their main meal at noontime. Supper was usually later at night. She had a point. Although I had heard that the meal habits had undergone changes. The long times devoted to dinner at mid-day were giving way to more like lunches in the U.S.. The trend was toward having dinner after dark.

"Keef, we still have a couple of hours before getting ready to go out. What was your dad doing during the occupation in Germany?"

"OK, let me read what my father had sketched out in the memo my mother had typed. I'll go over some selected parts. So, here it goes."

"Well, life was entirely different from the daily grind during combat. I was attached to the division's CIC unit. I was given an area to check out and control any subversive activities. There were none. No large cities were in my jurisdiction, only numerous villages and small towns. I screened some who had been arrested by the MPs for various reasons. Found a few German military who had merged into the civilian population without getting a military discharge. Turned them over to the MPs who took them to discharge centers.

"One day I was called to report to the G-2. He had received a phone call from someone in G-2 of the Third Army. They requested me to go there on detached duty to work with them on German military documents. I obtained a jeep and driver to take me to Bad Tölz, south of Munich near the Austrian border. After I was dropped off I started to walk toward Third Army Headquarters. An MP stopped me and told me I was out of uniform. I had not worn a tie. I told him that I wore what I had on me while with the Fourth Armored. He emphasized that this was a chicken shit outfit. Patton wanted everything in first class order. The MPs had to enforce his edicts.

"I spent two weeks in utter boredom. The people I worked with were nice. Instead of sleeping in barracks, I stayed in the office, which had washroom facilities. The work was dull. I don't know why I was picked to help them out. I suspect some higher-ups in Third Army G-2 were dissatisfied with the progress made in the review of the documents. So I was tagged. I really never found out the purpose of this research. I got extremely frustrated. I was used to action, not paper shuffling.

"Luck came my way after about two weeks. I was ordered to return to the Fourth Armored. My name had come up as being eligible to return to the U.S.. SHAEF had instituted a point system based on the length of time served in Europe plus extra credits for decorations. I had ample points.

"I checked in at headquarters with the G-1 who was responsible for assuring that the qualified individuals would be processed. However, in my case, there were complications. The G-1 needed my 201 file, the personnel records. Mine were at SHAEF because I was assigned there. The solution was for me to go to SHAEF, get my records, and bring them back. They gave me a jeep and a driver to proceed to Paris where the SHAEF records were located. I asked the G-2 to give me a letter, authorizing me and the driver to go to Paris to obtain my records, I thought I would need this in case I was stopped along the way. After all, it was unusual for a Fourth Armored jeep to travel all over Germany and France. To my surprise, I was never stopped. But the letter came in handy at SHAEF.

"After my return to the Fourth Armored, my papers were reviewed. I was sent to one of the Infantry Divisions, I believe it was the 79th, which had been alerted to return to the U.S.. I stayed with them for several weeks until trains had been secured to take us to Southern France, where we boarded a Liberty vessel to take us back to New York.

"I was discharged at Fort Meade on December 15, 1945."

Lucy thanked me for sharing my father's experiences in Europe. By then, it was time to go to eat.

I asked the doorman to suggest a place for dinner. Nothing elaborate; just good food. He directed us to a nearby place. When we were seated, I ordered *un menu a prix fixe*, a fixed price menu, which many popular French restaurants offer. We shared a meal of calf's liver with onions, potatoes *au gratin*, strings beans, and a mixed salad. When we ordered coffee, the waiter explained they usually served a demitasse of strong black coffee, but most Americans prefer the regular coffee, which they call *café au lait*.

When we returned to our room, Lucy asked me if I had any details on the March diary entry about the Hammelburg raid. She had read about it some years ago.

"Lucy, you and I are on the same wavelength. I also became curious about the details. I recall I asked my mother whether my dad had covered it in the compilation of his experiences which my mother had edited and typed. She said he had devoted several pages to it, but wanted her not to put it in the main body of the manuscript, which would cover only what he went through. As it was a significant event in his division's history, she should put it in an annex. When I examined what she had typed, I was fascinated." I began to read.

> "It became abundantly clear that this was Patton's personal baby. His motive to order the conquest of Hammelburg was really self-centered. He wanted to liberate his son-in-law, who was a PW in the camp. He never admitted this. Patton always maintained that he wanted to get the American PW's out of the camp before they could be moved elsewhere. He personally went to Division Headquarters when his initial order for the raid drew objection from the CG. Patton wanted Lt. Colonel Abrams, who was already a well-known and popular commander, to lead the mission. Even though Patton had cleared his intention of sending the task force with General Bradley, his superior, both his Corps Commander and the CG of the Fourth Armored objected. They were bent to proceed within the Third Army's operational area.

"Patton would not be deterred. He directed that the task force be activated immediately. The CG, Brigadier General Hogue, called Abrams to organize and command the task force. Abrams would only accept command if he could use his entire unit, Combat Command B, consisting of 3000-plus personnel of a fully equipped force. Hogue told him the Third Army had authorized only a smaller force of approximately 300 men.

"Patton decided to go to the Fourth Armored early in the morning of March 26. He went directly to Colonel Abrams, who told Patton he would only do this if he could take his entire command, with its heavy equipment, there. Patton told him only a small force would be involved. Abrams should be the officer in charge, but not go with it. Initially, Abrams had chosen Lt. Colonel Cohen, who commanded one of his infantry battalions. However, Cohen was ill and Captain Abe Baum, an infantry company CO, was ordered to organize and lead the task force.

"Baum's unit succeeded in reaching the camp. He took all PW's, including Patton's son-in-law, back with him. However, a sizable German force waylaid them after they had left the camp. Many of the task force soldiers were killed or wounded. Most of the liberated PW's were recaptured and returned to Hammelburg. Baum was severely wounded. The Germans were looking for him. He was hidden in the camp's hospital until Hammelburg was captured by American forces several days later."

Lucy thanked me. My father had noted that he did not have the full story. What he knew was from what he could get from various sources at Division Headquarters.

The next morning Lucy called the embassy. She would be there in about an hour. I returned to the room after breakfast to glance through the sight-seeing literature I had picked up in the lobby. I earmarked a couple of museums which were within walking distance.

Around noon I called Lucy on her cell phone. She said she was very busy. She had had a bite at the embassy's snack bar. She hoped to get finished when she had tied up some loose ends tomorrow morning.

I returned to the hotel around 5:30. Lucy showed up a short time later. She said that she had brought the Embassy problem under control. Apparently, the chief clerk and one of the senior secretaries had had a jurisdictional battle which escalated into personal enmity. Lucy felt that one of the women had to be removed; either sent back to the States or be transferred to one of the consulates. She believed she could wrap it up soon. Then she had a surprise. The chargé d'affaires appeared pleased when she outlined her findings. Just before her return to the hotel, he invited her to join him and his wife for dinner. Lucy mentioned an Army friend was with her on this trip. The chargé d'affaires suggested that Lucy bring her friend. He was most welcome. He gave her directions to his place, which was near the embassy.

After we got dressed, it was already past seven. Lucy suggested we should get on our way. We were expected at about seven thirty.

They had a terrific housekeeper who had cooked up a delicious dinner. I described the reason for my trip. I confided that, if I had not received the support of the Pentagon, I would not have undertaken this discovery tour all over Europe. I asked our host for the best place for a car rental. Lucy would take a few days leave and go with me. The chargé d'affaires suggested that Lucy should take advantage of the transportation available at the embassy. Having a car with diplomatic tags would be helpful in many ways. All she would have to do is sign a statement that all car expenses would be her responsibility. Lucy was most surprised and gladly accepted the offer.

When we returned to our room, we poured over the road map I had purchased to determine the best way to get to Bayeux, which was close to the invasion beaches.

Lucy completed her work the next morning and made her final recommendations. When she returned, we completed packing. The embassy car would be dropped off at the hotel. Lucy had already asked the doorman to call us. We decided not to wait and took our luggage to the lobby. Soon the doorman came in and helped us with our stuff. The car was a mid-sized American make, thus we didn't have to study the controls, had it been a French vehicle.

It would take us only a few hours from Paris to Bayeux. Getting out of Paris proved to be a struggle. There was lots of traffic. We had to stop a few times to make sure we were on the right road.

By the time we left the outskirts behind us we were getting hungry, but it was already mid-afternoon. We stopped at a bakery in one of the villages for a cup of coffee and croissants. The further we were from Paris, the lighter the traffic. Alongside the road were fields blooming with yellow plants. We later found out that they were colzo, also known as rape, part of the mustard family, a forage crop for animal feed.

We finally reached Evreux, the first larger town on our route. There was some sort of festival. Traffic was slow. We eventually reached the outskirts of Caen, the town where the British had had a lot of trouble getting through after the breakout from the invasion beaches. The Germans defended Caen stubbornly to limit further inland advances. We saw a large motel and decided to spend the night there.

The desk clerk recommended a restaurant near it. After taking showers and changing clothes, we went there. In comparison with Paris, the prices were reasonable. We had a leisurely dinner. We didn't get back to the motel until much later. We were both tired and had a good night's sleep.

In the morning we patronized the motel's coffee shop. We found out that breakfast was included in the daily rate. The waitress suggested we take their morning wake-up special, which turned out to be a substantial meal. We did not get back on the road until mid-morning and reached Bayeux around noon time. A pedestrian directed us to the Hotel de Ville (City Hall.) We stopped there to seek assistance in finding the address of the lieutenant's nephew. But the doors were locked. They adhered to the traditional 2-hour dinner break. A gendarme approached us, asking if he could help. In my broken French I explained we were seeking the address of a foreigner we wanted to visit. He said that all non-French residents had to register at the police station which was located across the street. We walked over. While it was open, it was manned only by a desk sergeant.

He suggested we come back later when the clerk who kept the records had returned. I asked him about a good restaurant nearby. He pointed to a place across the square which he visited every so often. Like most eateries in the provinces they offered a choice of three fixed-price dinners. We ordered vegetarian. Both of us were tired of hearty meals with meat. Also, the dinner we had selected featured white asparagus. The waitress said it was in season and locally grown. Instead of coffee we ordered tea. She laughed. Tea was seldom ordered, but they had a variety of tea bags to accommodate British tourists who stopped by after visiting the invasion beaches. Some of them were on the way to Paris.

After a leisurely dinner we crossed the square to reach the police station. We were directed to the clerk who handled the foreign residents' data. We introduced ourselves and showed him our diplomatic passports. He told us that there were not many foreigners in residence. He immediately identified who we wanted to see, gave us the address and directions.

Lt. Kaufmann's nephew lived in a nice house. It was probably owned by his wife who I had been told was financially well fixed. I rang the bell. An elderly woman came to the door. I explained that I would like to speak to the man in the house. Fortunately, she understood and spoke English. She said that he and his wife were at their summer home in southern France in the town of Grenoble. She gave me the address and phone number. I told her rather than call, we would go down there.

Then we returned to the police station to seek advice on the best route to take. We spoke to the clerk who had previously taken care of us. After driving to Utah Beach where my father had landed, and visiting the American cemetery, we wanted to head south, passing through some of the localities my father had listed in the diary. The clerk marked out some of the secondary roads on the road map.

As the sun did not go down until around nine, we had plenty of time to check out Utah Beach. I showed Lucy the area my dad's landing craft had come ashore. From there, we headed for the American Military Cemetery at Saint-Laurent-sur-Mer. It was one of several cemeteries maintained by the American Battle Monuments Commission which is located at the Pentagon.

Next on the list was the town of Saint-Mère-Église. A young man pointed out the church where the parachute of an 82nd Airborne paratrooper was still on the steeple when my father passed through. We stopped at a hotel at Avranches where we had dinner. Thereafter we took a walk through the town.

The next morning we bought some fresh bread and goodies for lunch. As we were leaving, the son of the owner of the hotel recommended we make a side trip to Le Mont Saint- Michel. Lucy was all excited, explaining to me it was a world famous monastery built on an island in the ocean. We got there early in the morning, but it was already full of tourists. To get to the monastery we walked on a causeway from the mainland. It took us almost two hours to take in the sights. Before we left we found a good spot for lunch.

Our next spot on the itinerary was the Brittany American Military Cemetery, near the town of Saint James. We were impressed with how well maintained it was.

Arriving in Vannes late in the afternoon, we passed an imposing building. I recognized it as the prefecture, the seat of the area government. I remembered that my father had joined the local FFI in liberations ceremonies there. He took photos. I waited to drive into the courtyard; however a gendarme did not permit us to enter. When we looked for a place to stay, Lucy wanted to be near the ocean. We drove to a suburb where a hotel was located on the bay. We looked it over. Lucy was not impressed. We spoke to a young woman with a little boy, and she recommended we should consider a new motel located at a sports complex in nearby Arrandon. Arrandon is a clean, prosperous suburb. We tried to eat at an attractive place, but it was not open. Some restaurants in France are closed on Wednesday, many on Mondays. We opted to eat at the motel where we stayed.

In the morning, the manager of the motel served us breakfast. I conveyed to him that I just wanted tea and toast. I had had a stomach ache during the night. His English-speaking ability was limited. Nevertheless, we had a lively conversation.

I showed him my father's 1944 photos of Vannes, including one in a jeep with two prisoners on the hood. I also told him the purpose of our trip. When we checked out, he surprised us by refusing to take any payment for the room and the meals. He said that it was a gesture of appreciation for my father's participation in the liberation of Vannes. He also urged us to return to the prefecture, but to walk in. Driving into the courtyard is prohibited.

When we went back to the prefecture, a gendarme directed me to the information office where the receptionist spoke some English. I told her what had happened the day before, showed her the WWII photos of the building, and asked for permission to take the same photos today. She said picture taking was not permitted. However, she appreciated the unusual circumstances. After she called the Prefect's office, permission to take the pictures was granted.

We then walked into the center of town and photographed the other scenes my father had taken in August, 1944. It was surprising easy to recognize the buildings, even after so many years!

Before we left, we exchanged traveler's checks and Lucy couldn't resist shopping (sweaters, etc.).

Finally, around 11 a.m., we pulled out of Vannes, heading for Redon. Again, we passed many fields planted with colzo, as well as beautiful orchards in full bloom. When we got near Segre we stopped at a gas station. The Fourth Armored had passed through this area on August 14, 1944. One of the pictures my dad had taken showed a group of people standing by the road. Neither the owner of the station nor his wife recognized anyone in the photos. We had our picnic lunch there, gassed up and went on to Le Lion-d'Angers and la Flèche in the Loire Valley.

The countryside was in a springtime glory. The road we were to follow (we tried to duplicate as well as we could the entries in the diary) was no longer in service. The new road passed through St. Calais. It was getting late, and Lucy wanted to stop. However, the accommodations we desired were not available in the small towns we passed through. Before we left on our trip we agreed to stay in a "good" place every night; room with a bath a must. So we had no choice but to push on to Orléans. We got there during the evening rush hour, heading for Olivet, a suburb. We looked for and found a first-class hotel. It was very modern and well-appointed. We checked and liked the accommodations. The dining room was inviting, so we decided to eat there. To make sure my stomach would not act up again, I stuck to a light supper while Lucy dug into the most delicious steak. She again feasted on large, white, tender asparagus which was locally grown.

Lucy wanted to see the Cathedrale Sainte-Croix d'Orléans. There the stained glass windows depict scenes from Joan of Arc's life. We encountered lots of morning rush hour traffic between Olivet and Orléans. A gendarme directed us to an underground garage near the cathedral. But I had noticed a small bar in front of which cars were parked. We found a space. While I got directions at the bar for our trip to Troyes, Lucy went into the cathedral. I joined her later.

We had our usual breakfast at the bar and then we took off, passing through Montargis and Sens. We had not bought anything for lunch. After we went through Sens, Lucy saw an Auberge, which looked like a real nice place to have lunch. When we went inside, we knew we were in a first-class establishment. The patrons were formally attired. The menu featured only full course dinners. Considering that I wanted to eat light (after my stomach upset in Vannes) and that this kind of meal would take 2 to 3 hours, we decided not to stay. So on to Troyes.

For the first time on the trip we had to feed a parking meter. A young woman showed me what coins to use. She also directed us to a nearby pizzeria. When we went inside we were pleasantly surprised. It was an old tavern where the pizza was prepared on charcoal in the fireplace-type oven. We ordered spaghetti and Vichy water. There was a jolly gathering of young people at the next table. When one of the fellows left, he kissed all the boys and girls. The young man saw us watching, and came over to our table and wanted to kiss us also!

Outside of Troyes we passed Lac et Foret d'Orient, Lake of the Eastern Forest, a regional park and recreation area. We did not have the time to stop.

We drove through to Bar-sur-Aube, Joinville to Domrémy, the birthplace of Joan of Arc. I checked the diary. On September 12, 1944, the Fourth Armored had gone into reserve in this area. It was primarily to wait for gasoline and equipment maintenance.

There were no hotels in the small towns we passed through. So even with darkness setting in we pushed on to Neufchâteau, the seat of the prefecture in the area. At a gas station the attendant recommended a first class hotel. We got a nice room. A delightful meal was served in the dining room. After dinner we did some window shopping in the rain. This was the first day on the trip it had rained almost consistently.

After we had returned to the hotel, I took out the map I had bought in Paris. We had just about reached the southern limits of my father's route. This was a good place to head further south to visit Lt. Kaufmann's cousin in Grenoble. We had been so preoccupied in following my father's footsteps that we had pushed the real purpose of our "tour de France" into the background. There was a secondary road from Neufchâteau to Dijon. We arrived there are around noontime. Lucy spied what looked like a cross between a formal eating place and a hamburger joint. So we pulled up there and walked in. To our surprise it was neat and spacious inside. In addition to hamburgers, hot dogs, and French fries, they also offered a luncheon featuring hamburger steak and vegetables. We also could not resist ordering a strawberry milkshake suggested by the waitress.

We continued on the road which merged into the main highway just north of Lyon. It was getting dark. We halted at a large motel on the outskirts. It proved to be a good choice. The room was more than adequate. For food there was a restaurant as well as a cafeteria. We chose the latter. It was not busy so we had a leisurely meal. The manager came by and asked us if we liked what had been served. He spoke English, explaining that he had he had been sent to the U.S. where the company was a part owner of the American chain.

We told him about the purpose of our trip. He left us for several minutes and returned with a map. He marked on it how we should precede to Grenoble. We should bypass Lyon by using the beltway around it and looking for the sign for the turnoff to Grenoble. It went through mountainous country. Although the distance was only between 100 and 150 kilometers or so, it would involve some slow and careful driving. He suggested we stop by the main police station in Grenoble to get directions. It was an old town which had spread out during the past 30 years.

Thanks to the directions, which were easy to follow, we reached Grenoble around noontime. As the manager had predicted, parts of the road cut through steep mountainsides. At one point it was one- way due to a blockage from a rock fall. When we reached the town center, I saw several government-types of buildings, including the police station. Parking there was prohibited except for official use only. I figured since we had diplomatic tags, I would avoid a ticket. As I got out of the car a gendarme approached me and pointed at the sign. I gestured toward the tags. He laughed. The spaces were for police vehicles.

I said, "OK, do you speak English?" He nodded. I gave him the paperwork with the nephew's address. He knew him and his wife. His wife owned one of the original dwellings, not far from the station. She was born here, and, in fact, was a volunteer in the mayor's office.

He said parking was at a premium in the downtown area. He then pulled out some sort of identification ticket for using one of the official spaces at a nearby municipal garage. After parking the car, I should walk behind the garage. The house was on the street behind it. I thanked him. His name was Charles. I should mention it to Babette, *la femme* of Hans Metzger.

The dwellings behind the garage were large structures, dating back at least 100 years. Lucy was most interested, telling me that they probably were constructed in the 19th century.

There was a no bell button at the door. A neatly painted sign in French and German directed us to a knocker on the door. A young woman answered. I suspected that she was probably a college student and would understand English. I introduced Lucy and myself. We were here to visit Babette and Hans Metzger. As we were conversing, a middle-aged woman appeared. The girl introduced us. Babette motioned us to come in. When we were seated in the parlor I explained that we had some questions to which we hoped Hans had the answers. I briefly described my father's experiences in World War II. Babette displayed a genuine interest. I clarified our coming to Grenoble was prompted by Hans' aunt in Oppenheim who thought that Hans would have the answers I was seeking. Babette knew of her, but they had never met. Hans was out of town. He had been invited to the Heidelberg University to give a lecture. He was to return either tonight or tomorrow. He had driven his car to the airport in Lyon.

Babette invited us for lunch. While we were eating the first course, cream of mushroom soup, I related the gendarme's assistance. Babette said they were old friends of Charles. I congratulated her on her big role in the mayor's office. She laughed. She was merely carrying on what her ancestors had started many years ago. Some of them had been on the city's various boards.

Then she inquired what Lucy was doing. Lucy shared how she had met me in the Czech Republic, and then we had renewed our friendship in Washington, where she was working in the State Department. From there on Lucy and Babette were a pair. They practically monopolized the conversation.

After lunch Babette inquired where we were staying. Lucy explained we had just gotten there and had not picked a place yet. Babette had plenty of rooms and would love to have our company. She instructed the young woman to get our luggage from the car. I went with her to help. When we returned, Babette took us to a large bedroom on the second floor, which Lucy had picked out from three guest rooms. Babette told us to rest up and come down around six. She wanted to show us some of the town while there was still daylight.

All of the travel for the last four days caught up with us. We were both pooped out. There was a shower between our room and another guest room. We were soaping each other and hugged each other. We dried each other quickly and hopped into bed. Lo and behold, our fatigued feelings had disappeared. We love each other ardently. Soon we fell into a deep sleep. We did not wake up until there were knocks on the door. I put on a robe and opened it. It was the young girl. She told us *Madame* wanted us to come downstairs when we were ready. I took my last clean clothes out of the bag. Lucy put on some of the stuff she had bought in Vannes.

I apologized to Babette about the mixture of outerwear I wore. This was my last clean outfit. Babette told us to go back upstairs and put all our dirty laundry on the floor. Her help would put it in the washing machine and dryer. I thank her for her thoughtfulness.

We took a leisurely walk through the downtown district. It was fascinating to hear about and see all the points of historic interest. Babette elaborated, in a mixture of French and German, on the rule Grenoble had played, particularly in the Middle Ages when it served as a transit point for traders coming up from the Mediterranean on the way to Lyon.

As it was getting dark, I invited Babette to join us for dinner at her favorite restaurant. The place was not far from her house. She was well known there. We ended up in a private alcove. Lucy and Babette indulged in cocktails while I tried a home-brewed beer. Babette ordered a selection of locally caught fish, *pommes frites* (fried potatoes made according to a local recipe) and selected vegetables. The waitress suggested that we try what they just got in, truffles, the rare deep-in-the-ground mushrooms.

After we made our way home, Babette took us to what she called her music room. There was a piano. Babette and Lucy played a few pieces. It was almost midnight when we called it a day.

We woke up late the following morning. Upon entering the dining room, there was a gentleman at the table eating a hearty breakfast. When we approached he looked up and smiled.

"Good morning, Hans. Glad to meet you."

"Babette told me all about you. I had also called my aunt in Oppenheim before I left Heidelberg. She laid out for me what you're after. But please sit down and join me. Babette is already at the mayor's office. They called her to handle some problems."

Turning to Lucy, he got up and greeted her. While we were eating he described the poor road conditions he encountered on the way from Lyon. "Babette told me you had had a similar experience." After breakfast we went to the parlor.

"Keef, I am curious. How did you become involved in all this research? After all, you are too young to have been in the war."

"I don't know how much your aunt laid out. Briefly, my father was on a mission at the end of the war to seize the German Army's intelligence data on the Russian Army. This information was at a place near Prague. At the same time, a German Army officer, your uncle, who had worked on this data, was traveling westward to surrender to the Americans. When he was questioned, he emphasized the existence and location of the valuable intelligence. However, my father had already seized the German intelligence information. It is probable that your uncle had previously advised American agents, who operated near

Prague, about it. Your uncle's alert may have helped to trigger my father's mission.

"I am trying to discover who actually ordered my father to engage in this. I believe that your uncle may have been aware as to when and whom the American agents had been alerted. It is significant that the raid took place contrary to the Eisenhower-Zhukov agreement that no U.S. action would take place behind the Line of Demarcation."

"Keef, while my uncle's official records are in Freiburg, he did write a draft on some of his experiences while he was with the Headquarters for the Eastern Front. My aunt gave me his writings. I have read them several times. They contain interesting observations, especially some critiques of his fellow staff members. However, there is absolutely nothing about his leaving his unit in Czechoslovakia nor anything about encountering Americans. He did not dwell on his journey to the American Army lines.

"I suspect that he had recognized that his alerting the Americans to the existence of these intelligence details would have political implications. He may have wanted to avoid being involved in any way with the American-Soviet rivalry. I further think that after he returned to civilian life, he pushed his war experiences consciously into the background. Many German veterans wanted to look toward the future, rather than relive the past."

I thanked him for clarifying what he believed was on his uncle's mind. While I was disappointed that there was nothing there to lead me to a solution of what I was after, I realized that I had to redouble my efforts in Washington. I had to persist until I found an answer. I couldn't believe that there were no documents somewhere which would clarify it.

Nodding to Lucy, I expressed my appreciation for Babette's and Hans' hospitality and for Hans' understanding and clarifications. We should get on our way. I asked Hans to phone Babette so that we might thank her. She came on the line. I related to her my lengthy conversation with Hans. "Lucy and I are most thankful for your taking such good care of us. We really have enjoyed our stay at your home."

While we were packing our suitcases, a thought came to mind. We still had plenty of time to complete our itinerary in France and then catch the return flight. As we were way down south, we could visit Switzerland. Through my father's side, I had a distant cousin who lived near Basel, right near the French border. After my father had died, I found the address in his papers and wrote them a note. A few weeks later I received a letter from them, inviting me to visit them. I had entered their information into my address book.

I turned to Lucy and asked her whether she would like it if we made a detour to Switzerland. She was surprised and wanted to know why I had thought about this so unexpectedly. After mentioning that we had ample time left, I described how I had come across the fact that I had distant cousins there.

"Keef, you never said anything about having family in Switzerland. Why?"

"Lucy, it just had not occurred to me. I never thought about them until now. I have not been to Switzerland. This was a good opportunity. What do you think?"

"I haven't been there, either. As you know, I accompanied John on many of his trips. But he never had any need to go there. I have always wanted to travel there. I have heard so much about it. Of course, I would love to make the detour! Meeting your cousins will be a bonus. Let's go!"

As we were saying our farewell to Hans and the young woman, she gave us a package of goodies to take with us. She told me that Babette had called her to prepare something for the road.

Lucy waited by the front door with the luggage while I got the car. Hans had marked on my roadmap the best way to proceed to Switzerland: Lyon to Beaune, then take a four-lane highway to Belfort, where we take a secondary road to Basel. Halfway between Beaune and Belford is the city of Besaçon, which would be a good stop for the night. We should get to Basel by mid-morning.

CHAPTER 13

SWITZERLAND

OUR RETURN TRIP FROM Grenoble to Lyon was much smoother than before. No road blockages and all daylight substantially reduced the time. I questioned Lucy about what had prompted Babette to prepare a care package. Lucy, when gossiping with Babette, had described our roadside lunches. Lucy thought Babette wanted us to maintain this practice.

About two hours after Lyon, we stopped at a picnic site to enjoy Babette's sandwiches. She also had included fresh fruit. After lunch, we resumed our journey. We reached Besaçon. There were numerous hotels in the outskirts, including one which was part of the chain where we had stopped for lunch on the way down. The room was not luxurious, but had everything we wanted. After we had refreshed ourselves, we ate in the cafeteria.

The next morning after breakfast, we ordered sandwiches and fruit for lunch. By around eleven we were at the Swiss frontier.

We had heard about the steep price of gasoline in Switzerland. We gassed up at the last French gas station. It was a busy place. There were quite a few commercial vehicles there. Looked like all wanted to fill up.

At the crossing, the Swiss customs guard noticed our diplomatic tags. He wanted to ascertain whether we were on official business. I told him we were tourists. In that case he had to charge us for use of the Autobahn. He wanted 30 *franken* for a pass, valid for three days. We explained that we had no Swiss money, so he took French *francs* instead. He also showed us how to get to Rheinfelden. After groping our way through Basel, we got onto the Autobahn to Zurich. We turned off at Rheinfelden and, sure enough, we saw a sign pointing to Magden, where my cousin and her family live. Magden is a village; in its center are a few shops, small hotels and well-kept farm houses. On the hills were villa-like new homes. We found my cousin's house, but nobody was home. We knocked on the door of the next house and explained who we were. They invited us in for coffee. My cousins were on vacation. We sat on their patio overlooking Magden and ate our lunch. Our friendly host checked around by phone to locate the place where my cousins were vacationing. He was successful. They were somewhere near the Italian border. He then found a telephone book for the place and called them up. My cousin was very surprised to hear from us and she invited us to come down to spend some time with the family. It was a four-hour trip by car over the mountains and we had to decline.

I asked her for a nice place to stay at Magden. She recommended a *gasthof* in Magden. Our host guided us down into the village to the hotel. When we arrived, the manager told us that she had just had a call from my cousin's husband who had made reservations for us. She put us in a nice big room with a beautiful view of the mountains. After a walk in the village, we had dinner in the main dining room. Lucy said it was served and prepared beautifully (veal covered with a fluffy sauce, lightly fried potato wedges, the beer from a long established brewery, ice cream with crusted nuts, whipped cream and liquor.) After dinner we asked the manager to recommend a short trip the next day (Sunday.) She suggested Lucerne and from there to a resort area on top of a mountain on the other side of the lake called Bürgenstock. We also explained to her that we had come to Switzerland on the spur of the moment and found that all the banks were closed, as it was a holiday weekend. She kindly loaned us $100 in Franken.

We drove on the Autobahn to Lucerne. There we took a leisurely stroll along the lake (Lake Lucerne or Vierwaldstättersee.) From there we went to the other side of the lake and slowly drove up the four miles on a very narrow road to the mountain peak on which Bürgenstock was located. There were several luxury hotels, shops and restaurants. The tavern which had been recommended to us, proved to be a pleasant, outdoor restaurant, extremely busy that day. Of course, Lucy found a store which was open and bought some little gifts. When we got back to Magden in late afternoon we took a walk, and drank "natural" water which was running in several fountains in the village. In the evening we had a light supper. The manager and her husband (who was also the chef) joined us for coffee.

The next morning, when we went to pay our bill, the manager explained that there was no charge for the room as we were guests of my cousins. She also urged us to drive through the vineyard area of Alsace which many visitors said reminded them of the scenery of the Napa Valley in California. So we decided to go through that part of Alsace before resuming our pre-planned route. After departing Switzerland via Basel, we entered France and headed north, driving parallel to the Rhine.

When we reached Colmar, we had a picnic lunch with the bread and cheese which the hotel manager in Magden had thoughtfully provided for us.

We then headed into the wine country. The scenery was gorgeous. We had beautiful weather. One particularly nice area was around the old town of Ribeauville. We decided to spend the night in this vicinity. A hotel near the town of Riquewihr was recommended. It was the hotel/restaurant. It was modern and very comfortable. The room we had overlooked the vineyards and had a little balcony. The restaurant in the hotel was not open because it was always closed on Mondays.

We decided to look for a place to have dinner in the nearby village of Zellenberg. At a winery, we were told of an excellent restaurant nearby. As it was small they advised us to make a reservation. This was a delightful place! We had a leisurely two-hour dinner, certainly one of the many pleasant experiences of the trip. For hors d'oeuvres we shared a French onion pie dish. For the main course Lucy had hot asparagus (large white ones) with ham, a local specialty. I had a boiled beef dinner which came with shredded vegetable salad. There were about six different raw vegetables grouped on one plate. It was delicious. For dessert we had raspberry glacé. We imbibed the local Riesling wine.

Heading westward toward Lorraine we passed through beautiful mountainous country through the towns of Koenigsbourg and Saint Die. When we approached Baccarat, Lucy told me this was the place where crystal was made. We stopped. While Lucy went shopping, I walked around to take in the local scene. I must have acquired the native look because some French visitors asked me where they could use the bathroom. I directed them to the *hotel de ville* which was nearby. After Lucy had bought a bunch of gifts we departed for Lunéville, the first location on the rejoined World War II route. From there we drove to Dombasle.

I noticed an elderly man sitting on a bench in the sun. We stopped the car to inquire if he knew the family I was looking for. I was prepared for a negative reply. After all it was a long time since the end of the war. But the man I had addressed said, "I think I know the family you are looking for! He took us to one of a row of modern houses which probably replaced the old farm dwellings. On the way, in my broken French, I tried to explain to him that my father had stayed on the family's farm for a few days during the war, that my father had been sick, and how they had fixed him some really good food, mostly rabbit dinners and Mirabelle (a potent liquor) and how all that had cured him of his ailments. He introduced us to a man who was the son of the farmer my dad had known. He spoke good English. Now we could really converse! As I started to explain my visit, his wife came down from upstairs. She was a very charming lady and a wonderful hostess. We ate a compote made from the mirabelle, a local fruit which looks like a cross between a cherry and an apricot. They wanted to give us a large jar of the fruit, but we only took them up on the offer of a bottle of Mirabelle liquor, made from the fruit. After spending a couple of hours with them, we took some pictures and headed on our way.

We had planned to stop off at Château-Salins, but we went on to Morhange. There we found a small hotel at the edge of town. During a walk near the railroad station, a gentleman told us where the best restaurant in town was. It was truly good. It took us almost 3 hours to finish our dinner. The different courses were interspersed with offerings of ices and fruit. After walking off some of the food, we drove back to the hotel.

It was raining when we left the next morning. We headed due west, crossed the Meurthe River at Pont-a-Mousson. In 1944, this was a grimy factory town, as my father had described it. Today it was a rather attractive little city with lots of new housing and light industry. In 1944, my dad had passed through Nancy and Metz, but we decided to bypass both because of the traffic congestion and the inordinate amount of time it would have taken.

We were now heading due north, which was the direction his division took during the war in an effort to relieve Bastogne. We passed through Pagny. At Jarny we stopped for breakfast. It was rather cool. The coffee and croissants hit the spot! By the time we reached Longwy the sun was out. It turned into a beautiful day. We stopped at a sporting goods store to buy a racing cap for my neighbor. The owner spoke good English. He told us that they had another store in Naples, Florida. Before we left Longwy, Lucy found a large combination grocery and soft goods store. We purchase our usual bread and cheese for lunch, and also bought a number of cotton aprons to take home.

Then onward into Belgium. When we arrived in Arlon, I was unable to locate the hospital where my father had gone in to take a bath and change clothes. As we approached Bastogne, I looked for three villages his division had bivouacked in. We found two of them. The third had disappeared when they put in new roads. Arriving in Bastogne about noon, we found an old Fourth Armored Division tank in the center of the town as a monument to the liberation of Bastogne. We had our picnic lunch and walked around. Then we headed east toward Luxembourg. As we still had plenty of time, we decided to go to Vianden, a resort town on the Moselle River. It was a beautiful drive through the Ardennes area in northern Luxembourg. We arrived in Vianden early in the afternoon. We looked for, and found, a hotel which had been described in a newspaper article I had read. It was a charming place. We were told that originally it had been a monastery. This was the first time on our trip that we ran into a gathering of Americans. Before the evening meal we took a sunbath on the porch of our room overlooking the garden and mountains. People told us this area is called the Switzerland of Luxembourg. The dinner in the beautifully appointed dining room was excellent.

In the morning we walked up to an old castle, the Burg Vianden. It was being restored. Then we took another walk through Vianden, a very clean and pretty town. Lucy found a shop featuring Chinaware. She bought some coffee mugs for people in her office.

We took off around 11:00 a.m. Driving to Diekirch, we looked for a store which was supposed to have lace curtains that Lucy wanted. We found the place, a grocery-variety store combination, but they had no lace at all. There was a cafeteria next door and we decided to have some lunch.

Time had flown by. It was time to return to Paris and then head home. There was a good road south toward Metz. From there, a major highway leading west directly to Paris. We arrive there late in the evening. We went to the same hotel we had used before. We got up early the next morning and drove to the embassy. The marine at the gate suggested we parked the car near the building entrance. We wanted to say goodbye to the chargé d'affaires, but he was on a field trip with the ambassador. However, his administrative assistant was familiar with our car arrangement. She had me sign a statement that there was no damage.

Lucy suggested that instead of returning via Reykjavik, we should check whether there was a direct flight to Dulles. The administrative assistant called the travel coordinator about this. She stopped by, telling us there was a direct flight later in the afternoon to Dulles. If we wanted to do this, she would make the changes. There would probably be some extra charges. She would forward the bill to the State Department. I asked her to only add this on Lucy's bill. The airline should send my part of the additional charges to me directly. The administrative assistant went downstairs to the cafeteria with us. As we were eating, the travel coordinator brought us our new tickets. The embassy would provide a car to take us to the airport.

The plane was crowded. The travel coordinator had suggested that we choose business class. We agreed. When we had boarded, we were glad that we upgraded. We had a dinner which was not the greatest, but, as we were starved, we gobbled it up. Thereafter, we decided to do a postmortem of our "tour de France." We made the following observations, which I wrote down for Bob MacMerial and Jennifer. It was as follows:

"All transportation arrangements worked out well. Hotel accommodations and meals were better than expected. Contact with people in all countries was very pleasant. We were impressed by the courtesy-of-the-road attitude of the French drivers. Responses to requests for directions were freely given and always helpful. When people became aware that my father had been in France with the American Army during World War II, we could feel in many cases a special regard.

Taking a picnic lunch almost every day enabled us to maintain our schedule. We had brought along an insulated plastic bag which kept our supplies fresh. We ate most of our dinners in the dining rooms of the hotels. Food and service were always good. We noticed that the dining rooms were well patronized by the locals. Most establishments offered *le menu touristique*, a fixed price menu for a full course dinner. There are usually at least three menus to choose from, at different price levels. Usually this was a much better way to have a full meal at a lower cost than ordering *a la carte*.

The number of English speakers we encountered was small, but we managed to get along. Laundry was no problem. We washed out small pieces of clothing at every opportunity, and dried them overnight on a small line we had brought along. To summarize, the trip was thoroughly enjoyable."

The flight was smooth. We nodded off soon after dinner. After arrival at Dulles at midnight we took a cab to Lucy's place. I told the driver to wait while I helped Lucy with her luggage. When I got home, I did not check everything as I usually did upon returning from a trip. I went to bed promptly and fell asleep.

CHAPTER 14

THE DC SHUFFLE

IT WAS AROUND ELEVEN in the morning. I was just about getting up after a good night's sleep when the phone rang. It was Eloise.

"Eloise, what's the idea of waking me up?"

"Keef, are you OK? It's late in the morning."

"Yes, I feel fine. Got back late last night from three weeks in Europe; had to tie up some loose ends. Also went to Switzerland on the spur of the moment. I have some distant cousins there, on my father's side. But now I have given up trying to locate the origin of the order for the raid in Europe. I have exhausted all possible sources there. My hope is that the answer will be in my father's files somewhere in the Pentagon. Did you discover how I might obtain access to them?"

"Keef, that is exactly why I am calling. Your dad's papers are probably in a storage facility for classified stuff they won't release. In spite of all my connections I was unable to ascertain where this facility is. Nobody will tell me. Because it involves data from all over the Pentagon, The JCS has final say over who may examine them. Touch base with JCS. Question your contacts there and keep your fingers crossed."

"Thanks, Eloise, I will get right on it. By the way, how is your relationship with your friend in the IG office progressing?"

"Keef, you are still the nosy guy. And as I had mentioned to you previously, we are about ready to get engaged. But right now I am pissed off. I am not talking to him to teach him a lesson."

"Eloise, ease up! Think of it like a Latin saying: *Amantium irae amoris integration est.*"

"Keef, what is this? Translate."

"It means, "Lovers' quarrels are the renewal of love.""

"Where did you pick this up?"

"My mother. Don't know where she found it."

"Keef, I like that. I will use it. Thanks!"

After I got dressed, I made a house inspection. Everything was in order. I had done a thorough cleanup before I left. There was nothing to do except a little dusting. My neighbor had piled the mail on the kitchen table. I walked next door to thank her. She told me that this time I had left my house in good shape there had been no need to send the cleaning woman over. She talked about having heard from her niece in Chicago, whom I had met just before my trip to Europe. She was going to be in Washington for a special education teachers' convention later this month. She would stay with her. Her niece expressed a desire to go downtown for dinner after her meetings were over. She was wondering whether I might want to go with her. My neighbor nixed this. I guess she figured Lucy would not like it. She would try to arrange for someone else. She asked me if I had a friend who might fill in. I thought Henry could be the guy.

When I returned home, I e-mailed him. He responded that he would give it a try, and to let him know the day before. I called my neighbor. My partner, a single young fellow, was willing. I gave her Henry's e-mail address. She could stay in touch with Henry.

My next order of business was to call Bob MacMerial. He answered the phone himself.

"Bob, how come you picked up the phone? Did you fire Amy while I was gone?"

"Keef, I told you before that Amy is catching on. I think she is on par with Eloise. How was your trip?"

I gave him a summary, including the stopover in Iceland and the sojourn to Switzerland. I didn't mention anything about Lucy. I expressed my frustration about not getting more information from Hans Metzger, the German lieutenant's nephew, after having gone all over France to locate him way down south.

"Bob, the only thing left for me to do is to check my father's files at the Pentagon.

"Remember my contacting Eloise some time ago to ask her to find out where the files are now? I don't recall whether I told you what Eloise was able to uncover. Anyway, it was not much. Somebody, she would not identify who, thought the files were put into storage. This individual did not know where. He indicated the documents there were highly classified. Eloise suggested I should request assistance from my contacts at JCS. Perhaps they would help me out on this.

"Inasmuch as the CG of INSCOM is aware of my efforts regarding the origin of the raid and authorized my devoting time to this, it would be a good idea if you let INSCOM know that I will be working at the Pentagon with the DIA (Defense Intelligence Agency) and the JCS. In case somebody at the Pentagon calls INSCOM as to what this was all about, they should be prepared to respond."

Bob agreed. He would call the INSCOM chief of staff to bring him up to date on the results of the trip to Europe. "I will emphasize that the last thing you can now do is to find your father's records. A contact at the Pentagon recommended that you seek assistance there from people with whom you have previously worked at DIA and JCS. I believe if INSCOM gets an inquiry, it will provide an opportunity to relate that INSCOM supports you."

Bob asked me whether he should alert his contacts at the D/A. I did not think it was necessary. They know I worked with DOD on the missile business. As far as they are concerned, this still may be a part of that same project. Bob requested that I keep him up to date. I told them I would start on it tomorrow.

After lunch I called Lucy. She was glad to hear from me and had a lot to tell me about what was going on at State. She would stop by this evening. I should not prepare anything. A coworker had told her about a place downtown where one could pick up fully prepared meals. She would stop by there on her way here.

When Lucy arrived, she put two cardboard boxes into the microwave. To avoid dishwashing we placed the contents on paper plates and used plastic silverware. The food was tasty. One box contained sliced roast beef, the other vegetables.

For dessert I took ice cream sandwiches out of the freezer. As everything was disposable, we dumped it all into the garbage can.

When we sat on the couch, I told her about my neighbor's niece. Lucy thought I was reading too much into it. The girl probably just felt strange to head downtown alone. Well, I still felt there was more to it. At any rate I had contacted Henry to take my place. Lucy chuckled. She said I just wanted to get credit for avoiding any entanglement. Then she gave me a deep kiss, but she moved away and began to describe her recent State Department experience.

"Keef, I got into a bureaucratic tangle. After I had submitted my travel documents for reimbursement, they called me to the audit office. First of all they wanted to know why I did not stay at the hotel the embassy uses. I explained that that was where the cab driver dropped me off. The receptionist there assured me they would meet the price of the other hotels. I offered to pay the difference, but the auditor said that it was not necessary. The charges were in the ballpark.

"Then he asked as to why I needed an embassy car for three weeks. I responded that my boss had approved my extended leave. I had not requested the embassy car. The chargé d'affaires urged me to take it, provided I paid all the expenses. He urged me to take advantage of the offer as it would facilitate my travel. Diplomatic tags would avoid road taxes and expedite any assistance I might need from authorities. The car was available, so it was not an imposition. I suggested that the auditor could get in touch with the embassy on this. He admitted he had contacted the European political section. They told him the embassy has plenty of leeway on matters like this. He was new in the auditing game. My trip was his learning experience "

I laughed. "Now we know that no matter which Federal Agency you work for you have to put up with no end of regulations."

After she had finished her tale, I moved over and hugged her. She claimed it was getting late and had to leave soon, but, I could not help myself. I held her tightly and soon I noticed she was getting into the mood. When she peeled off my shirt, I got all excited and we had a pleasant encounter.

Before she returned home, Lucy said that she had mentioned, at her office, that she was looking for some volunteer work. A fellow employee suggested she look into the Tragedy Assistance Program for Survivors (TAPS.) It extends support to survivors of wives, husbands, children, parents, brothers and sisters, battlefield buddies and sweethearts of those who died while in military service. Through a national network of volunteers it provides assistance to them. It has been in existence for over 20 years. It is supported by corporations and individuals, including ranking military as well as members of Congress.

She checked it out with friends in the Pentagon. Everyone endorsed it. They pointed out that this is a not-for-profit organization. Lucy went over to their headquarters in Arlington, Virginia. They gladly accepted her offer. She believed it would be a rewarding experience.

After Lucy left, my thinking concentrated on my next steps. The search at the Pentagon was a matter of making the right connections. I was fortunate to have succeeded in getting the CG of INSCOM interested. If I would be able to arouse the curiosity of somebody in DOD, my search could get started. I would initially approach John Mosen, the security officer at JCS, with whom I had had a good working relationship in the past.

After breakfast the following morning, I called John. I would not have been surprised if he was no longer there. When we last talked he indicated he was thinking of retiring. But, I was lucky; he was still there.

"John, this is Keef. Long time since we last saw each other."

"Keef, glad to hear your voice. I have often thought about what ventures you have gotten into. A few weeks ago I came across a DOD memo that said they had tagged you to investigate some security problems at the missile command. How did this go?"

"It's a long story, John. I will tell you about it later. The reason for my call is that I need your advice on how I should proceed on my search for my father's files on his raid into Czechoslovakia. When are you available?"

"I am free this morning. Why don't you come over? You can drive here. One of our key employees is on leave. He has a reserved parking space near the front entrance. Just ask the guard, who will stop you at the parking lot, to direct you to the JCS parking area. Another guard there will guide you to the space."

"The weather was favorable, inducing me to drive through Rock Creek Park. I took Memorial Bridge. A back way took me to the Pentagon lot. Since 9/11 the security was very tight. After showing my identification, I ran around the parking lot until I found the JCS location. After the guard looked at my identification, he pointed toward a vacant spot which was not far from the entrance. Inside, my credentials were checked once more. This time it was a Navy shore patrol. I questioned him if this spot was always manned by the Navy. He said, "No, like everything in the JCS, the four services rotated around in all non-professional spots. This, of course, reflects the membership of the JCS staff, comprised of Army, Navy, Air Force, and Marine Corps personnel."

I boarded an elevator up to the JCS floor. Now I was in familiar territory. As I stepped out, there was John.

"Keef, it's good to see you. Welcome on board!"

He whisked me through another security checkpoint until we reached his office. I gave him a rundown about why I had approached him. He promised he would clear the way for me as much as he could. He congratulated me on the missile command job. He had been ready to retire last year, but JCS persuaded him to stay at least for another two years. To help him make the decision, they managed to convince the personnel types to get him a promotion. In order to accept it, a special provision was inserted into his job description; that he would serve as the special adviser to the Chairman on inter- service security matters.

We drifted into personal topics. I asked him about his wife. She was getting along well. To keep busy, she volunteered at a hospital in Fairfax. He wanted to know whether I finally had found the right girl and exchanged rings. I told him about Lucy. I elaborated on how we met when I was in the Czech Republic. Last year we renewed our acquaintance in Washington. John was thrilled about how this all happened. Then he looked at his watch. "Let's go and visit with General Hepsterall. He wants you to stop by."

The general was expecting us. He knew I had been busy. A friend in the SEC/DEF office described my working for the DOD on the missile site problem. He was laudatory about my accomplishments. When the general asked what I was up to now, I summarized my European trip.

He said, "I talk to the CG of INSCOM quite often. He filled me in on your data search regarding the raid and how long you have been exploring who had ordered it. He would like the JCS to help you. So I realize this is really your final effort to get to the bottom of this.

"My recommendation is that you approach the DIA. John has good contacts there who should steer you to the right people. Keep John up to date. I will also mention it to the Chairman, who asked me the other and day what you were doing since the conclusion of the missile business."

John took me for lunch at the Executive Dining Room. Since his promotion he has access to it. We both ordered the low calorie special, which was mostly salad and fruit. We lingered on, gossiping about family life. When I left mid-afternoon, John promised to e-mail me the details about my upcoming visit to the Defense Intelligence Agency.

By mid-morning the following day, John's e-mail arrived. I should go to the office of the Director of National Intelligence at Tysons Corner. The best way was the beltway. DIA maintains an office there. It took me about 40 minutes. After checking my credentials, I was directed to the third floor. A receptionist took me to an officer who maintains liaison with the DIA, which had an office here. They used it every so often to coordinate some paperwork. No one was in today.

I told him the reason for my visit and asked him whether his agency had knowledge about the storage site. He had heard of this place, but was not familiar with it. Perhaps someone in the main office of the DIA would be able to help. He had suggested to John, when he talked to him about my visit, to contact the DIA Executive Officer. I knew it was at the Joint Base Bolling-Anacostia, quite a distance from Tyson's Corner. I couldn't get there before the afternoon. The best route was to go back to Washington, drive along the Mall and Pennsylvania Avenue, and take the bridge across the Anacostia River. It would probably take one to two hours, depending upon traffic.

I asked him to call the DIA, letting them know that I would be there this afternoon. When I mentioned I would like to stop for a quick lunch, he suggested going downstairs. There was a snack bar which had a good selection.

It took me almost two hours to the DIA building. There was no guard at the entrance, but upon entering, one had to go through a screening device similar to those at airports. After showing my identification to the receptionist, I was directed to take the elevator to the top floor, where the executive officer would meet me. She would call him that I was on the way. As I stepped out, a lieutenant colonel greeted me. After we reached his office, we had a friendly conversation.

"Mr. Keefer, I have been acquainted with John Mosen for a long time. You may know of his receiving a big promotion recently. John described your efforts to get the details on your father's adventures in Czechoslovakia in 1945. What a story!

"After John's call, I checked with several longtime employees as well as one historical unit. I came out with zilch. Your father had an office with us when we were still at the Pentagon. He checked with some of our people every so often, mostly with one historian. Unfortunately this individual retired some years ago. He was really the only one who knew what your father was working on.

"I have checked with both our director and his deputy; neither had anything. They had heard that there was a storage facility for important historical data, but they had no knowledge of who had jurisdiction or where it was located.

"I am sorry I am unable to provide some leads. The only way for you to sniff this out is if you can persuade the JCS Chairman to take a personal interest."

I thanked him. I would talk to John Mosen and hope that he would be able to open some doors for me.

After battling the rush hour congestion for almost two hours, I finally got home. All this running around had worn me out. I took a couple of hours of rest. I felt better. While I was lying on the couch, I took an inventory of everything I had tried. Before I approached JCS, was there anything else I could tackle? In retrospect, the lengthy trips to France, Germany, and the Czech Republic were inconclusive. I finally had to accept that Europe proved negative. I theoretically put on a dunce cap to contemplate if there was nothing else for me to go after before I involved the JCS. To no avail. I had made exhaustive attempts to get something at the National Archives, the CIA, and Army historians.

It then occurred to me that there was one thing I had not thought of until now; among the dwindling senior members of the OSS Society, the successive organization to the WWII Office of Strategic Services, there may be someone who knew something.

I had been a member of the society for a number of years. I became acquainted with its president, Charles Pinck. We met and talked every so often.

I decided to give him a buzz. I was lucky to reach him. I knew he was extremely busy. Besides running the organization, whose membership consisted of OSS operatives of WWII and individuals who are with the Special Forces Operations Command (SOCOM), Charles was raising funds for a permanent OSS Society home.

I asked him whether we could meet for lunch. He was all tied up, but would keep it in mind. I then told him I was making progress on the book we had previously discussed. I asked him whether there were any members who had served in Czechoslovakia at the end of WWII. Charles responded that he had recently checked the membership records in order to answer an enquiry about OSS activities in Czechoslovakia. He only found a few of such members still alive. None could recall anything other than their activities supporting the Czech Resistance. He would ask if they were aware of any U.S. Army actions beyond the Line of Demarcation. Charles sympathized with me. Perhaps I would eventually dig up something at the Pentagon.

I was not very hungry. I just heated up some leftovers. All that driving took a toll. I felt very tired and hit the hay early. Around one o'clock in the morning I woke up. I felt very uncomfortable from my neck down to the belly button. I went to the bathroom and noticed while I was walking the pain did not disappear, but eased up. The same thing happened when I sat on the couch. Finally, after remaining in an upright position for some time, the discomfort went away. I returned to bed and slept soundly.

Bob MacMerial called just after I had washed the breakfast dishes. He wanted to know how I made out with the DIA. I gave him a rundown of a frustrating day. Everyone had recommended I should approach the top level of the JCS. I would call John Mosen later to get the ball rolling. When I related about last night's distressing episode, Bob laughed. I interrupted, questioning what was so funny. He apologized. He did not mean to trivialize it, but it had reminded him of his father-in-law who had had the same thing. It is no longer a problem for him. "This condition is known as acid reflux. It is caused by incomplete digestion of food. Usually comes with age, but is known to occur in some people in middle age. You fight it by taking a pill when you feel it coming on or when you wake up with it. It is a medicine called ranitidine. It has been used for many years. I will call the Doc I use on the Post. He will mail you a bunch. He has plenty of samples. I am sure it will work for you in case you need it again."

I was just about to call John Mosen when Lucy got on the line. "Keef, where were you all day yesterday? I couldn't reach you."

"I was at the Defense Intelligence Agency locations at Tyson's Corner and Anacostia. They are quite a distance from each other. So I spent a good part of the day driving, sometimes in stop-and-go traffic. I did not get anything beyond what I already knew. I'm now ready to go after the real McCoy, the JCS. They have control of access to the stored records of all the services which had not been released for various reasons."

"Keef, I hope you will succeed in the final run of your lengthy journey. Good luck with the Pentagon bureaucracy!"

"Thanks, Lucy. Did you know anything about acid reflux?"

"I do. My father had it. I don't remember at what stage of his life. He eventually sort of outgrew it. Occasionally, he relied on a pill his doctor had prescribed. Why do you ask?"

"Last night I woke up with this awful feeling. I had to get out of the sack. It went on for a couple of hours. I mentioned it to Bob MacMerial this morning. He was sure I had a bout of acid reflux. The Fort Meade medics will send me a medicine which has been used for many years. Perhaps it was a one-time occurrence. At any rate, if it happens again, I will have to take the magic pill."

"Keef, you are too young for this. If you watch what you eat, it may never come up again. It's nothing serious, don't worry about it."

"Lucy, somebody told me that frequent sex will prevent it. Are you coming by tonight?"

"Keef, nobody has ever claimed this; you're pulling my leg. I hope we may see each other later in the week. Take care!"

Next on my list was to contact John Mosen. He was not in his office. Shortly thereafter, though, he called me back. He was at home. His wife was not feeling well. It was just a bellyache. She will be OK. I summarized my DIA experience.

"John, I need to turn to you again. I have to get ahold of my father's research at the Pentagon. It is stored someplace at a facility in Virginia. Yesterday, they suggested that the key is to approach the JCS Chairman for access. Do you believe he is approachable?"

"Keef, I am sorry that you didn't obtain any new data at the DIA. But checking with them was necessary. I had discussed your dilemma with General Hepsterall. Now I will go back to him. I will get his reaction regarding approaching the Chairman. I believe inasmuch as the Chairman is aware of your past efforts on DOD assignments, chances are good that he will be sympathetic. But we will see. I will discuss this with General Hepsterall. As you know the General had suggested approaching DIA. Now that this has not panned out, he may very likely support going to the Chairman. I will let you know about Hepsterall's reaction."

"I called Bob MacMerial again to keep him current on what I was doing. Bob thought that Hepsterall would probably recommend to the Chairman to authorize your access to your father's files. Bob speculated that INSCOM's interest in your search, and the fact that the CG of INSCOM and Hepsterall have a friendly relationship, will help immensely. I would keep Bob abreast after I had heard from John Mosen.

John rang me early the next morning. He had had a very productive conversation with Hepsterall. He subsequently approached the Chairman on this. The Chairman would like to discuss this with you before he decided. Hepsterall wants you to stop in at about 1400. You can still take advantage of the vacant parking space.

I left home around one. Went through the park at Memorial Bridge again. After going through all the security checks, I arrived at the JCS offices just before two. John took me to Hepsterall. He recommended that I present the Chairman with a summary of my searches both in Europe and here. Don't say anything about why your father's records aren't locked up. JCS did not arrange this. The Chairman knows that INSCOM has supported you.

Hepsterall then escorted me to the Chairman's office. We had to wait about 10 minutes before we met with him. Hepsterall introduced me. The Chairman invited me to explain how I came to investigate the raid.

After I briefly outlined my involvement, I went on to describe my efforts over the past few years. I had now come to the conclusion that nothing has been released over all these years because of the state of U.S.-Russian relations. "I believe my father worked on this puzzle extensively. His files were in the Pentagon when he died and are now stored in a Pentagon facility. General Hepsterall had recommended that I check with the DIA. The only thing I found out worthwhile was that the papers are probably at a storage site somewhere in Virginia. The DIA staff claimed not being aware of its location. I believe they know, but do not have the authority to release it. I want to finish this job, and I need your help to obtain access to the facility."

"Mr. Keefer, I am sorry you had such a lengthy and frustrating experience. General Hepsterall had apprized me of the support you have received from INSCOM. He had done some checking before he saw me on this. Apparently, there is lots of information in storage which should be released. Several years ago, a Pentagon task force was activated to review these records and recommend those which should be released.

"Due to the steady reduction in personnel in the military and the demands to address our current problems, this effort has a low priority and, in fact, has stalled. I have asked John Mosen to obtain comments from several classification experts. They concluded that in this day and age there are no valid reasons not to release your father's papers. John will make the recovery arrangements."

"General, I am most grateful for giving me the time to present my case. Finally I visualize the end of a long journey."

After departing from the Chairman's office, I thanked General Hepsterall for his support. John suggested I come for breakfast at his home tomorrow morning. He would take me to the location where the papers are.

Early the next morning I was on my way. It was in the middle of the rush hour. It took me over an hour to get to John's place. Breakfast was at the table. John's wife had already left for her volunteer job. He had mentioned to her about my settling down with Lucy. Naturally, she was curious about it. He told her as much as I had related. John said we were driving west to the site near Flint Hill, still in Virginia. It may take one to two hours, depending on traffic. I was not to discuss with anyone any details about it. He would not stay there with me.

I followed his car. We arrived at a large, unmarked building. There was only one car parked near the entrance. John believed it belonged to the manager. A woman opened the door after John had rung the bell. She knew John. He probably had been there before. After he introduced me, she suggested I follow her. She had located my father's papers and had placed them in the room next to her office. John departed for the Pentagon.

The manager took me to her office. We chatted a while. She had been there for over a dozen years. During the first few years, there were lots of visitors from the Pentagon. At that time she had an assistant. Nowadays, there was not much activity. She had been busy retrieving the records which the task force had identified until they suddenly had stopped. She had made a cursory review of my father's papers. Thus, she had some insight on the reasons for my coming there.

I went next door where there were several boxes were on a table next to a desk. The manager had eased my task by separating the files in two packets according to date and origin. This would save a lot of time.

The first bunch I picked were the War Department and European Theater documents on the raid of the cave 30 miles south of Prague during February, 1946. I made a careful review. The operation was launched by the headquarters of the European Theater and was to be coordinated with the American embassy in Prague and the Czechoslovakia military. However, there were no prior contacts with either of them. The papers offered no apology. The only reference to this was that that Czech liaison officer at headquarters had been notified about sending a task force to the cave. The War Department papers asserted that the Pentagon had not been consulted.

As I reviewed the documents, I came to the conclusion that there were certain similarities with my father's operation in 1945. Nothing was released on the 1945 incident. The 1946 incident was covered by a paper trail because the Czechs seized three participants and raised a diplomat stink. The Pentagon instructed the European Theater to trivialize it, claiming that only historical documents were seized. Washington sought to downplay what happened, ordering initially there was to be no publicity, retention of the documents captured, maintain cordial relations with the Czechs, and avoidance of complications with the eastern ally. Without naming them, it meant the Russians. Thus it is likely that the materials in the cave contained data the Russians would have been interested in. It is noteworthy that this aspect was only hinted at in the exchanges between the War and State Departments.

My father made the following comments on the first set of documents. "In both the 1945 and 1946 operations the identity of who issued the original directive has not been released. While nothing at all has surfaced on the 1945 action, the 1946 incident had to be accounted for because it was discovered and had received publicity. It is significant that the European Theater received instructions from the Pentagon on how to handle this. The sensitivity created by the publicity on the 1946 operation stirred up Washington, even Eisenhower, who headed the Pentagon at that time, was briefed on it. Washington felt it needed closure. On February 23, 1946, the State Department released an innocuous statement:

DEPARTMENT OF STATE
FOR THE PRESS   FEBRUARY 23, 1946
No. 131

On February 11, 1946, an American military detachment from the American occupation forces in Germany entered Czechoslovakia and proceeded to remove to the American zone in Germany a number of documents which were found concealed in a hillside south of Praha. The detachment sought these documents because they were informed that the documents would throw light up on the pre-war plans of Hitler and give information as to the conduct of the war by the NAZI government.

Although this American detachment entered Czechoslovakia with passes issued by the appropriate Czechoslovak liaison officer, this expedition had not been given approval by the Czechoslovak government, which has protested this action. The American government has expressed its deep regret to President Benes for this incident and has ordered an immediate return of the documents to the Czechoslovak government.

"This statement was drafted jointly by the State Department and the Pentagon. Prior to its release, the Pentagon notified the European Command: 'In conference with the State Department yesterday, February 19, it was proposed that the U.S. make apology on manner in which detail was carried out. This to be made in such a way as not to jeopardize position of Theater Commander in Europe.'

"There is likely to be a connection between the 1945 and 1946 raids. Whoever tipped off the U.S. on the data in possession of the remnants of the German Army Headquarters for the Eastern Front may have revealed the existence of the material hidden in the cave. The mission to enter the cave at the same time of the 1945 action could not be carried out since the Red Army units were already in the area. Colonel John Haskell, the OSS officer in Moscow, worked with Maj. General John Deane, head of the U.S. Military Mission in Moscow on this. As early as May 1 Deane was advised by SHAEF that the Red Army would advance to the Line of Demarcation, which was a considerable distance beyond the area in which the cave was. Once the Russians had withdrawn their forces from Czechoslovakia, the cave mission was activated.

"In both these incidents, nothing has been released on who gave the order. How the Army became cognizant of the existence and location of the targets is unknown. However, this source must have been the Czech underground. How and when this was conveyed to the Americans was probably through contact with OSS operatives. They were the only U.S. military near Prague to receive the data. It is noteworthy that the Pentagon had the dominant role in the return of the cave documents. This did not take place until they were microfilmed. It is also probable that not all documents were sent to the Czechs.

"Why the 1946 incident was conducted without the planned Czech participation is not difficult to answer: the approach of the Cold War."

While I was reading my father's comments, my belief was reinforced that the source for my father's raid had to be in Washington. I wondered whether my father would have agreed. The role of Eisenhower in both raids while he was still at SHAEF is difficult to assess. My father's take on this was not clear. Thus far his records are murky. He was speculating whether Patton had had any input. Apparently he was intrigued by comments which had been attributed to Colonel Koch, Patton's G-2. Koch was known to have actively sought information not limited to the Third Army scope of responsibility. It is well known that Patton himself was anxious to advance as far as Prague. When Eisenhower proposed to temporarily go beyond the Line of Demarcation, the Soviets strongly objected. Eisenhower then dropped the idea to go beyond the Line.

By that time plans for the raid near Prague had been finalized and were implemented. At the same time, the cave situation would also have taken place. But with Eisenhower's agreement not to go beyond the Line of Demarcation, it was dropped from being attempted in this timeframe. It is possible that it would have occurred in spite of a possible confrontation with the Red Army in the cave area. However, Eisenhower went on record to strictly adhere to the Line of Demarcation. My father's action near Prague was considered less risky since Russian units had not yet reached there.

When I glanced at another batch of material, I saw more documents dealing with efforts to advance toward Prague. This was a good time to stop. It was getting late. It would take me a long time during the rush hour to get to Silver Spring. I stopped by the administrator to tell her I was calling it a day. I would see her in the morning. She suggested I should get there are around 10 o'clock.

After I had a quiet supper, I needed to relax. I called Lucy. We had a lengthy conversation. I told her that John had taken me to the site where I found an amazing amount of data my father had been working on. I promised to give her a detailed rundown later.

CHAPTER 15

DIGGING DEEP

I LEFT AROUND EIGHT in the morning. Did not take time for breakfast. Just drank some orange juice. After I crossed into Virginia, I stopped at a bakery, picked up some rolls, cream cheese, and jam. When I arrived way past ten, the administrator scolded me for being late. She sat down, ate, and chatted for a while. She mentioned that she was separated. Things just had not worked out. She wanted to know whether I was single. When she escorted me to my father's papers, she brushed against me several times. Before my Lucy days I would have taken the hint. While she was no spring chicken, she was fairly attractive. But now this was in the past. To avoid any future plays like this, I casually mentioned I was engaged to an old friend. She was startled, but I believed she had a ladylike character. It seemed to have worked. She stopped playing with me. She realized she had to look for greener pastures elsewhere.

The next folder was labeled "Patton - Koch". It dealt with my father's obsession that somehow Patton was involved with this raid. He noted that he went over all of Patton's papers, including his biographical information. He did not find anything at all. However, he was not satisfied. He found out that Colonel Koch, Patton's G-2, had considerable leeway granted by Patton. My father's persistence pointed him to the Army War College in Carlisle, Pennsylvania, which had custody of Koch's papers. Through a Pentagon contact, he connected with Carlisle. He was lucky to find somebody there to check Koch's notes from May

1945 which were annotated by Koch's biographer. He noted Koch's efforts to go outside Patton's area to gather data on the German Army. Nothing specific was covered. Much was devoted to Patton's efforts with Bradley to get the OK to go as far as Prague. Bradley tried to obtain Eisenhower's approval, but it was not granted. My father commented on Patton's role, stating his preliminary conclusion was that he had had no role in mounting the raid.

The next folder was labeled "Washington-London Politics." It was a collection of my father's notes, not organized as to subject or time frame. There was a series of messages from April 23 to May 7 between London and Washington concerning the advisability of the Army's advancing to Prague. Most were between Churchill and Truman. General Donovan, Chief of the OSS, also was involved. While he was technically on the Pentagon staff, he also operated independently. His last correspondence with Roosevelt took place in early April, 1945. It was uncovered after Roosevelt's death. The messages between Churchill and Truman had been released by the Truman Library.

Churchill's pressure on Washington to allow Patton to proceed to Prague ended early in May 1945. On April 30, Truman advised Churchill about halting the Army's advance at the Pilsen-Karlsbad area. Truman stressed in this letter that "I shall not attempt any move which I deem militarily unwise." Churchill was aware of Eisenhower's position to limit the penetration in Czechoslovakia. General Donovan also got into act. On May 2 he had sent a report directly to Truman warning that the U.S. would be faced with Soviet ambitions in Europe and Asia after the war. According to an unidentified source, early in May Donovan took action to obtain the vast and invaluable intelligence the German Army had collected on the Red Army.

There was a note on the margin of this entry indicating that my father was surprised that Donovan apparently was the instigator of the timing of the raid. He was going to look into this further.

I picked out a folder at random. It was labeled "Presidential Libraries." It seems that my father had contacted them for information pertaining to Czechoslovakia in April-May 1945. The first set covered the response from the Truman Library. There were four entries, all about Prague. A memorandum from State to Truman on April 23 included a paragraph concerning a note received from the British Foreign Office about the desirability of the liberation by the U.S. Army. An April 30 message from Churchill to Truman stated, "There can be little doubt that the liberation of Prague and as much as possible of the territory of Western Czechoslovakia by your forces might make the whole difference in the post-war situation in Czechoslovakia."

Another message from Churchill to Truman on May 6 emphasized that "we must earnestly consider our attitude towards the Soviets and show them how much we have to offer or withhold." This message also urged that its contents be restricted between Truman and his Secretary of State and not "become matters of departmental circulation."

The above looked like it was Churchill's response to Truman's communication on April 30 which described Eisenhower's position that after the defeat of Germany, "… if at that time a move into Czechoslovakia is then desirable our move would be on Pilsen and Karlsbad, i.e., limited to the western part and not further toward Prague."

Data provided by the Eisenhower Library summarized a message of May 7 from Churchill to Eisenhower in which the Eisenhower is urged not to let his (Eisenhower's) directive (SCAF-349) "… inhibit American forces to advance to Prague if your troops have not met the Russians earlier."

A State Department publication, "Foreign Relations of the United States, Diplomatic Papers, 1945, Vol. IV Europe" provides an interesting note: "The American diplomatic mission to Czechoslovakia could have a radio transmitter and necessary personnel and that radio equipment and an operator might be obtained from the OSS." My father wrote on the margin that "the reference to the OSS pertains to Eugene Fodor's team which was in Prague. It was in radio communication with the OSS office in London as well as with American Planes flying in this area. Fodor probably obtained information on the Intelligence Section of the German headquarters which had surrendered to Czech partisans south of Prague."

In another comment my father wrote about the possible involvement of the State Department's representative at SHAEF. "Their input into the military decisions dealt with civil affairs, military government, psychological warfare, intelligence, and post-war plans. Ambassador

Robert D. Murphy was the political advisor at SHAEF. He was in constant contact with the State Department and participated in promoting the Army's search for German intelligence on the Russians. Whether he had anything to do with the raid cannot be established. He may have had a role in the raid.

My father further noted that the Cold War was emerging in April, 1945. This was recognized by British and U.S. officers at SHAEF as well as in the Pentagon. Decisions were made to prepare for the Cold War.

It was getting late in the afternoon. I had perused the last folder the administrator had pulled for me. I stopped by to say *au revoir* to her, thanking her for facilitating my task. She escorted me to the door. As she turned to me, I gave her a hug. She responded with a kiss. I did not let it linger and turned away saying I had another appointment.

On the way back I gave Lucy a buzz. I briefly described my sojourn to review my father's Pentagon files. She wanted to hear more about it. Instead of heading for Silver Spring, I should stop by at her place. She had lots of leftovers from last night. They had celebrated her roommate's birthday. Four of her friends had brought plenty of goodies. I told her that traffic was horrible. I would not be there for a while. She said she was on her way home. This would give her plenty of time to freshen up. I urged her not to take a shower until I arrived. She laughed. "You are in an air conditioned car. I think you need a warm-up."

It took me almost two hours. When I knocked on her door, she pulled me in and gave me a hearty kiss. I noticed she wore a light slip-on which I had not seen on her before.

She became aware of my appraising look, saying, "Nothing doing now. The food is ready."

After a leisurely meal, she poured some brandy and urged me to tell her all about the Virginia trip.

I did not say anything about the aggressive administrator. I went right into the gist of my father's Pentagon papers. Lucy was impressed about all the footwork he had done. The data in his files gave me a more complete picture about the raid and all the events surrounding it. Lucy wanted to know what else I could do before pulling the curtain on this.

I responded, "That is exactly what I want to discuss with you. On the way back from Virginia, when I was stuck in traffic, I made some notes on what I had learned from all my travels and from reviewing my father's document collection."

Lucy was anxious to hear my deductions and conclusions.

We settled on the couch and, after Lucy had refreshed our drinks, I took out my notes told her my thoughts.

"First of all, I should emphasize that two questions triggered the intensive research; 1) who specifically ordered the raid, and 2) how did the notion to seize the German intelligence on the Russian Army evolve?

"Despite years of research, no definitive answer to both items was found. However, in going over my extensive travels, responses from interviews of high ranking professionals associated with the CIA, DOD, and Presidential libraries, I was able to reach logical and rational conclusions.

"Concerning the origin of the raid, General Donovan, the head of the OSS, had a leading role. Donovan was in Europe in the spring of 1945. He was in London early in May 1945. The central office for OSS operations in Europe was located in London. Early in May 1945, Donovan took action to obtain the vast and invaluable intelligence the German Army had collected on the Red Army. Information on Donovan's activities at this time was found in his communications with FDR. Donovan was an old friend of Roosevelt and had sent him data directly periodically. Most of the contents of Donovan's notes have been released, but some were not.

"Fodor's OSS team, while in the Prague area on May 8, 1945, was in contact with OSS in London. Fodor's discovery of the German collection undoubtedly triggered the raid. There are no records on how Donovan's order was transmitted to the Fourth Armored. It came through regular Army command channels. It must have originated in SHAEF. The Fourth Armored was selected because it was the closest unit to the location of the German intelligence data. Due to the tight time frame, the order probably came directly from SHAEF to the Fourth Armored, by-passing normal procedures through intermediate headquarters.

"Furthermore, it makes sense that Donovan had urged the OSS staff at SHAEF to assure that the order went directly to the unit closest to the proposed action. A review of the Twelfth Army Group, Third Army, and XII Corps files at the National Archives was negative. There was nothing on it in Patton's personal diary. The Fourth Armored was Patton's favorite division. He would have written something if he had been involved.

"No reports were found on a Pentagon directive to SHAEF concerning being on the lookout for German intelligence on the Russian Army. According to a high ranking officer at the CIA, based on his professional knowledge, he believed there was a presidential directive, verbal or written, to the intelligence services on the pursuit of any leads on Soviet intentions in the post-war period.

"The OSS officer who headed the American Military Mission at Tito's headquarters in Yugoslavia stated that he had received a directive from the American headquarters in Italy (AFHQ) to collect information on Soviet forces in the Balkans. He recalled that this order originated with General Donovan. He believed that the policy to secure Russian Order of Battle data was made early in 1945 in Washington."

When I was finished, Lucy agreed with my conclusions on the two questions which prompted me to find the answers. What kept puzzling her was that I had not come across any official records. From her years of experience in working in the government, she agreed with me that are times when normal procedures are ignored. She also concurred with my assumption that there were some references which were kept out of the public eye for geopolitical considerations.

"I guess I still have to make a final report to my CG at Fort Belvoir. I also have to send a memo to the Chairman of the JCS through John Mosen."

While we had coffee and cake, she turned to me with a serious look. "Keef, I think now that you will no longer be preoccupied with your father's experiences, we will have more time for each other."

"Lucy, I was under the impression that you had become my number one priority. Have I been negligent?"

"No, Keef, I didn't mean to imply that. Rather I believe we have reached a point in our relationship where we should dwell more on our future."

"Lucy, I agree with you 100%. I thought I had conveyed this to you on our trip."

"Yes, there was an implication of this, but shouldn't we seriously contemplate a happy future together?"

"Lucy, you are absolutely right. We will be together forever. We should eventually tie the knot!"

Then she pulled me over and, once again, we became one.

CAST OF CHARACTERS

(in order of appearance)

Name	Rank/Title	Location	Description
Kevin Keefer (Keef)	CWO	Fort Meade, MD	Chief Warrant Officer, Investigator, Army Military Intelligence Service (MIS)
Bob MacMerial	Lt. Col.	Fort Meade, MD	Commanding Officer, MIS Detachment
Alicia Gouperz	Ms.	Orlando, FL	Former Commanding Officer, MIS Detachment, Lt. Col., Contractor, U.S. Army
Eloise ---------	Sgt.	Pentagon	Formerly with MIS Detachment, Works at Pentagon
Amy ----------		Fort Meade, MD	Administrative Assistant, MIS Detachment
Bill Keefer	Mr.	Fort Meade, MD	Father of Kevin Keefer (deceased) Agent MIS Detachment
Henry Kelly	SA	Fort Meade, MD	Special Agent, MIS
Carla ----------		Prague, Czech Republic	Producer, Film Company

John O'Rancher	Col.	Prague, Czech Republic	Army Attaché
Lucy O'Rancher		Washington, DC	Personnel Office, State Department
Eduard --------	Uncle	Prague, Czech Republic	Czech Underground Activist and Anezka's Uncle
Anezka ---------		Prague, Czech Republic	Niece of Czech Underground Activist, Uncle Eduard
Jennifer Keefer		Atlanta, GA	Daughter of Kevin Keefer
James Hunter	Sgt.	Orlando, FL	U.S. Army Reserve
--------- Smythe	Maj.	New York City	Army Advisor
Allan Graham	Agent	New York City	FBI Agent
Alice ---------		Brooklyn, NY	Computer Consultant
Al King	Lt. Col.	Fort McPherson, GA	Attached to G-2
Annette Moez		Orlando, FL	High School Teacher
Carrie Hunter		Richmond, VA; Orlando, FL	Computer Consultant, Sister of Sgt. James Hunter
Annabelle ---------		Orlando, FL	Motel Receptionist
--------- Alters	Maj.	Potsdam, Germany	Executive Officer, German Army History Office
Albrecht Kaufmann	Lt.	Oppenheim, Germany	Order of Battle Specialist, German Army, Eastern Front (deceased)
Alois Hepsterall	Brig. Gen.	Pentagon	Executive Assistant to Chairman of Joint Chiefs of Staff

Anna Kaufmann	Frau	Oppenheim, Germany	Sister of German Lt. Albrecht Kaufmann (Order of Battle Specialist)
--------- Slank	Capt.	Fort Leavenworth, KS	Aide to the Commanding General
Hans Müller	Insp.	Passau, Germany	Police Inspector
Franz Eppenstein	Doktor	Freiburg, Germany	Ph.D. Researcher, Bundesarchiv
Maria O'Neal		Offutt Air Force Base, NE	Administrative Officer, Missile Command
George Mizells	WO	Offutt Air Force Base, NE	Warrant Officer, Investigator
Paul Kerriko	T/Sgt.	Offutt Air Force Base, NE	G-2, Air Force Missile Command
Carolyn Smithfield		Bellevue, NE	Student, Girlfriend of T/Sgt. Paul Kerriko
Abigail "Abby" Mizells		Omaha, NE	Wife of George Mizells
Joyce Keefer	Mrs.	Silver Spring, MD	Mother of Kevin Keefer (deceased)
John Mosen		Pentagon	Security Officer, Joint Chiefs of Staff
William Donovan	Maj. Gen.	Washington, DC	Director of Office of Strategic Services
Eugene Fodor	Lt.	Prague, Czech Republic	Team Leader, OSS
Babette Metzger		Grenoble, France	Wife of Hans, the Nephew of Lt. Albrecht Kaufmann
Hans Metzger		Grenoble, France	Nephew of the Lt. Albrecht Kaufmann

Printed in the United States
By Bookmasters